Also by John Lawe

Pure Evil

Deadly Consequences

Right to Kill

by

John Lawe

The Kinler Mystery Series

Right to Kill

Copyright @ 2016 by John Lawe

This is the first trade paperback edition January 2016.

Cover design by Design Point, Inc.

ISBN: 978-0-692-37144-2 (sc)
ISBN: 978-0-9972467-0-4 (e)

Library of Congress Control Number: 2016901903

Printed in the United States of America

Available from Amazon.com, Kindle and other retail outlets.

Acknowledgements

I wish to acknowledge the contributions and encouragement I received from my Oregon Christian Writers' critique group. I am thankful to Linda Nathan, Logos Word Designs, LLC, for editing services and Design Point, Inc for the cover design.

Chapter 1

"What's out there?" Matt peered over his glasses at his wife.

Seated across the booth, Anna tilted her head and pressed close to the window to see behind him, outside the restaurant. "Ohh—aww. She needs a hug."

"Who?" He stole a quick glance back over his shoulder. "Can't see. That poster's in my way."

"I know, almost blocks me too."

Matt tried another peek but his arm bumped his coffee cup. "Ouch." He scooted down the bench to avoid the hot spill. "Whoops."

"Clumsy." Anna dropped her napkin in the puddle to stem the flow. "Be more careful."

"Who needs a hug?" He blotted the damp, dark spot on his trousers with a napkin while he scanned the room for their waitress.

"Some ladies outside—down near the entrance," Anna said. "They're too close to the building for you to see. Maybe when they move out to their car."

A waitress arrived at the end of their booth. "Somebody made a mess." She tossed a fistful of napkins in front of Matt and dropped her rag in the middle of the table. Dressed in jeans, her sweatshirt read "Detroit Lake" in big letters across the front. "I'll be right back."

Matt dried the bench while Anna used the rag to sop up the puddle on the table. With wet napkins and the rag piled on the end, Matt moved back to the wall and across from his wife.

Their waitress returned, a pot of coffee in one hand; a pad and pencil filled the other. "Ready to order?"

"We're waiting for another couple," Anna said.

"I could use a warm up." Matt slid his empty cup toward the waitress. "Please."

After she poured, the waitress gathered the wet debris and left.

Anna leaned forward and kept her voice low. "Now, don't look, but those two ladies outside? The older one was crying."

Tight against the window, Matt attempted another glance back over his shoulder.

"Careful." She guarded his cup with her hand.

"I still can't see. Do you recognize them?"

"Don't think so. The younger one maybe." Anna cradled a cup in her hands.

"There's Allen." Matt waved to his friend through the window.

In the parking lot, Allen struggled to ease his large, heavyweight-wrestler body out of the passenger side of a subcompact.

"Why didn't they come in his car?" Anna asked.

"Beats me."

"I'm so happy for them. Beth's been alone a long time."

"Yeah, but he's been a bachelor a long time." He picked through the bowl of creamers to find an unflavored half and half. "Surprised me the other day—he's so private. Told me, except for his grandpa and his old wrestling coach, our friendship's been the longest one he's ever had."

Anna's eyes tracked their friends outside. "You guys met—what—three, four years ago?"

"Almost five. After his grandpa died, he'd bounced around in foster care until after high school."

"How old was he when his grandpa died?"

"Eight, I think."

"Being uprooted, moved around, maybe he didn't have a chance to form friendships."

"Or learn how."

"You're a good teacher." She checked on their friends. "She looks small beside him."

"Almost anybody would. You're five-six and you look small next to him. She's as tall as you."

"She's taller, five-eight—Oh!" Anna lowered her voice. "Beth stopped to talk to those ladies. She hugged the older one."

Matt sipped his coffee. "Maybe she'll tell us what's going on." He shifted and raised his arm to catch Allen's attention as he and Beth entered the restaurant.

A retired FBI agent, Matt worked as a part-time private investigator out of Allen's office. He enjoyed the game, but expenses from his cases often exceeded income. Matt scooted closer to the window and slapped the bench for his partner to join him.

Beth slid in beside Anna. "Been here long?" She flipped her dark hair behind her shoulder.

"Nah," Matt said.

Allen leaned against his partner. "Do I smell a new coffee cologne?"

"Had an accident." Matt patted the damp spot on his trousers.

"Accident?" Anna snickered. "More like a bath."

"Not that bad." Matt adjusted his glasses.

"Detroit Lake" appeared, tossed menus on the table and left with a drink order.

"Why'd you drive?" Anna asked. "Allen's car has more room."

"That's what I told her," Allen said.

"It was my turn," Beth said. "Besides, I wanted to show Allen where my husband drowned." She paused, spread a napkin on her lap and met Allen's eyes as she folded her hands on the table. "I needed to."

Allen reached across the table and covered her hands with his. "We both needed to."

Beth studied Allen's eyes and, with a slight smile, nodded.

"Good for you," Anna said, "let it go." She touched Beth's arm.

"You're right." Beth fussed with the napkin in her lap. "Took years before I could come up here, but when my daughter returned she wanted to see where her dad died. I brought her up. We come back every now and then."

The waitress returned and left with their order.

"Before I forget—" Anna motioned toward the parking lot. "Who was the lady you hugged out there?"

"Ohh … poor lady, Lucille Duffy." Beth glanced out the window. "Her husband just died in an accident. She's devastated. Her daughter was with her. Carmen. They'd been to a memorial service."

"Should I know them?" Anna asked.

"Maybe." Beth placed a teabag in her cup. "Carmen used to do nails in my shop. Lucille dropped by sometimes."

"What kind of accident?" Matt asked.

"Traffic. He drove through a guard rail and landed in the river." Beth poured hot water into the cup. "Upside down." She jigged the teabag from a string.

"Up toward Marion Forks?" Matt asked.

Beth nodded. "Whitewater." She blew at the steam and sipped.

"I think I read about it in the paper," Matt said. "He was alone at night. No witnesses. Some speculated he fell asleep or had a heart attack."

"Lucille believes someone killed him—ran him off the road." Allen leaned with his forearms crossed on the table, "That's what the daughter told me."

"The sheriff investigating?" Matt asked.

"Oregon State Police," Allen said, "They do accidents on highways."

"Lucille doesn't think they're investigating," Beth said. "That's the main reason she's upset. She believes they don't care."

"The daughter said her dad had been getting threatening calls at night." Allen glanced at Matt.

Beth drank from her tea. "Tom just retired. He'd been with the highway department almost forty years." She stared at the cup and gave a slight nod toward the window. "Worked Highway 22 out there—

from here to the summit most of that time. He knew every twist, turn and bump. It's hard to imagine he'd just drive off the road."

"Harder to understand why the State Police wouldn't investigate," Matt said. "She must be wrong."

"Carmen says some detective told them the Medical Examiner believed Tom died of a heart attack—either before the accident or caused by it," Allen said.

"With the threatening phone calls, you'd think they'd take a closer look at things." Matt frowned.

"Does Lucille have anybody?" Anna asked.

"She has the house here in Detroit and goes to a little community church," Beth said. "Carmen lives down in Stayton. Her husband works for the fire department there."

"I gave the daughter one of your cards," Allen said. "Told her to call if they needed anything."

"My card. Why not yours?"

"I'm too busy. Got a big trial coming up and this attorney demands a lot from me."

"Dump him."

"Can't. I need the income. I'm not independently wealthy like you."

"Yeah, that's why I drive an old, brown Ford pickup." Matt motioned toward the parking lot. His wife often teased him by referring to his private-eye work as an expensive hobby.

"Now, now," Anna said. "Let's not fight, you two. You don't even have a client."

"Good point," Matt said. "What's this big trial of yours?"

Allen leaned back. "Defendant's a scum. Tried to burn down a house. The DA charged him with attempted murder because the owner was asleep inside, but he did manage to get out."

"How can you defend somebody like that?" Anna asked.

"I don't." Allen eyed Anna for a moment. "I gather information and report back to my client, who also happens to be this vermin's defense attorney."

"What if he gets off?" Anna asked.

"If the prosecutor can't convince a jury—" Allen grabbed a fry. "I can't help that."

Anna frowned and picked at her salad with a fork.

"Honey, he's not saying the guy will get off." Matt patted Allen's shoulder. "This happens to be the way our justice system works—or not."

Allen chewed as he nodded. "This guy's admitted the arson, but he's fighting the attempted murder." He glanced at the ladies, placed his forearms on the table and cleared his throat. "Look, I work for attorneys who defend people accused of crimes. The attorneys are my clients. They ask me to get information, find someone or do an interview and I do it. I don't fudge the facts—report what I have." He shrugged. "Sometimes it helps them, sometimes it hurts."

"I understand," Anna said. "Makes me mad when bad guys get off because of some lie or technicality."

Allen smiled. "Well, I give my attorneys the straight truth, unaltered—leave any shading or twisting to the professionals."

"Lawyers do love nuances and lies, spoken and unspoken." Matt wiped his hands on a napkin and tossed it on his plate. "Does this defendant have a record?"

"Uh-hmm." Allen hurried to swallow. "Minor one. He worked as a mechanic at the state motor pool until he got caught stealing tools. They fired him and he was convicted on a misdemeanor theft charge. Ninety days in jail and couple years of probation."

"Does he say why he tried to burn a house down? Who owned it?" Matt asked.

"I've never heard the why." Allen set his hamburger on the plate and grabbed a napkin. "The house belonged to a lobbyist who also owns another house in Lake Oswego. When the legislature is in session he lives in the Capital, but his family stays in Oswego."

"What's the firebug's beef with a lobbyist?" Matt sipped from his water.

"I'm not privy to information like that." Allen leaned back and glanced at his partner. "If I were to engage in wild speculation, this had something to do with some union issue."

"Union issue?" Matt cocked his head and peered over his glasses.

"Can't get into client information." Allen smoothed the napkin bedside his plate. "But this lobbyist has been a thorn in the side of public employee unions for a long time. The attorney I work for is with a big, high-powered law firm—Leach, Philcher, Hannibal. They do a lot of work for unions. Most of my cases involve union grievances and contested firings. The firm represented this guy after he torched a supervisor's car and later when he got fired for theft." Allen tapped his thick finger in front of Anna. "I didn't work those."

She smiled.

"Was he employed when he did this arson?" Matt asked.

"No, unemployed."

"Wonder why your big law firm represents a poor mope like him."

"I don't care about him." Anna locked her eyes on Matt. "What are you going to do about Lucille?"

"What do you mean?"

"Matt, she needs help." Anna placed her hand on Beth's arm. "Doesn't she?"

With a hesitant nod, Beth said, "She … yes, she probably needs help. At least … someone to talk her through the options—explain things."

"I don't want to butt in, if she hasn't asked for help." Matt brushed a hand back over his thinning hair. "Besides, you lined me up to check on the filbert farmer for that couple at church."

"Yes, I remember. But I wish you'd call him a hazelnut farmer."

"Same difference."

"Hazelnut sounds better, more romantic. You remember 'Dreaming of a White Christmas—roasting on an open fire'."

"Filbert rhymes better with farmer."

"See what I have to put up with." She smiled as she leaned against Beth's shoulder. "Yes, honey. I did tell them you'd help." Anna straightened up. "But I need to find out what they want. Their friend owns the farm next to theirs and a stranger's been hanging around."

Chapter 2

"What! You got some critter cornered under there?" In their living room, Matt dropped to his knees, stretched prone and peeked under the recliner. "Just your bone. No varmint." He forced his arm under the chair and flipped the bone clear. Eddy pounced and pranced off with the prize clamped in his teeth.

"He's a strange one." At the dining table, Anna flipped a page on the newspaper. "Sam doesn't obsess over things like that. I suppose any Border Terrier could have a hang-up or two."

"Or three. Eddy's primal instincts are a bit different. Drove me nuts the other morning. You weren't up, but he had a dust ball cornered under the computer desk and wouldn't let me rest until I fished it out."

"What'd he do with it?"

"Nothing. Sniffed it, but he left me alone." Matt settled in the chair across from his wife. "I had to dig deep in the old papers to find the story. What do you think?"

"Not much we didn't already hear." She combed fingers through her dark, curly hair. "Nobody saw the accident. A trucker stopped, but the river was too high and swift to do anything."

"Pavement was dry." He leaned forward to savor the smell of fresh coffee as he gripped the carafe to pour. "A cold night, but the paper reported no ice."

"I read the weather forecast for the Oregon mountain passes. It's going to be wet up around Detroit today. What time do you meet Lucille?"

"I told her mid-afternoon."

"I've left several messages for Eric and his wife." She raised her palms.

"Maybe concern for the filbert farmer has waned." He blew on his coffee before he sipped. "I hope so."

"I'm sorry if I've kept you too busy lately."

"It's okay." He reached across to touch her hand as he smiled. "But your busy doesn't pay very well."

With a smile in her eyes, she said, "Good thing we have your pension so you can pay rent on your desk."

"I don't think Allen would evict me." He swallowed the last gulp and carried the empty mug to the sink. "I've got to do our taxes too."

Anna rose from the chair and faced Matt across the long granite island between the dining room and kitchen. "If I hear anything about the farmer, I'll call or text you."

◆◆◆

Later, a steady rain and a string of eighteen-wheelers slowed Matt's progress. Above the dam and along the lake, stained berms of snow lined both sides of the highway. The past winter had been one of record snowfall. Matt figured the residents of Detroit were ready for an early spring.

"I'm here." Matt pressed the cell phone to his ear as he entered the driveway at Lucille Duffy's home.

"Is she alone?" Anna asked.

"Don't know yet. One car—lights on inside."

"I hope she's got someone to lean on. I finally talked to Eric. The farmer he's worried about is Delbert Hines."

"Wait, let me get so I can write. Okay."

"Delbert's eighty-seven. Always lived alone—never had family around. The farm's up near Dundee."

"Dundee? How's Eric—that's a long way from here. Where do Eric and his wife live?"

"This gets complicated," Anna said. "I'll explain when you get home. Eric and his wife retired from farming and bought a place on the Santiam River. Their son took over the farm and he's the one who told them about problems next door. Apparently, some guy moved in with the old man. This stranger won't let anybody talk to Delbert and claims to be a nephew."

"Sounds like they better call the sheriff or senior services. Don't know what I could do."

"Somebody asked the sheriff to do a welfare check. Delbert told the deputy everything was fine."

"Oh, honey." He sighed as he ran a hand back over his thinning hair. "This sounds like another one of your rabbit trails—not sure if I can help."

"I'm sorry. Sounded more serious when I talked to Eric and his wife at church. But, Matt—I told them you'd look into it."

Matt leaned back against the headrest, closed his eyes and kept his thoughts to himself. "It's okay. We'll sort this out when I get home."

The old cliché about things not always being as they first appear flashed in his mind. As an investigator, he had found the observation to be true. He'd learned to steel himself against forming conclusions before he had all the facts. Far too many times, investigators had jumped into a case with a preconceived notion and failed to remain objective. Matt fought the tendency to assume facts as a short-cut to solve a case or answer a question.

With the truck door closed, he headed for the front porch. Fir trees towered around the small, single-story house. Dark, stained siding blended with the forest scene. Smoke from the chimney hung and drifted above the brown metal roof. Matt touched the doorbell button under a hand painted placard that read "Tom & Lucille."

Through a narrow opening, Lucille examined him with raw, puffy eyes. "Mr. Kinler?"

Matt nodded.

She opened the door. "Come in, please."

Matt followed her into a living room dominated by a panorama of Detroit Lake through a windowed back wall. "What a wonderful view." He faced the sliding glass door. "This is due west?" He motioned with his arm.

"Close." A sad smile. "Tom ... loved this place." Lucille moved toward an easy chair beside the fireplace and plucked a tissue from a box. "It'll be much nicer when the reservoir fills this spring. Please sit."

The fire crackled as warmth and the scent of burning wood filled the room. Matt placed his notebook on the coffee table and settled on the end of the couch near her. "I'm glad you called," Matt said. "Beth told me of your tragic loss. I'm sorry the Lord called him home so suddenly."

A slight nod as Lucille wiped her nose and dabbed at her eyes. "Thank you."

"I understand you have a church fellowship to support you up here."

"Yes, they've been generous with meals, their time and support." She shifted and leaned on the arm of the chair. "But I called you to find out who killed my husband. I want the murderer held responsible."

While grief remained near the surface, Matt recognized Lucille had entered the stage where anger often follows a tragic loss. "Mrs. Duffy, I'll be glad to help if I can. Please understand I'm not a miracle worker. But if I can determine the why, how or who of your husband's death, I'll do my best."

She locked eyes on him, set her jaw and replied with a low, steady voice. "Find who killed Tom."

"I'll try. To start, I need you to tell me what you know. All I have is from the newspaper story."

"Ha. No reporter talked to me." She pressed her lips together before she continued. "Whoever killed Tom had to be from the State Employees' Union."

"How can you be so sure?"

"Because he stood up to them. They harassed Tom when he was an employee and, after he retired, the harassment got worse."

"Why after he retired?"

"My husband was outspoken, Mr. Kinler." She wrung her hands. "He didn't have much formal education, but he was smart. Loved to think and talk politics. Tom didn't like being forced to join the public employees' union. He spoke out against his dues being used to support liberal politicians and causes. They finally reduced his dues by an amount supposedly spent on political activity. He called the calculation for the reduced amount 'fiction'."

"But they kept after him?"

"Oh, Tom might have retired, but he didn't quit." Lucille's eyes gleamed as she lifted her chin. "He found a group of people who planned to put an initiative on the ballot this fall to amend Oregon's Constitution. If it'd pass, government employees in Oregon would no longer be forced to join unions. Dues couldn't be taken from a paycheck without an employee's permission."

"I'm not familiar with this initiative business."

"Me neither. But Tom called himself a Chief Petitioner. I think there were two others. He was working with these people to gather signatures on a petition to get the measure on the ballot. They had to have something short of a hundred thousand signatures by July."

"Do you have the names of the other people he worked with?"

She nodded. "I supported my husband, but I didn't go out and work with him much."

"So why do you believe somebody from the union caused your husband's death?"

"Killed him!" She glared at Matt.

He raised his hands. "Forgive me, I don't doubt what you say, but I'm in the habit of choosing my words carefully."

She rubbed her face. "I understand." Hands dropped to her lap, "The thought of them getting away with murder makes me angry." Lucille's reddened eyes focused on Matt. "For weeks before he died, we got telephone threats once or twice a day—one of those always in the middle of the night. They told him to stop the petition or else."

"Did they say they'd kill him?"

She leaned back and shook her head. "They never said what. Just they'd get him if he didn't stop."

"Same person call?"

"Tom thought so, but I didn't hear most, just the ones on our answering machine."

"Do you still have the messages?"

"Yes." She bounced out of her chair. "I almost forgot. Be right back."

Matt made notes as he waited for her return. Why hadn't the detectives investigated or seized the answering machine? Maybe his detective friend, Pasqual Trudeau, could explain.

Lucille plopped the machine on the coffee table beside his folder. "You take it, keep it. I don't want that man's voice in my house." She returned to the easy chair.

"Why'd your husband go out that night?

"A guy who used to work with Tom left a message. He claimed to have information on the union guys behind the phone calls. My husband went to meet him at Marion Forks."

"Did he tell you who called?"

"He might have. I don't remember. The call's on there." She waved at the answering machine. "The last…" Words stumbled in her throat. "…last call."

"What'd the detective say—did you talk to one?" He examined the old machine.

"Yes. He told me my husband died of a heart attack." She touched a tissue to her eyes. "Tom fought high blood pressure. His father died with a bad heart in his fifties."

"The detective didn't want this?" He tapped the answering machine.

She fished a business card from the drawer in the end table and passed it to Matt. "I didn't tell him about it." Lucille shrugged. "I was drained, too upset—didn't think to tell him what I've told you."

Matt studied the card. "An accident investigator—not a homicide detective." He tucked the card in his notebook. "Lucille, I promise I won't let them overlook anything as they investigate Tom's death."

Chapter 3

Matt slammed the truck's brakes. The tires stuttered on the wet pavement. There was no traffic in his rearview mirror, so he backed up several feet to let the minivan out of the diagonal space. He was courteous as always, but today he needed to park in front of the courthouse to watch for Pasqual Trudeau. He let the engine idle and cranked up the heater to ward off the cold of the miserable rainy, windy day.

Trudeau promised to find him during the grand jury's morning break. The detective's habit of being late or missing occasional appointments frustrated Matt, but he had learned to trust Trudeau who was all business and a straight shooter, traits Matt tried to cultivate in his own conduct.

The short, skinny detective appeared in the main entrance and moved a few paces to the side. He turned up the collar on his tan windbreaker and adjusted his brown hat before he lit a cigarette. Matt smiled as Trudeau scanned the vehicles along the curb. He couldn't remember the detective wearing a pork pie hat. The scene reminded him of a skinny Popeye Doyle from one of his favorite movies, *French Connection*. Trudeau spotted Matt, hurried out to the curb and hopped in on the passenger side. The smell of stale tobacco smoke filled the cab.

"Nasty day." Trudeau shuddered and rubbed his palms together. "What's up, Kinler? I don't have much time."

Condensation formed on the windows. Matt lowered his window a few inches, selected full defrost and cocked his head to face his friend. "You said you might get a peek at the Duffy autopsy, but what I really need is advice on how to handle what I learned from his widow yesterday."

Trudeau leaned forward to stick his hands in the warm air blowing at the base of the windshield. "Sad case. My contact in the ME's office says Duffy died of a heart attack. Probably dead before he hit the river. No water in his lungs."

"The widow thinks somebody killed him," Matt said.

"If she has anything to back her up, she'd need to tell the State guys—the accident investigators."

Matt nodded. "Said she was pretty upset the first time they came by. Didn't tell them why she thought someone killed her husband."

Trudeau withdrew his hands, leaned back and studied Matt. "She'll have to go through the hoops if she has anything." He wiped his chin and lips. "Man. I've got an infant death and another homicide back to back. I'm swamped."

"I've never worked with the State Police. What happens if their accident fatality turns into a homicide?"

"I think the accident file just gets passed on to the homicide detectives—about all."

"The investigator will need to talk with her again. She was confused the first time."

"She must've told you something they need to hear."

"She did. Would you pass her information on to them? I've never met this investigator." He passed the investigator's business card to Trudeau. "Maybe you can tell him I'm not some 'nut job'."

"I won't lie for you, Kinler." The detective smirked.

"Okay." Matt grinned, "Guess I deserved that."

"I've met him. He's new. What'd the widow have to say?"

Matt described Tom Duffy's contentious history with union leaders, his role as a petitioner on the ballot initiative and the threats Duffy received in weeks prior to the accident.

"Lucille gave this to me." Matt tapped the answering machine on the seat between them. "Last call was from Gerard Crum. He told Tom to meet at Marion Forks. Crum said he could identify the person who'd been threatening Duffy."

"Does she know Crum?"

"Didn't at first—but she thinks he worked with her husband. He's crippled with a stiff leg."

"This for the State guys?" Trudeau moved the machine onto his lap.

"Theirs to keep. I made a copy of the recording."

Nicotine stained teeth showed in his smile. "So she's a client of yours?"

"Told her I'd nose around a little."

"If you hear anything of interest, you can give me a call."

"Always have."

"I'll pass this along." Trudeau hoisted the answering machine from his lap, "They'll be delighted to get this."

The untidy detective hustled up the courthouse steps and stopped outside the entrance to grab another smoke. Matt waited for a break in traffic before he backed out.

With the wind and rain, he decided to forego the freeway. A slow trip up River Road would be more bearable than a drive through the blowing rain and froth whipped up by the trucks on I-5.

In Newberg he pulled over to call Eric's son for directions. He picked up the trail to the filbert farm on Highway 99W through Dundee and followed a series of farm roads to Eric's place. Eric, the son, told Matt he wasn't a junior because he had a different middle name than his father. To avoid confusion in the family, the son became "Little Eric" and his dad "Big Eric."

Matt spotted the sign for Spaniel Century Farm and turned onto the fence-lined lane. He parked at the bottom of a hill in front of a tidy manufactured home. Also well kept, another dwelling up on the hill appeared every bit the style of a century old farmhouse.

"Little Eric" strode out on the porch with a grin, in bib coveralls and a short-sleeved t-shirt. Matt couldn't remember the last time he had seen a forty-year old with the face of a child. Eric loomed large, as large as Matt's partner, Allen.

As Matt reached the bottom step, he said, "Like I said on the phone, your dad told me you'd show me where Delbert lives."

"Yeah, okay." The man lumbered off the porch, brushed past Matt and climbed in the passenger side of Matt's truck. Cordialities and small talk weren't Eric's forte.

The simple directions didn't require a tour guide, but Eric warmed to the task. Minutes later, Matt drove onto Delbert's property. "You're much bigger than your dad. Should I change your name to 'Big Eric'?" The graveled lane led through a hazelnut orchard.

The big man laughed, but during their brief acquaintance "Little Eric" found everything funny. The laugh, as he inhaled, had an odd "yuk-yuk" sound.

Matt hit the brakes in front of an old, weathered, white farmhouse. There were no lawn, flowers or ornamental shrubs; the gable roofed house sat in the middle of a hazelnut orchard. The lane continued beside and beyond the two-story home. Across the lane from the house was a wide three-sided building with a shed roof; it was large enough to house farm equipment. A new Class A motor home parked across the front of the shed with a twenty-foot runabout on a trailer.

"Not the kind of toys Delbert would buy. Maybe one of them mid-life crises." The "yuk-yuk" again.

Matt surveyed the area for any sign of life before he moved to the front door. Years of foot traffic on the painted porch had worn a path of bare wood. He eased the screen open and rapped on the door.

"Come in." From inside, the weak, raspy voice of an elderly man.

Matt moved aside and held the screen door for Eric.

"Hey, Delbert."

Delbert Hines strained to focus on his visitors. "Eric? That's you?"

"Yep." The laugh again. "Brought a friend to see you."

"Nice to meet you, Mr. Hines. I'm Matt."

The old man studied Matt and raised his bony arm. "You the man wants to buy my farm?"

"No, just wanted to meet you." Matt shook the puzzled man's hand. "I didn't know you were selling."

Delbert shifted in his overstuffed chair and slid one leg off the footstool. "My grandson, he's a nice boy."

"Grandson?" Eric asked. "I thought you had your nephew here."

Delbert blinked dull gray eyes. "He's a nice boy."

Matt whispered to Eric. "Talk farm stuff. I'll look around."

Clutter filled the living room, but nothing struck him as a safety hazard. In the kitchen, one day's dishes filled the sink, but no rotten food or vermin littered the counters. Matt leafed through a stack of mail by the telephone. Banking and investment mail had been ripped open, but personal correspondence remained untouched. Matt selected several items to borrow and return later.

Two bedrooms behind the kitchen had been used. He returned to the living room where Eric and Delbert waited. "Did we straighten out whether we have a nephew or a grandson?" Matt asked.

"Nope." The laugh.

"Let's go outside." Matt led Eric out to the truck. "Have you seen two guys here or just one?"

"One, and that guy told me he's a nephew. Only thing, Mr. Kinler—we don't think Delbert ever married. As far as we knew, he didn't have family. Can't figure a grandson or nephew."

"Go inside and get the old man. Let's take him over to your place where he'll be safe until we figure this out—shouldn't be here alone."

While Eric worked with Delbert, Matt examined the RV and boat and made notes of all the identifying numbers he could find.

By late afternoon, a lady from senior services had a care provider scheduled to take Delbert to an elder care facility to be evaluated. A sheriff's deputy had taken the information on the boat and RV and located the dealer. Delbert Hines' signature appeared forged, but Delbert wasn't much help.

Outside Eric's house, Matt called Anna and briefed her on what had happened. The rain had paused, but the dark, laden clouds remained.

"I'm glad you checked on him," Anna said. "Who knows what would've happened. Did this nephew show up?"

"Not as far as we could tell, but I can't see Delbert's place from here. I didn't know what to expect from this nephew or whoever he is. We had to get the helpless old man to a safe place."

"If he used Delbert's money for those big toys, who knows what else he did."

"I grabbed correspondence from his bank and mutual funds. The sheriff's office and senior services will salvage what they can."

"This kind of thing makes me sick. So cruel."

"I agree, but we've done the triage and he's going to get the help he needs."

Matt pocketed his phone as he approached Eric's porch. The flash, sound and force of several explosions caused him to stumble forward onto the steps. He caught his fall on the porch, regained his balance and twisted back to see what had happened.

Eric rushed outside and joined Matt as a ball of fire, smoke and flying debris rose in the dark sky above where Delbert once lived.

"Holy moly!" Eric said.

"Someone's probably called, but better get 9-1-1." Matt stared at the smoke and flames, as he smelled fumes from the disaster. A sickness quivered deep in his stomach as he realized what could've happened.

"They had lots of calls"— the laugh—"I also called the deputy." He waved a business card.

"Wish I could get closer to see what happened over there," Matt gazed at the huge cloud above the orchard. "The fire department's bound to close off any access."

"I could get you closer." Eric pointed to an outbuilding behind his house. "Scoot across my pasture in the ATV right up to Delbert's orchard."

The bench seat had been built to hold a driver and passenger, but designers didn't anticipate one the size of Eric. Matt clung to the edge of the seat as they bounced across the uneven field.

When Eric stomped the brake at the fencerow Matt tumbled to the ground. Firefighters shouted back and forth with barked orders, responses and warnings. He cleared the fence and crouched to peer under the limbs and billows of smoke to capture a view of the house. The smoke, fumes and heat compelled him to shield his face as he crept closer.

Eric slapped Matt on the shoulder from behind and spoke close to Matt's ear, "Too hot for me. I'll wait at the fence."

Matt crouched close to a tree, pulled his jacket up over his head and formed a peephole to study the scene. The farmhouse was a total loss, and flames engulfed the equipment shed. Smoke swirled from the tires on an old truck near where the RV and boat had been parked.

Chapter 4

"He'll never realize how close he came to death."
Matt kicked his running shoes to the side, tossed the
cell phone beside his plate and grabbed the carafe.

"Who, Delbert?" Anna yawned and rubbed her
eyes. She tightened the sash on her robe and slid into
the chair across from him.

He nodded. "I just talked to the deputy—a real
go-getter." He poured for her and topped off his mug.
"I expected him to be home asleep, but he's stayed on
the case. He's young but must be running on fumes."

"Did he have anything new?" She snatched his
last piece of cinnamon toast. "I'll leave that bacon for
the dogs."

"All preliminary, but he's pretty sure of arson.
Fire started with dynamite and propane tanks made
into bombs hidden in the crawl space. I told you how I
felt the explosions clear over at Eric's."

"My first thought was natural gas."

"Me too, until they told me he didn't have
natural gas. He used oil for heat and electricity for
cooking."

"Thanks to you, Delbert wasn't home—or
he'd be dead."

"Part of the plan, I think. The deputy told me,
off the record, that about thirty minutes after they
froze the old man's accounts, wire transfer requests
poured in from a Las Vegas bank. The bad guys had

sent them in Delbert's name, but nobody fell for the forged requests."

"Whoever's behind this planned to clean him out," Anna said.

"I think the phony nephew had the house wired to blow with the old man inside after he cleaned out the accounts. We came along and ruined his plan. When he discovered Delbert gone—he set the house to blow anyway and took off with the RV and boat."

"I shudder at the thought of that house wired with you inside." She eyed him as she held the mug against her chin.

"Probably a close call." He offered his hand across the table. She embraced his hand with hers. He said, "A lot of people get hurt when men engage in dark deeds. I'm thankful God spared me."

"Me too." She blew a kiss and released his hand. "Do you think the pass will be clear for you guys today?"

"Wet, but no snow."

"Are you sure you have to do this? You could turn the hazelnut farmer's letter over to the sheriff." She smiled.

"The filbert farmer?" He smirked, shifted sideways and crossed his legs. "I could but, Honey, I can't let this rest. This guy has to be stopped."

"Our friends were appalled when their son called to tell them what happened to their old neighbor. They'll feel better after the police catch the bomber. Worried about their son, 'Little Eric'."

"Well, I forgot about the letter until I called Allen this morning. Found it on the counter beside my phone where I emptied my pockets last night." He drank from the mug. "After I told Allen what happened, he got all ramped up ready to go over there with me. Besides, this trip may answer a lot of questions."

"If this guy's the bomber, I hope you'll have enough sense to back off." She rose from the table and stretched her arms.

"You know me." He peered over his glasses.

"Yes. That's why I said that. Did you feed the dogs?"

"If I hadn't, they'd be complaining instead of sacked out."

She moved to the throw rug in front of the door to kneel where Sam and Eddy sprawled. "A dog's life—not a care in the world." She ruffled their ears.

"I need to get out of my running clothes and shower before Allen gets here."

"I'm surprised he's going with you—his big trial and all."

"Me too, but today he's free."

"If we didn't know him so well, we'd probably never notice the change in him after he received that scrapbook," Anna said.

"Not to mention his interest in Beth."

"It's amazing how God works. Forty-five, an avowed agnostic, and one day a stranger walks in and hands him a scrapbook kept by his old wrestling coach. God smacked him head on."

"Before, he liked to debate with me, now we talk."

"I guess you weren't such a good debater."

"I'm a dandy debater." Matt smiled as he stuck his chest out. "Things just happen on God's schedule, not mine."

She smiled as she rose. The dogs followed her into the kitchen. "I'm glad you're both going. He's got enough sense to keep you out of trouble."

♦♦♦

Matt glanced at the truck's clock and figured they'd be in Sisters before noon, if he didn't get stuck behind more big rigs. With Detroit Dam on his right, he tensed as he watched for the start of the passing lane.

Once clear of the eighteen-wheeler, he sped along the open road. Carved into the steep mountainside, the highway ran high above the reservoir. Sheer rock faces broke through the evergreen forest in places on his left. On the right he caught glimpses of the huge manmade lake through openings in the trees.

"Did you finish the letter?" Matt asked.

"Yeah." Allen stuffed the folded paper into the envelope and tossed it between them. "Fredrick Hines had a falling out with Delbert and wants to patch things up."

"Doesn't say how they're related."

"Could be dad, brother or nephew, didn't say."

"Notice the postmark?" Matt tapped the letter.

Allen grabbed the envelope, studied the mark. "Six months ago—so what?"

"Found a lot of unopened mail at Delbert's. I snagged this envelope because of the last name in the return address."

"From the way you described him—Delbert's beyond caring."

"He is." Matt lapsed into silent thoughts of an old man, alone, drifting into dementia. "When my grandfather passed away he didn't recognize any of us. Sad."

Through the trees he caught glimpses of the lake bottom exposed by the reservoir's seasonal low. Stumps covered the barren basin where evergreen forest once stood.

Signs announced their arrival in Detroit. With tourist season months away, the small town lacked the summer bustle.

"There's the shop for the highway department." Allen leaned forward to study the complex on Matt's side of the road. "I'd guess Duffy worked out of there before he retired."

"Have to be—wonder if they've replaced the guardrail yet?" Matt asked.

"We'll know soon enough."

An hour later in Sisters, Allen studied the screen on his cell phone, "Take the next right— house should be third down on the left."

"Here we are." Matt wheeled over to the curb across from the address.

"Without house numbers it'd be hard to find someone here," Allen said.

"Do look alike, three, maybe four house plans." Matt opened the door. "Let's talk to Mr. Hines."

The single-story house with wood siding and composite roof had the hint of a yard with brown grass. Matt strolled up the token driveway and followed a short walk to the front door. *Tidy*. Matt poked the doorbell.

"Nice smell, pine and juniper," Allen said

The man in the doorway leaned on a cane, seventy, give or take a few years. "May I help you?"

A full head of white hair and beard surrounded the puzzled expression on his tanned face.

"Fredrick Hines?" Matt asked.

"No. He passed away several months ago. Maybe I can I help you. I'm his son, Henry."

"Oh, I'm sorry. I didn't know."

"Thank you, but he'd been sick for years. He's at peace now." Henry shifted his weight and repositioned the cane.

"Are you related to Delbert Hines?"

The white eyebrows shot up. He rocked, unsteady. "We—I thought he was dead. Dad sent him a letter and we never heard back."

"No, he's alive." Matt said, "May we come in?"

◆◆◆

A rain-snow mix pelted the windshield as Matt drove over the summit of Santiam Pass in the late afternoon.

"Back in civilization, I'll do a work-up on this Dave Smith," Allen said.

"Got to be a phony name and a thief to boot."

"Yeah, but since Henry told us Smith had been arrested in Deschutes County for driving under the influence, I'll track him down."

"Think we'll turn this over to my Yamhill deputy friend. Let them track Smith down—probably turn out to be his bomber. Henry said he'd handle Delbert's affairs."

"Well, since I'm started," Allen said, "I'll finish the DUII record check for Dave, whoever he is. My curiosity won't let me quit."

Matt braked for a sharp downhill corner and shook his head. "Interesting how all this started.

Henry hires the Smith guy to do some home repairs. The repairman pilfers personal papers. Then Delbert has a long lost nephew show up and the old man becomes an easy mark for a thief and killer."

"At least Delbert's got family who'll see to his care." Allen crossed his arms and leaned against the headrest. "Henry's the reliable sort."

The highway snaked down the western slope of the Cascade mountain range. Matt used headlights as they passed through the tall, dark evergreen forest. A light rain fell.

"You remember Murphy, my old wrestling coach?" Allen asked.

"Yeah, the scrap booker."

"That's him. I got an email from his son, the missionary." Allen closed his eyes. "He bought a house in Florida."

"After being in the Philippines for so long, they needed a warmer climate," Matt said.

"Yeah, but I think their kids live down there. Also close to his mission's headquarters."

"You've got one incredible story to tell, partner. If he hadn't gone through his dad's stuff when he got back to the states, he'd never have found the scrapbook. Without the news clips on your wrestling exploits, he'd probably never have found you."

"Yeah." Allen lowered his arms and opened his eyes. "But—he did. He told me Murphy kept several journals on different kids—his favorites. I'm the only one he'd found so far. I told him I'd help if he wanted."

Matt glanced at Allen. "God reached Murphy through his missionary son then grabs your attention through Murphy's journal."

"I'm surprised he kept a journal on me." Allen fixed on the road ahead. "He wrote what he'd planned to tell me, but died before he could."

"You got his message."

Allen nodded.

A comfortable silence settled as they traveled, each occupied with their own thoughts. Soon, Allen fell asleep.

Matt followed a long-haul truck, impatient for the next passing lane. He thought of Tom Duffy. The man worked this road, day and night, under all conditions. The way the accident happened on the way to meet a former co-worker didn't make sense.

The sign read Marion Forks. In a split second, Matt decided. His foot to the brake and an abrupt turn disturbed Allen's nap. "Let's make a pit stop," Matt said.

Allen yawned and wiped his face with his hands. "I'll need to wake up."

Matt left his partner in the truck and strode toward the entrance. Inside, he found the gift shop empty and vacant stools lining the counter. Smells of fried food and sounds of clanging cookware spilled out of the kitchen. In the main dining room, one couple occupied a table at a back window with a view of Marion Creek behind the restaurant. He tried to remember the last time he'd been in this place. Artist Ray Eyerly's scenes of Oregon still adorned the walls. The wood paneling, furniture and trim created a lodge like atmosphere. A stone fireplace and the moose head mounted on the wall added to the ambiance. He couldn't remember moose in Oregon. *Oh well. Nice touch.*

"You waiting to be seated?" Allen joined Matt at the dining room entrance.

"No. Just thinking. Guess we choose our own."

"Have you seen any hired help?" Allen asked.

"Not yet. But that couple has food." He nodded toward the occupied table.

A young man emerged from the kitchen with a glass coffee pot in hand. A dishtowel hung over his shoulder. A stiff leg impaired his movement. In his late twenties, the waiter passed and swept his free hand across the room. "Take your pick—be right with you."

Matt chose a table across the room from the other customers.

"Why'd you stop here?" Allen asked. "I had a good nap going."

"This is where Duffy was headed. Thought I'd take a look."

The waiter dropped menus on the table then offered and poured coffee. "I'm just filling in. Gabby'll be back in a few minutes."

"You do the cooking too?" Matt glanced at the white cap.

"Oh, yeah, forgot." He eyed the bill on the hat. "Been training me since my accident." He slapped at his stiff leg. "Only job I could find."

"What happened?" Allen asked.

"I crashed on my dirt bike. Crunched my knee."

"Can't replace it?" Matt asked.

"Doc said he could, but I tried rehab first. I had a seasonal part-time job with highways, but didn't have insurance when this happened. I can't afford surgery now—too expensive."

Matt studied the young man. "Did you work up here with Tom Duffy?"

His eyes darted from Matt to Allen. "N—no." He shuffled sideways, "Ga—Gabby'll take yer order." He hobbled from the dining room into the kitchen.

"Better corner him before we leave," Allen said.

"What I'm thinking—he fits our Gerard guy."

Minutes passed as several customers arrived for early dinner and seated themselves. The couple by the window prepared to leave, but the waiter hadn't returned.

Matt slid out of his chair and moved to the front where the trainee fled. He peeked inside the kitchen. No movement; he called out, "Gerard?"

No answer.

A commotion near the main entrance caused Matt to back away from the door. The expression on the face of the stocky woman did not invite questions. She stormed past him and into the kitchen.

"Gerard!" she shouted.

Matt poked his head back in the dining room. Every customer stared as he motioned for Allen to follow. In the lobby, he placed cash by the register and hustled outside. Dusk.

"Take it Gerard's gone." Allen caught up with him.

"Hoped I'd get a glimpse of his ride."

"Last name is Crum, right?

Matt nodded.

"We'll find him."

Chapter 5

"Right there." Matt hit the brakes and swerved onto the right shoulder. The truck fishtailed in the loose gravel. Rocks pinged on the fenders and underside, but he avoided the ditch. "Don't tell on me."

"My lips are sealed." Allen feigned zipped lips.

"I want a closer look." He moved the truck off the highway, punched the button for hazard lights and killed the engine.

"Won't be much here. They replaced the damaged parts." Allen pointed at the new section of guardrail ahead of them on the left side of the road.

"You can stay, I'll go." Matt grabbed a flashlight under the seat. "There's another one in the glove box."

Guardrail lined both sides of the highway. The narrow right shoulder forced him to pick his way through the ditch outside the rail. Allen grumbled behind him.

Matt stopped across from the new section installed along the riverbank. With a hand on the metal barrier, he shined the light on the scraped and marred pavement. Except for the repaired section, a snow berm remained packed along the base of the guardrail on both sides of the highway. He'd need to find photographs of the accident to learn the snow depth, road conditions and other details. Maybe when the investigators released the accident report.

"Don't think there's been much snow since the repairs." Matt motioned toward the berm on the other side of the highway. "Lot of melt since the accident."

"As long as we're here, let's do a crime scene walk through," Allen said.

Matt checked traffic before he vaulted the guardrail and sprinted across the road. He worked both sides of the rail from each end of the repaired section and returned to the truck empty-handed.

Minutes later, Allen climbed into the cab and handed Matt a white fiberglass rod. One end had a metal fitting attached.

"What's this?" Matt examined the rod.

"I don't know—broke off of something."

"Wonder what this white stuff is." Matt rubbed his fingertip over a rough spot on the metal fitting. "Here's where it broke off."

Allen accepted his find and studied the white mark. "Road paint, maybe. This rod's like the ones I've seen on the ends of snowplow blades."

"Could be." Matt propped his elbow at the bottom of his window and raised his hand to his cheek. Hazard lights flashed in the darkness. "Where do you think they hauled the damaged section?"

"Straight to the recycle yard would be my guess."

"I'll have to ask. Accident with a fatality— maybe they kept the rail to reconstruct what happened," Matt said.

"Who'd do the reconstruction, the highway department or the State Police?"

"Trudeau said State Police, but he wasn't sure if they'd do much for an accident with a single vehicle." Matt started the engine and switched to headlights. "If the shop in Detroit's open, let's do a snoop around."

Sparse weeknight traffic allowed them to reach the road maintenance shop without delay. Matt entered the paved yard and veered right to avoid notice by anyone from the office in the large, rectangular, metal building. As he passed several large bay doors, he glanced inside the only one that remained open. A backhoe was inside, but he didn't notice any employees. When he reached the far end he pulled in beside a State truck, concealing them from anyone back in the office.

He joined Allen near the tailgate. "Let's mosey around the outside of the building. Might find the section of guardrail."

Alert for movement, Matt headed across the yard. "Do you see anyone?"

Allen shook his head. "No noise either."

"Surely someone's here." Matt gestured toward the open bay.

They moved along a row of snowplows, backed and parked against the fence. Matt slapped Allen's arm. "There." He gripped the fiberglass rod mounted on the end of a snowplow blade.

"Wait, stay back. Let me get a picture," Allen said.

"Probably don't need one, not enough light anyway."

"Better than nothing." Allen held his cell phone to frame the shot.

"Hey, thought I heard voices." A stocky man in coveralls approached. "Public's not allowed in here—you cops?"

"No." Matt faced the man. "Somebody said the guardrail from Duffy's accident had been hauled in here. Thought we might take a look."

"Nope, hauled off to recycling." The man wiped his hands with a red rag. "You can't be here."

"We're going." Matt tugged on Allen's sleeve and headed for the truck.

The man followed.

"Why'd you ask if we were cops?" Matt asked over his shoulder.

"Don't know—he snapped some pictures," the man said.

Matt spun back. "Did you work with Tom?"

A hesitant nod, no eye contact—the grease-stained hands worked the rag.

"His wife told me about the accident," Matt said.

"Lucille." The man cleared his throat. "I went to the memorial; Sanford's my name."

"You work with him very long?"

Eyes averted, he twisted the rag. "Long time … good man."

"What I'm told, but I heard not everybody liked him." Matt studied the shorter man.

"Are you … did she…?" Sanford shuffled his feet and glanced toward the office. "Lucille said she was going to hire someone." He eyed Matt for a moment.

"Told her I'd help answer some questions." Matt shoved his hands in his jacket pockets. "You work the night shift alone, Sanford?"

"Days usually. I had to do some catch up tonight."

"You got a last name? Maybe we could talk sometime. I'm Matt Kinler."

"Stanley. Sanford Stanley. But … I, ah … don't get me involved in this."

"Involved in what?" Matt jerked his hands out of his jacket and crossed his arms.

Sanford glanced toward the office and checked the yard.

"You afraid someone will see us?" Matt asked.

"I'm not a brave man, Mr. Kinler." He scuffed the sole of his boot on the asphalt. "I don't want trouble. Wife's disabled. I need this job. I keep my head down and my mouth shut."

Matt grabbed Sanford's arm. "Let's get out of sight." He caught a strong whiff of motor oil and grease as he led the soiled man into the shadows between his truck and the department's vehicle. "Tell me what's going on, Sanford. Just between us, no notes. I'll forget your name after tonight."

Sanford removed his cap and wiped his forehead with the rag. "I—I don't … I ah … Lucille's right. Tom was killed. I don't know who did it." He replaced the cap and craned his neck to glance around.

"If you were me, where would you go to find the killer?" Matt leaned against his truck.

"Highway Department." Sanford's eyes darted up to meet Matt's. "The union." He worried the rag in his hands.

"So … someone caused the accident?"

Sanford nodded. "I think they forced Tom off the road with a snowplow."

"How do you know that?"

"I came to work the morning after Tom died, but I hadn't heard anything yet." He swiped a hand across his forehead. "I ah … had to do a little work on a backhoe over by the gravel pile. Somebody had parked a snowplow back there—one end of the blade got all banged up—white streaks on it. By the time I got back in the shop, the supervisor had called a meeting to tell us about Tom."

"What about the snowplow?"

"I didn't have time to inspect it when I noticed the damage. Nobody else knew anything." Sanford shrugged with his palms out. "Couple of us drove up to see where Tom went over the side. When we got back, the snowplow was gone."

Allen spun away and opened the door on Matt's truck. He retrieved the rod and raised it in front of Sanford's eyes. "Do you recognize this?"

Sanford gripped the rod. "One of those guides off a snowplow blade. Lose 'em all the time."

"We found this one near the accident," Allen said.

With a pensive face, Sanford returned the rod.

"Don't know if you saw the white marks on the metal fitting," Matt said.

Sanford stuffed his hands in his pockets and hunched his shoulders. "Tom's truck was white."

Matt shot a glance at Allen, who studied the metal end in his hand. "Sanford," Matt said. "You told me the killer might be union. Why?"

Sanford shuffled his feet. His head swiveled as he shifted to check the yard. "Mr. Kinler, I … I don't … I can't lose my job."

"I'm not asking you to name anyone. Just explain why a union guy would hate Tom enough to kill him."

Sanford tugged the rag from his pocket and muttered, "Money."

"Did you say money?" Matt asked.

"Money and power." He wrung the rag with his hands. "Wherever Tom worked he tried to persuade employees to quit paying the full amount of their union dues. Said we should refuse to pay for the political stuff."

"Could you do that?" Matt asked.

Sanford nodded. "Tom did it."

"I think it's called the 'fair share'," Allen said. "A union member can reduce his dues by filing for an exemption from paying the portion of dues used for political activity."

"I never filed," Sanford said. "I pay the full amount, about seventy-five each month."

"Almost a thousand a year; too bad you can't quit the union," Matt said.

Sanford peeked out from under the bill of his cap and locked on Matt's eyes. "That's what Tom was working on, and the union wanted him stopped."

"Was everybody in the union out to get him?"

"No, just the leaders." He eyed his boots as he spoke with a soft voice. "Anybody I worked with liked Tom, but we kept our mouths shut."

"One more thing before we go, did you ever work with Gerard Crum?"

He shook his head. "I know who he is."

"Where's he live?"

"Not sure—Stayton maybe." He glanced up. "Saw him in Detroit with one of the union guys."

"Recently?"

"Back a week or so, with 'Bully Boy'."

"Bully Boy?"

"Everybody calls him that—William Boyd is his real name." Sanford flashed a sly smile. "He thinks it's a compliment."

"Where's Boyd work?"

"The shop in Salem."

"Does he come up here much?" Matt asked.

"Nope."

"He came up here about a week back," Allen said. "How close to Tom's accident?"

Sanford's jaw dropped and he stroked his chin. "Close—might've been same day—not sure."

Chapter 6

"Heard you on the phone down here." Anna swept past, arranged a coaster on the end table for her coffee and tucked herself on the couch. She flipped the bottom of her robe to cover her bare legs. "I love the fire, so cozy."

"Needs another chunk of wood, but I couldn't drag myself over there." Matt pressed the mute button on his TV news. "Had my new deputy friend on the phone." The recliner creaked as he raised the back. "Told him what we learned over in Sisters—Dave Smith, DUII, all that."

"Have they made any progress?"

"Not a lot. Delbert's thriving." Matt chuckled.

"What's funny?" She sipped from the mug.

"Not funny really—sad. A detective went to interview him about the nephew—who's probably our Mr. Smith. But Delbert thought the detective was his nephew. Thanked him for selling the farm and asked when they were going RVing."

She sighed. "He's safe now. I'm glad you found family to help him."

"Deputy told me something interesting. Crime lab's not through yet, but there were three bombs under the farmhouse. Each had a five-gallon propane tank, a can of gas, dynamite and a timer with an electric match."

"What's an electric match?"

"Igniter is another name. Anything that makes an electric spark. They can be homemade, pulled from an appliance or gas barbecue, or bought. People who do fireworks use them all the time."

"Makes me sad to think people spend time thinking up ways to make bombs." She drank and placed the mug back on the coaster. "I'm glad that's behind you. Let's talk happy things. I have lunch in Salem with Sophia."

Near the front of the recliner, Eddy whined with his nose pressed to the floor.

Matt bent forward and tipped the footstool up on one side. Eddy dove for his bone and strutted off. "Dog drives me nuts." He dropped the footstool. "I'll be in town too. I have that appointment with the director of Tom Duffy's petition drive."

"Allen going?"

"No. His trial's started. I need to call—bring him up to speed."

◆◆◆

Blocked. The mob clogged the sidewalk and spilled out into the street to snarl traffic. Matt flipped the turn signal off, drove straight through the intersection and searched for an alternate route. When he'd called to confirm his appointment Marion Walters hadn't mentioned demonstrators massed in front of her office.

The radio announcer on his favorite AM station gave the time. He could join Anna in the business district for lunch and return later. Maybe the rally would be over. Better yet, kill time in the courtroom gallery at the trial for Allen's arsonist. No, he'd told her before twelve. He'd find a way to keep his word.

Within sight of the golden pioneer atop the State Capitol Building, Matt circled the blocks near Walters' office. The organized and boisterous crowd marched in front of the building used by Worker Independence Now, a non-profit organization. Earlier, Matt had left a message on her answering machine. The announcement used the acronym WIN.

He approached the protest from the opposite direction of his first attempt. An empty space behind a large charter bus allowed him to park within a few blocks of the picketers. His pickup occupied one space while the bus tied up half a dozen. On the sidewalk, Matt spotted the bus driver beside the open door of the charter. The crowd noise carried to where Matt parked, but he didn't understand the chants.

"What's the ruckus?" Matt stopped on the sidewalk abreast the driver.

"Nothing." The heavyset driver glanced at Matt. "Just another union rally."

"Must be something." Matt waved a hand toward the news van. The satellite dish on the roof provided backdrop for a reporter postured with a microphone to his lips. Another man shouldered the camera and fixed a bright light on the reporter's face.

"Oh, I suppose." The driver crossed his arms. "I do several of these a week—routine for me."

"You bring them here?" Matt's attention focused on the distant activity.

"Not all of them. About half."

"How long do they hang around?"

"Two, maybe three hours." The driver lifted his cap, brushed his hair back and replaced the cap. "March in a circle—shout things, somebody'll give a speech. That's when you know they're about to break up."

"You have done this a lot—from around here?" Matt asked.

"Naw." He crossed his arms again. "Come down from Portland."

Matt cocked his head. "That's where your demonstrators come from?"

"Oh yeah. Pick 'em up at the union hall. They get ten dollars an hour, free lunch and one of them purple t-shirts."

"This a union bus?"

"Naw. I'm with the charter company. We're non-union, but they hire us. Cheaper for 'em."

"Any idea why they're here?"

"Naw." He thrust his chin toward the crowd, "I think something about workers having to join unions and pay dues." He shrugged. "I don't care as long as they pay me that green union money."

"And you do this several times a week?"

"Yup. Las' week they did minimum wage at a McDonald's in Beaverton and a Walmart over in Gresham." His midsection jiggled as he chuckled. "Over at Walmart, they got their free lunch at Mickey D's."

"And you haul this same crew around to every rally?"

"Pretty much."

The distant chants died down and the crowd formed around a pickup parked at the curb. In the truck bed, a woman blabbered into a bullhorn on some theme Matt couldn't follow. The news people moved the camera equipment closer to the speaker. A tall, barrel-chested man joined the woman in the truck and raised his hands above his head. The noise level jumped with hoots and hollers from the crowd. With the bullhorn to his mouth, the man in a purple shirt spoke. The crowd grew quiet. Demonstrators and news cameras pressed closer and focused on the speaker.

Matt seized the opportunity, hustled up the street and slipped past the crowd to the WIN office. He found curtains drawn, the door locked, and a piece of cardboard taped over the glass in the door. Matt tapped his pen on the glass. A young woman peeked out as she lifted a corner on the cardboard.

"Matt Kinler. I have an appointment with Marion Walters."

She disappeared and the deadbolt clunked. Her rapid gestures in the open doorway conveyed an impatience to secure the door.

He brushed by the keeper of the door. A little over five feet, she had shoulder-length red hair, a pale, freckled complexion and worry in her eyes.

"Alone?"

"Yes." She locked the door. "Marion's at the Elections Division office."

"You have a name?" Matt surveyed the low-budget furnishings: folding tables and chairs, and butcher paper taped on a wall with tally marks and printed notes made with a black, felt-tip marker.

"Darla." She settled on a chair in front of the only desktop computer. A desk phone beside her station at the table completed her office equipment. Half of her five-foot table had stacks of forms, some blank, some not. Pamphlets piled on the end had "WIN Right-to-Work" in bold white letters over a background of blue and red stripes.

"This how many signatures you've gathered?" Matt studied the tally marks.

"Each mark is one hundred. I have to add what we've done today."

"May I?" Matt slapped the back of the only padded office chair. Without objection, he settled at the other folding table designated for the executive director. A nameplate, laptop and desk phone comprised Marion Walter's equipment.

"How long do you think she'll be gone, Darla?"

"Usually she's gone less than an hour." She cast a worried glance at the front door. "But today she may stay away longer. She didn't expect the crowd out there."

"Understand that. My lucky day too. You work full-time?"

"Yes, sir. Temporary, until the signatures are all turned in. I worked for Elections, but lost my job with budget cuts. I'd met Marion when she came to Elections … liked her. She offered me a job when I told her I was being laid off."

"Happy for you." Matt crossed his legs and drummed his fingers on the table.

"I'm hoping to get another job with the State. This one won't last long."

"Don't give up, you'll find one." His empathy increased as she gripped the mouse near her keyboard. The monitor towered above her. The table was too high, the chair too low; she appeared small.

"I need a job. My husband deserted me … my daughter and I live with my mom."

"Hang in there, you'll find something." Matt rose and moved to the front door to check on the crowd. The big, purple shirt continued to yammer. "Think I could find her?"

"Probably. Election's office isn't too far—couple blocks over." She grabbed a sheet of paper. "Here's the address."

"There a backdoor?"

"Yes, behind me." She pointed a thumb back over her shoulder. "At the end of the hall."

"What's she wearing?"

Darla smiled. "You can't miss her. Silver haired, eighty year-old lady in a bright red blazer and black slacks."

"I can work with that." He slipped out the rear exit and headed for Capitol Street. Distance and sounds of traffic smothered the noise of the crowd and the bullhorn.

A block from his destination, Matt spotted Walters as she scurried out of the building. Head down, she set a rapid pace away from Matt and toward the State Capitol Building. She rounded the corner at Court Street and disappeared behind the office building. He quickened his strides to catch the spry lady.

When he reached Court he caught a glimpse of the silver hair and red blazer as she crossed the street and headed toward the front of the Capitol. He sprinted across Court in the middle of the block. As he reached the sidewalk, a crowd of school children blocked his view, spilling out of school buses parked in a line across the front of the building.

More than one hundred middle school children fanned out on the sidewalk and the expansive stairs that led up to the main entrance. The silver head of hair bobbed through the mob of active visitors. Students ran and walked in every direction. One chaperone had reached the top of the stairs and herded a group of boys down from the narrower section to join groups being organized on the sidewalk.

By the time Matt reached the first bus, the crowd had thinned along the curb. He hurried along the line of buses. Clear of the mob scene, he found Marion Walters. She had settled on a bench at the far end of the sidewalk and squinted at the screen on her cell phone. Matt slowed as he approached.

Chapter 7

Traffic whizzed past as Anna moved to the curb on Liberty Street. She turned, faced the Reid Opera House, adjusted the purse strap on her shoulder and waited for Sophia. Her friend couldn't resist a temptation to shop. Anna preferred to wait outside and enjoy the noonday sights and sounds of the city. Besides, it saved her money.

Among other things, Sophia Taylor had been a con-artist and burglar until sheriff's deputies arrested her in one of Matt's cases. Slapped around by life's circumstances, desperate, Sophia fell on her face before God. She had Matt's business card and reached out for help. Through a series of events Anna had become her counselor and mentor.

Reluctant at first, Anna accepted the role, unsure she had the knowledge and wisdom needed. After all, Sophia had a past with experiences foreign to Anna's well-ordered life. Their relationship began with phone calls and emails. Now they met for lunch on a regular basis.

Sophia had accepted Christ as her Savior and changed her life's priorities before their friendship developed. The nature of the relationship morphed into mother-daughter, with Anna the mother Sophia never had. Anna offered stability, acceptance and common sense to a woman troubled by guilt, loneliness and insecurity.

"You didn't buy anything," Anna said.

"Couldn't make up my mind." Sophia joined Anna near the curb. She was taller, in her mid-forties, and trim; her shoulder length hair had returned to the natural dark brown. Sophia still drew glances and some eyes that lingered.

"Maybe next time." Anna took her arm. "Let's head for the parking garage. I need to get you back to work."

"My boss won't care." Sophia had learned to be a legal assistant. Matt found her a job as an intern with a Christian lawyer. Later, she gained a full-time position. "I've told him how important you've been in my life."

"Not me—God. I'm thankful to be a spectator as He works in you."

"You know what I mean." Sophia clutched Anna's arm.

They strolled toward Salem Center and the parking garage. Queued to cross the street with the light, a boisterous foursome spilled out of an eatery onto the sidewalk in the next block. In tights and t-shirts, the two young woman left nothing to the imagination. Their hairstyles screamed for attention, one a lime green Mohawk and the other black, collar length with hot pink streaks. The animated couples rounded the corner and headed down the sidewalk away from Liberty.

"We can go." Anna tugged on Sophia, whose eyes followed the colorful young women.

As they crossed the street, Sophia spoke. "Makes me sad. Brings back my shame for how I rebelled against God."

"We all have regrets, but you're forgiven. You're at peace now."

"Oh, I know. I'd like to grab those girls and shake some sense into their colorful heads."

"Would that have worked with you?" Anna placed a hand to Sophia's back.

"No." Sophia smiled. "Maybe God will get their attention like He did for me."

"Something to pray for."

As they headed out of the parking garage's third level, Anna slammed the brakes to avoid a collision. "Goodness. She backed out like she wanted to get hit." The old brown subcompact headed down the exit lane in front of them.

"Who'd do that? Wouldn't make sense," Sophia said.

"That car's seen better days."

"Thinking about those girls with the bad hair…" Sophia shifted sideways to face Anna. "When I accepted the Lord I thought all my problems would go away. I don't remember if someone told me that, but it's what I expected."

"This driver's acting weird." Anna hit the brakes again to allow more distance from the brown beater. "I've heard others say things about their problems going away—mine didn't."

"I've changed," Sophia said. "Different priorities—my life has purpose—no longer futile."

"Our faith does give us a perspective on what is important in life—you develop wisdom. Compare where you were with where you are now. You make better choices." Anna touched Sophia's arm.

"You came into my life at the right time, Anna."

"His timing worked for both of us." Anna paused at the sidewalk before she followed the brown wreck into the street. "Good. After the light up there, I'll be rid of this nutty driver."

"My life's been filled with hardship—trials. Most of them my own fault," Sophia said. "You've helped my resolve, to be content in tough times … to be thankful and mindful of God."

Anna stomped on the brake. "Oh! No!" She pushed herself off the steering wheel and checked on her passenger.

Sophia scrambled to right herself.

Steamed, Anna jumped out to confront the driver.

The battle-ax in a purple t-shirt with butch-cut hair swung her fleshy arm and slapped the rear bumper. "What're you doing, you little twerp? I just bought this car and now you've trashed it."

Anna forced herself not to speak her mind. The car had been trashed before this. She saw dents or scratches, but those didn't appear fresh. Red tape covered a broken taillight. The front of her minivan had no damage. The license plate had been creased, but Matt could fix it.

"Lady, can't you talk?" The nose ring was larger than her nose.

"We're blocking traffic." Anna spun away from the obnoxious woman's face. "Let's exchange insurance information and get out of the way."

"Oh—" The driver grabbed the back of her neck. "I need a doctor." She held her neck and plopped her forehead on the roof of the brown car, moaning. "You've made me late to work—I'll get fired."

"Good grief." Anna rushed to her van, grabbed a copy of her proof of insurance card and wrote her phone number on the back. She said to Sophia, "This isn't going well."

The Amazon had her insurance information ready when Anna returned. Holding one hand on the back of her neck, and with a grimace on her face, the woman exchanged slips of paper and said, "My attorney will be in touch."

Fuming, Anna summoned self-control and stomped back to her minivan. She sped around the other car as the woman shouted and made obscene gestures.

"Sorry for the delay." Anna extended her hand. "You upset? Why'd you hide your face when she screamed at us in your window?"

"Not upset." Sophia shifted to face forward. "I didn't want her to see me. I met her in jail—Hazel Humphries."

"Oh, my. What was she in for? Murder?"

"No. I think identity theft or check fraud. I stayed away from her. She threw her weight around."

"I experienced some of that."

◆◆◆

"My, you are a good detective." Marion Walters jumped up to greet Matt. "I just read Darla's message." She raised her cell phone. "Says you're on the way over here to find me."

"I have. The union mob sure messed us up today."

"You don't know the half of it. Here, have a seat." Marion Walters moved to the end of the bench. "Darla says they're still out front. We'll talk here."

"They rally out there a lot?" Matt settled beside her.

"Not a big group like today, just a handful usually. But they always harass the crews I send out to gather signatures."

"Must be hard to get signatures. What do they do?" He leaned back with hands in his jacket pockets.

"Usually shouting, name calling—some have thrown hot coffee and splashed our petitions. One guy ran up and scribbled on some pages filled with signatures. They know Elections won't take petitions that are defaced." She tucked the cell phone in her blazer pocket.

"Unions must be against free speech." Matt scanned the youthful crowd on the steps. "Can we talk about Tom Duffy?"

Marion's eyes flashed with anger as she studied him. "Unions support their—free speech. You disagree with them, they'll silence you, if they can..." She paused and lowered her eyes. "...Silenced Tom."

Matt slipped his hands from his pockets and leaned forward with elbows on his knees. "Take it you think union's behind his death?" He cast her a glance.

"I talked with Lucille." Marion crossed her legs and pressed her hand over the crease in her slacks. "I can't prove it, but they wanted to shut him up. They've been doing all they can to stop my petition drive."

"How could your petition fail?" Matt straightened and shifted sideways to make eye contact. "Could they do that?"

"There are three ways my drive can fail. I don't get enough signatures, I withdraw the petition, or all three Chief Petitioners resign or die." Her eyes locked on his, "I'm the last Chief Petitioner, Mr. Kinler."

The determination and intensity in her eyes drew Matt to her cause. He nodded. "Tom was one of your petitioners. What happened to the other one?

"She's a CPA." Her eyes followed the crowd as adults and young students milled around on the steps. "Divorced, single mother with three teenagers at home. When the telephone threats started, day and night, she resigned." She shook her head slowly as she fixed her eyes in front of the bench. "I don't blame her—she has a lot to lose." Marion thrust her chin out and glanced at him, eyes narrowed. "I'm eighty-five. I have a bad heart." She touched her chest. "I've got nothing to lose."

"Could I replace Tom as a Chief Petitioner?"

"Too late. After the petition cover and signature sheets have been approved for circulation, we can't add Chief Petitioners. At least one of the original Chief Petitioners must remain throughout the process." She raised her hands.

"What if something happened to you?"

"They'd dump the whole thing and someone would have to start all over—another two-year delay."

"You need to have protection."

"I do. Mr. Browning." A twinkle in her eyes as she pulled her blazer open for Matt to catch a glimpse of the gun in her shoulder holster.

Chapter 8

"Counselor!" The circuit court judge hammered his gavel. "The jury will disregard." He peered at the bailiff over thick-framed glasses. "Escort the jurors to the jury room." To the attorneys, he said, "Gentlemen. My chambers." The judge spun his chair and stormed from the courtroom. The scolded prosecutor led defense counsel through the door to meet with the judge.

Allen remained at the end of the table near the defendant. Without jail coveralls, Hershel Timms appeared civil in a too roomy sport coat and his hair combed. Tattoos defaced his neck and hands. Allen didn't understand tattoos. Some professional wrestlers wore tattoos when he was in the game, but the practice had no appeal to him.

He studied the back of Hershel's left hand. "What're those lines on the back of your hand and down your fingers?"

"Flames." Hershel showed both hands. "Not done yet. When I get a chance he's going to add red and yellow colors inside the outline." A prominent forehead over deep-set, pale eyes and a grin with missing teeth diminished his first impression. In talks with Hershel, Allen had been underwhelmed.

"Don't let the judge see those." He tapped the table beside the man's wrist. "And don't paint the flames until after the trial." Allen had no compelling interest to help Hershel, but the man hadn't shown the sense needed to help himself.

Hershel cocked his head to study Allen with a puzzled expression. After a moment, the puzzled face faded into a slight grin. "Ohh, I get it."

"I hope you do." Allen leaned back. His eyes lingered on the wall clock behind the judge's bench. The trial recessed before eleven o'clock in the middle of the prosecutor's opening. The court clerk shuffled papers at her desk. A deputy, arms crossed, waited against the wall.

He wondered if Hershel ever had a chance at life. Allen remembered his rough childhood. A father he'd never known. A mother who didn't care for him. His grandfather told him she had a sick mind. After college, a social worker helped Allen in an unsuccessful search for her. They found his mother's trail in and out of institutions, in and out of the state, but no mom.

He loved his grandpa, but lost him due to complications caused by diabetes. Dumped in foster care at eight, his anger raged. With daily arguments and fights, he was headed nowhere good. Murphy rescued him in elementary school. Warm tingles rippled in Allen's neck and back as he smiled at the memory.

A burly math teacher, Murphy also coached for a youth wrestling league. Every day after school he worked Allen and the other boys to the point of exhaustion. Allen remembered how he'd arrive for class each morning too tired to make trouble. The sport channeled his anger and taught him self-control.

During his last year in college, Allen had won the league's heavyweight championship. Murphy, God rest his soul, had cheered for him in the stands.

The most influential people in his life had always been men—a grandfather, Murphy and Matt. His early experiences with women made him uneasy around the fairer sex. The relationship between Matt and Anna had introduced him to what could be and then he met Beth.

The attorneys hurried back into the courtroom ahead of the judge, who reached the bench as the bailiff called, "All rise." A clap of the gavel and the court adjourned for an early lunch. The deputy ushered Hershel out of the courtroom.

"Win or lose?" Allen scooted his chair to face Lloyd Faire, his client and Hershel's defense attorney.

"We won this round." Faire organized papers on the table and stuffed them into a worn leather briefcase. "The Deputy DA got a royal tongue lashing. After the judge ruled to keep priors out, he thought the prosecutor had tried to hint at a prior history and plant the idea in the jurors' heads."

"He might have." Allen had investigated the details of Hershel's prior arson arrest as he prepared for this trial. Before Hershel had been fired for theft in the State's motor pool, he had torched a supervisor's personal truck. Because his co-workers also hated the supervisor, they gave Hershel an alibi. The Grand Jury dumped the circumstantial case.

"Probably won't matter," Faire said. "The judge pressed the prosecutor to finish the State's case this afternoon."

"He's cracking the whip." Allen followed Faire out of the courtroom.

He activated his cell phone as he entered the hallway. Outside on the street he checked for messages as he headed for the car. Seated behind the wheel he grabbed his sack lunch and tapped the number for Beth.

Small talk had become comfortable for him. When they ventured into topics of their future Allen locked up, lost for words. He'd never told anyone, but he feared rejection. Maybe a legacy left by his mother.

Parked on a street, beside the courthouse, Allen nibbled on a sandwich and people-watched as he told his lady friend of the trial.

"Whoa, wait a minute." Across the landscaped grounds, Allen studied a driver in a truck parked in front of the courthouse.

"Something wrong?" Beth asked.

"No. I think I recognize somebody, but he's nearly a block away. Need him to move—yeah. Remember the waiter up at Marion Forks I told you about?"

"Yes."

"He's here." The stiff-legged gait made Gerard Crum easy to spot.

Allen noted the Dodge pickup Crum left and watched the young man use the handicap ramp to enter the courthouse. He finished his call and lunch before he hustled over to write down the license plate number on the truck. Time didn't allow him to search for Crum because he had to get back to Hershel's trial.

Delayed by a cluster of people at the security gate, Allen missed the resumption of the prosecutor's opening statement to the jury. Inside the door, he paused to pick up the rhythm of the courtroom.

Spectators in the gallery concentrated on the speaker rather than notice him. Two rows behind Hershel, Allen spotted a familiar profile. When the prosecutor stopped for a drink of water Allen hurried down the aisle and moved behind the defense table to his chair. He glanced back into the audience as he settled to confirm his suspicion.

"The defendant admits he set the fire." The prosecutor had moved from the podium into the well and faced the jury. "The evidence in this case will prove Hershel Timms set the fire with the intent to kill the owner in his sleep."

Faire gathered his notes to speak as the prosecutor cleared papers from the podium. Allen seized the moment to tear a page from his notebook. He scrawled "Gerard Crum" and slid the paper on the table in front of the defendant.

Hershel flinched recognition and questioned Allen with his eyes.

Allen leaned close and whispered. "Do you know him?"

With a nod he whispered, "His brother was in jail with me."

"What's the brother's name?"

"Richard Crum."

◆◆◆

"How many more signatures do you need?" Matt leaned against the backrest and scanned the mob of middle-school students as they yelled and romped on the steps in front of the Capitol building. He picked out a handful of chaperones based on height and vigilant eyes.

"Don't know exactly. Maybe thirty, forty thousand." Marion studied her cell phone screen.

"Can you get that many by the deadline? July, isn't it?"

"Easy, if the unions would leave us alone. They won't—so it'll be close."

"Too bad you have to put up with all the harassment."

Marion crossed her legs and gazed toward the tops of the fir trees that towered above the far side of the building. "I, and my late husband before me, have worked to get different measures on the ballot for a long time. It's a lot harder now than when he was alive."

"Why's it harder?"

"Liberal politicians and their union backers. They don't want us common folk to make policy through the initiative process. Don't like voters passing laws. Almost every session they add or change the rules we have to follow to get a measure on the ballot."

"Are you through the worst part?"

"No, just the hardest. We had to get the Secretary of State and the Department of Justice to approve a title for our measure. That's the one printed on the ballot. We filed our paperwork and offered our suggested title—'Abolish Mandatory Union Membership.' After they finished, the title changed— 'Modification to Union Membership Rules.' We sued to have it revised and lost in court. They've got the deck stacked against any proposal from conservatives."

"Title alone doesn't tell a voter much."

"That's the point. Unfortunately, most voters are too busy with their own lives and don't do much research. If they're confused or don't know what a measure on the ballot would do, they'll just vote no."

"Swimming upstream the whole time." On the far side of the stairs, several boys caught Matt's attention as they jockeyed for position to take selfies in front of the large relief sculpture of Lewis and Clark with Sacagawea.

"After the title battle," Marion said, "we have to endure the worst stage, with all the union threats, taunts and harassment. Then, once we meet the deadline and turn in our signatures we have to watch them disqualify hundreds—thousands of signatures on technicalities. I try to turn in a lot more than we need—thousands more."

Three men descended the steps from the entrance of the State Capitol. Two men abreast wore dark business suits. A third, built like a football linebacker, followed, dressed in a black leather blazer and dark trousers. The animated conversation between the suits calmed as they faced each other near the front of the relief sculpture and a short distance from the schoolboys. The short, stocky suited man passed his briefcase to the taller, slender man as they talked.

The leather clad man jumped forward to assist the shorter man light a large cigar. A cloud of smoke billowed and hung above their heads. "Do you recognize those men in front of Lewis and Clark?" Matt asked.

"Hmm, don't think—wait the taller man in the suit is the House Speaker's Chief of Staff. I don't know the others."

The boys began to chant, but Matt couldn't understand their words. The linebacker with a shaved head stepped forward and scowled as he spoke to the students.

"Guy talking to the kids. He's a bodyguard."

"How do you know?" Marion asked.

"Trust me—I know."

Matt spotted a boy's hand shoot above his classmates' heads. The hand appeared to wave a cell phone.

The blocky man lurched toward the boys as they fled and fanned out running from their pursuer. A boy in a dark green windbreaker headed straight for one of the school buses. The pursuer closed on the boy until a woman half the size of the linebacker jumped in his path and screamed, "Stop."

Blocked, the boy hidden, the bus driver stationed in the door, the bodyguard retreated to his employer.

Matt's eyes tracked the three men near the sculpture. After a quick exchange, the Chief of Staff retreated up into the Capitol building with the briefcase. The short suit and bodyguard headed for a black luxury sedan, too far away for Matt to identify.

"I'll be right back." He hustled out to the curb and arrived in time to see the large, black Mercedes sedan with blacked out windows pass. Matt noted the license and returned to the bench.

"Why are you interested in those guys?"

"No reason. Just curious. Good to know the major players around here." Matt settled on the bench.

Chapter 9

Matt spotted the familiar boy with the dark green windbreaker in a line of students. Chaperones zigzagged like sheep dogs to organize students to board the buses. He sprang from the bench.

The lad laughed and joked with classmates as they waited in line. Matt approached. "Hi young man." The boy stood just under five feet tall. "I saw that man chase you over there." Hands in his pockets, Matt tipped his head toward Lewis and Clark. "What was that all about?"

"Nothing really." The boy squinted and displayed braces as he grinned. "We yelled, 'cancer, cancer' at the man with the cigar. The big guy said, to shut up." The boy showed Matt his cell phone. "I got their picture and the cigar guy shouted, 'Get the picture!' We ran."

"Can you show me?"

The pint-sized boy worked with his phone and displayed the image for Matt.

"There a problem here, Sammy?" The shouter's name tag read "Mrs. Marple, Seventh Grade."

"No problem," Matt said. "I just asked him why the man chased him and his friends."

"Well, that's my job, Mr. ah…"

"Kinler, Matt Kinler." He faced the boy. "By the way—Sammy, could you e-mail that picture to me? I'll give you ten bucks."

"What are you, some kind of pervert?" Marple forced herself between Matt and Sammy. "Do you have any identification?"

Matt displayed identification as a private investigator and handed her his business card. "Please, calm down, I just want a copy of the picture he took of those men."

"Excuse me." Marion had followed Matt and witnessed the teacher's alarm. "Mr. Kinler is my assistant. We'd like a copy of the child's photo. If you're uncomfortable sending it to Mr. Kinler, send it to me."

Marple studied the diminutive, silver haired lady and eased away from Matt. "Well, I suppose that'd be okay." She aimed her forefinger at the boy's phone, "But—just that one, Sammy. None with you or your classmates."

Transaction completed, and Sammy ten dollars richer, Matt left with Marion at his side.

"Can I walk you back to your office?" Matt asked.

"Delighted. Darla sent a text. The demonstration's wrapped up over there."

◆◆◆

Allen fought to keep his eyes open as the trial droned into the afternoon. He slipped a pen from his pocket and doodled in his notebook to stay awake. The prosecutor rescued him when the next witness entered the courtroom. Through the gallery and into the well, Hershel's intended victim strode up near the bench ready to be sworn.

Baxter Bauer adjusted the microphone as he settled into the chair on the witness stand. Middle-aged, with a full head of dark hair and wire-framed glasses, he responded to the prosecutor's questions. With Bauer's answers he was introduced to the jury.

A lobbyist for twenty years, Bauer and his family lived in their primary residence near Portland. During annual legislative sessions, he often stayed alone in a second house they owned in south Salem.

"Mr. Bauer." The Deputy DA referred to notes on the podium. "I want to take you back to February 27th last year when you had a fire in your Salem house. Were you inside when the fire started?"

"Yes. The downstairs family room, asleep in my recliner."

"Do you remember what time it was when you discovered the fire?"

"Not the exact time, but I'd guess between three and four in the morning. Three-thirty maybe."

"Do you normally sleep in the recliner?"

"No—not usually." Bauer glanced toward the jury and shifted in the chair. "When the legislature is in session there's a lot of pressure—stress. I have a hard time sleeping and I also suffer from acid reflux. My restless nights are part of the reason my wife stays in Portland."

"You've been lobbying twenty years." The prosecutor stepped away from the podium and faced the jury. "Has lobbying always been stressful?"

"N—No, just the last three or four years."

"What has made your job stressful in recent years?"

Faire jumped to his feet. "Objection! Not relevant, Your Honor."

"Overruled." The judge tapped the gavel. "The witness may answer."

Bauer leaned toward the microphone and cleared his throat. "Threats. I've received threats, night and day."

"Can you identify who made those threats?"

"No. All anonymous, some by mail, notes posted on my door, but most by phone."

"Do you know why you've been threatened?" The Deputy DA returned to the podium.

"The people threatening want me to stop lobbying for right-to-work legislation."

"If you don't stop, what do they threaten to do?"

"Objection, Your Honor." Faire remained seated. "No relevance to charges against my client."

"Overruled. Continue." The judge rocked back in his chair.

"Until the fire last year, I didn't know." Bauer glanced at the jury. "Always said they'd get me, never specific."

The prosecutor introduced a telephone threat Bauer had recorded on his answering machine. The judge allowed the recording to be played for the jury and the audience.

"If you know what's good for you and your family, stop the right-to-work bill. Pull it or you'll be sorry. Support union workers—not scabs. Stop or we'll get you."

Allen forced himself to remain placid as he heard the familiar voice. The threat, the words—all similar to those recorded on Tom Duffy's answering machine.

"Do you know who is responsible for these threats?"

"No. Not the person, but it has to be someone connected with unions."

"Objection!" Faire flew out of his chair as the witness completed his statement. "Opinion, Your Honor. There's no evidence of union involvement."

"Sustained." The judge tapped the gavel. "Jury will disregard reference to the union. The record will show the witness does not know the identity of the person who has made the threats."

The prosecutor leafed through his notes. "Mr. Bauer, on the night of the fire, were you ever in the upstairs bedroom?"

"Yes, I turned the lights out and went to bed after the eleven o'clock news. But my indigestion flared up and kept me awake. Around midnight, I went downstairs. Helps me to be upright in the recliner."

"Did you turn the lights on when you went downstairs?"

"I don't think so—usually don't."

"What alerted you to the fire?"

"The sound of breaking glass woke me. I ran out of the family room and heard more glass break upstairs. From the bottom step I could see light flicker on walls upstairs, like from flames. That's when I smelled smoke. I grabbed my cell phone and ran outside."

"Did you see anyone?"

"I thought I saw someone running away, but it was too dark."

"Your witness." The prosecutor left the podium to allow for cross-examination.

Faire remained behind the table for the defense as he stood. "Mr. Bauer, do you know the defendant?" He motioned for Hershel to stand.

"No."

"Have you ever talked to Mr. Timms?"

"No. I don't believe so."

"Has Mr. Timms ever threatened you?"

"No. I don't believe so."

"The defense has no further questions, Your Honor."

Next, a Salem neighbor of Bauer's testified of her observations on the morning before the fire. On a dog walk, she observed a pickup with lawn maintenance equipment at Bauer's house. It wasn't the normal day, and it was a different man and truck, so she wrote down the license plate number. She didn't recognize Hershel seated at the table for the defense.

Motor vehicle registration records, introduced as evidence by the prosecutor, listed Hershel as the registered owner. Allen peeked at the plate number he took from Crum's truck—the same. He glanced back into the gallery. Gerard had left.

Allen resumed doodling as the crime scene investigator worked with the prosecutor to introduce evidence recovered. Routine stuff for an arson fire until they introduced items found in the crawl space. Propane tank, five-gallon container of gas, timer and dynamite grabbed his attention. Allen stopped the doodles.

"And how long had this bomb been under the house?"

"We were unable to determine that, but not a long time—no dust."

"Was the device set to explode?"

"Yes. Three a.m. on Thursday, February 27 last year."

"Were you able to determine why the device failed to detonate?"

"Yes. A defective igniter."

"You testified earlier of the Molotov cocktails used to set the room upstairs on fire that night. Why didn't the heat and flames cause this propane bomb to explode?"

"A little luck. The firefighters suppressed the fire in the second floor bedroom before the heat and flames reached the device under the house."

"Refer to the diagram of the floor plan on the easel." The prosecutor grabbed a pointer and moved closer to the exhibit. "Where under the first floor was this bomb located?"

"The bomb had been placed directly under the base of the stairs."

The Deputy DA tapped the pointer on the spot in the diagram for the jurors. "Do you attach any significance to the location?"

"Whoever placed the bomb intended to block anyone from getting out alive."

"Objection!" Faire jumped to his feet. "Your Honor, please strike. Opinion, not evidence."

"Sustained. Strike—jury will disregard."

The latent fingerprint examiner didn't help the defense. He testified that Hershel's palm and fingerprints were found on parts of the propane bomb.

Allen scribbled a note as a reminder to check on how often the cops find propane bombs in Oregon.

Chapter 10

"Watch out! They'll eat you," Matt said.

"Ha, I'm too old and tough." Allen shut the car door and stooped to tussle ears on the greeters.

Matt left his Adirondack chair and leaned on the porch rail. "You're early."

"I wanted to go over some things before I meet Beth for lunch." Allen climbed the steps.

"Take Anna's chair. I'll get you a mug for coffee."

"Little chilly for sunbathing."

"Yeah, but sunny and dry. Keep your coat on."

When he returned Allen had a lap full of terriers. "Enough guys." Matt shooed the dogs before he settled in his chair.

"Where's the wife?"

"Ran into Lyons. Do some errands—pick up mail."

"To think, people pay for forest smells in a package and you have them au naturel." Allen inhaled deeply as he held the mug against his chest and gazed out across the canyon. "If I lived here, not sure you'd see me in town much."

"We love to sit out here. Our sanctuary." Matt swept his hand across their panorama. "This stand of old fir trees gives us privacy while we enjoy this great view."

"Anna could start a business—design cedar homes like yours."

"Don't give her ideas." Matt stuck a thumb back over his shoulder. "Besides, the river rock chimney's my idea."

"Okay." Allen drank from his mug. "You said you had an appointment today."

"Yeah, the lobbyist in Lake Oswego—wanna go?"

"Can't. The jury's out and I'm on a one-hour leash."

"Finally caught up with the trucker who found Duffy." Matt hoisted the carafe from the table between their chairs. "He called from a truck stop near Pendleton, I think he said."

"Did he tell you anything interesting?" Allen offered his mug. "Just a warm-up."

"Nothing about the accident we haven't heard. But, something curious." Matt enjoyed the warmth as he gripped the mug. "He remembered a snowplow headed toward Detroit before he arrived at Duffy's accident. Estimated the plow to be a quarter mile from where the truck went into the river. Hard for him to believe the driver didn't see anything and stop."

"Hard for me too. Was the plow damaged?" Allen asked.

"Only got a glimpse. Lots of curves up there—too dark."

Allen sipped. "Too bad you didn't get to sit in on the trial."

"Yeah, wished I could've heard the recording the lobbyist made of the threats."

"Matt, I'm convinced the voice is the same as the one on Duffy's tape."

"Maybe the lobbyist has a copy I can borrow. Don't think we want to ask the union lawyer to rummage through his discovery material."

"Yeah, probably not a good idea."

"After we talked about your trial, it got me thinking." Matt sipped from the mug. "Hershel set the bomb under the house and the igniter failed. Do you think the Molotov cocktails were part of the original plan or did he put them together when the bomb sputtered?"

"If you knew Hershel, you wouldn't ask." Allen stared out across the canyon. "He's not smart enough to think in terms of back-up plans."

"Whoever put him up to it must have."

Allen said, "I can't prove this, but somebody sent him with a plan to make sure no one survived. They told him where to place the bomb under the bottom of the stairs and gave him the cocktails to block the upstairs windows with fire."

"Cold, partner. Hershel must have no conscience."

"Whoever sent him has no conscience. I'm not sure Hershel has the cognitive skill to realize the implications of what he did. To him, if he followed instructions, he'd get money. Simple as that."

"Pathetic. Not the first time an evil guy finds a simpleton to do his bidding." Matt shook his head. "Depressing. Let's change the subject. I talked with my Yamhill deputy friend. Told him how your defendant put his bomb together. He's sure the bombs used to blow up Delbert's house had a similar design."

"Except for one thing," Allen said. "Hershel's didn't work."

"Good point. Like you say, Hershel's not ready for prime time." Matt swigged the last of his coffee. "Shoot, only two out of three of his fire bombs hit windows and he was probably right under them."

"If you'd met him, you'd know he's not big league," Allen said. "I told you I'd do some research. I discovered we don't have a lot of bombings around here. In recent years, only these two incidents combined propane with gasoline and dynamite."

"There's some connection between Delbert, the lobbyist, and Duffy." Matt said. "Same type bomb used at the filbert farm and the Salem house. Same caller threatened Duffy and the lobbyist."

"Hershel's the only one we've identified and there's nothing to connect him to Duffy or Delbert." Allen poured a refill. "But we do have Gerard Crum driving Hershel's truck and he made the last call to Duffy."

Matt said. "And Hershel and Gerard's brother were in jail together—Richard's his name."

"Too many moving parts to make sense of things," Allen said.

"At least we got parts now." At the sound of tires on gravel, Matt left his chair and waved to Anna from the handrail. The dogs scrambled down the stairs into the yard. Anna parked her minivan beside Allen's car.

"Allen—before you go." Matt glanced back over his shoulder. "I have a license plate for you to run down."

"Where from?"

"A big, fancy, black Mercedes. Keep forgetting to give it to you."

Anna stomped up the stairs, arms full of purse and mail. The dogs cued on her mood and stayed clear. On the porch, she greeted Allen as she fished a letter out for Matt. "Read this while I take my stuff inside."

Matt leaned with his back to the rail as he read. "We're being sued. Damage to the car, loss of wages and medical expenses."

"You don't seem surprised," Allen said.

"Nope. Not from the way Anna described the accident."

"I am so mad!" Anna marched out of the house. "Our insurance company wants to settle." She snatched the letter from Matt.

"Did you talk to our agent?" Matt asked.

"Yeah, he's the one who told me."

"When was that?"

"Ten minutes ago—on my way from the post office."

"While driving? Hope you had your seatbelt on."

"Matt." She swatted his arm with the letter. "Stop teasing, I'm not in the mood for your dumb humor."

"Did our agent have a settlement figure?"

"Thirty-four thousand."

"Little over half of the fifty-nine in the suit," Matt said.

"Insurance companies always want to settle," Allen said.

"It's not right, Allen." She put her arms around Matt. "What are you going to do about this?"

"Me? What can I do?"

"Fight them. This is so wrong." Anna stepped away and ticked off figures on her fingertips. "She'd get five thousand for a piece-of-junk car, four thousand for a nothing job—she's an ex-con for crying out loud. On top of that, twenty-five thousand medical for a fake injury."

"Remember, lawyers get their cut. She'll only realize about three grand," Allen said.

"Still six times what her destruction derby car's worth." She fixed her eyes on Matt. "Fight this Matt—find a way!"

"Don't know what I can do. The insurance company's in the driver's seat on this."

Anna moved to Matt's Adirondack and slumped back. Eddy jumped on her lap.

"This reminds me of a guy I met sometime back," Allen said. "He was a fraud investigator for NICB."

"What's NICB?" Anna asked.

"National Insurance Crime Bureau, an organization funded by insurance companies. I'd forgotten about them." Matt bent over to grab his mug and poured a refill.

"Do you think he could help?" Anna asked.

"Not sure," Allen said. "I know they work insurance fraud cases with the cops. Maybe he'd have a suggestion for us. I met him when I had a wealthy client who bought a Lamborghini. Turned out to be stolen and the seller had vanished. This investigator had a sting going with the cops to break up the car theft ring."

"Did they?" Matt asked.

"I think they did, but it didn't help my client—he lost the car and a lot of cash."

"Maybe I should call this insurance investigator. We have all the information on Anna's accident and our policy stuff," Matt said.

"I've got his number at the office. I'll text you." Allen pried himself out of the chair. "I need to go or I'll be late for lunch."

"If I need you when I'm up in Lake Oswego, will you be available?"

"Yeah, as long as I can help while I'm on jury watch." Allen stopped at the bottom of the stairs. "By the way, I ran Hazel's plate. Uses the last name, Boyd, and had an address off I-5 near that amusement park south of town. Google shows some kind of RV campground there."

"Good to have when we need to chase her down."

Matt settled in Anna's chair. The sound of Allen's car in the driveway faded. "Guess I better get going too. I'll need three hours for my roundtrip, plus time with Bauer."

"The boys and I'll wait dinner," Anna said.

"I shouldn't be too late."

"Matt, I sure hope the insurance guy can help us stop Hazel from cashing in on fake accidents."

"Me too. I'm as upset as you about this, but I'm not going to get my hopes up. Insurance companies invite these little scams. They'd rather settle claims they think are small so they don't spend money on lawyers and time in court. Attorneys who represent the Hazels of the world recognize easy money, snag the small claims and negotiate settlements."

"But Hazel's accident's a sham."

"She's either hoodwinked an attorney or she's hooked up with a crooked one. I've heard of insurance frauds where they have a network of tow companies, body shops, doctors, lawyers, all in cahoots."

"Matt, we have to do something."

Chapter 11

Dead-end street, fourth on the left, Matt stopped against the closed gate in the driveway entrance. The short driveway to the gate left the back of his truck in the street. He glanced both ways for traffic. As instructed, Matt called Baxter Bauer.

Privacy slats woven in the chain link gate and fence combined with trees and bushes to conceal the house and property from view. Without directions, the house would've been hard to find. The street had no sidewalks. Overgrown rhododendrons lined the curb in front of the fence. Other properties along the narrow street had manicured yards, mailboxes and house numbers, but not the Bauers'. A "Keep Out" sign hung on the gate beside alarm company warnings. Not what he expected at a Lake Oswego address.

Bauer in jeans, tan polo shirt and sneakers held the gate open long enough for Matt to drive inside and park behind a dark gray subcompact. The pale green, single story bungalow had a gable roof. The dwelling had the same fifty-plus-year appearance as neighboring properties, but it needed more attention.

"We can talk inside, Mr. Kinler. The wife took our three kids on a field trip to OMSI, the science museum, this afternoon. We're homeschoolers."

In the house, Bauer used his foot to clear a path through the toys and removed children's books from an overstuffed chair. "Have a seat. Sorry for the mess."

"Your classroom?" Matt asked as he sat.

"Classroom, living room, family room, you name it." Bauer cleared space in a wingback chair. "This was supposed to be temporary until the builder finished our Salem house."

"Pretty tight quarters for a family of five. Don't mind me asking—what changed?"

"Long story." Bauer wiped his forehead and brushed fingers back through his hair. "The short version—union antics."

"Do we have time for the long version?" Matt asked.

"I'm not sure where to start." Bauer leaned back. "I had an uncle who'd been a lobbyist for a long time. When I enrolled in college he gave me a job in his Salem office. After graduation, I stayed and he mentored me. I ... I took over his business after he passed away." He cleared his throat. "My aunt and uncle had no children ... treated me as a son." Bauer shifted in the chair and crossed his legs. "They were wealthy and owned a lot of property around here. When my aunt passed away, I inherited this place—all their holdings."

"Did you inherit the Salem house?" Matt asked.

"No. My wife befriended a group of mothers who home school down there. We bought the property and found a builder. That was about four years ago." He tossed his hands.

"Builder finish on time?"

Bauer nodded, "He wasn't the problem. The trouble began when a client retained me to lobby for the passage of a right-to-work law. Almost overnight, activists from the public employees' union targeted my family and me. Telephone threats started, night and day, and demonstrators marched in front of my home.

"A nightmare, Mr. Kinler—absolute nightmare. My wife packed up the kids and moved across town to her parents. Put our nice, big house near the country club on the market—sold within a week. But, my wife wouldn't move to Salem until the union harassment stopped."

"How'd you end up here?"

"My in-laws live in a gated community so the demonstrators didn't bother them much—stood around the entrance with signs sometimes. I had this place, and property records list my uncle's trust as the owner. We didn't want to burden her folks too long so we moved here. Crowded, but I have a security system and the unions haven't found us yet." He wrapped knuckles to the side of his head. "The trust pays utilities and we use cell phones."

"All for right-to-work laws—quite a hardship on you—and your wife."

"Mr. Kinler—" His eyes narrowed as he fixed on Matt. "I believe this is one of the most important public policy issues of our time—corruption of our representative form of government."

"Union membership?"

"Not union membership in private businesses; the problem comes from power wielded by public employee unions."

"What's the difference?"

"When unions negotiate wages and benefits with a private employer two sides are at the table, the employer, who pays, and the employees' union rep. When public employee unions negotiate, there are also two sides, the public employees' union and some faceless government manager. The taxpayer, who pays the bill for any agreement, has no voice."

"But we elect politicians to our state legislature, city and county governments, school districts and so on. Don't they have a say?" Matt asked.

"Sure, but they're either corrupted, bullied or intimidated by the unions. You've heard the saying about money being the 'mother's milk of politics.' Well, the public employees' unions have mega gallons of milk. All from the mandatory union dues paid by public employees.

"If an elected politician opposes any union effort, unions will turn on the politician. They won't support a reelection effort and usually help an opponent."

"Hardball politics," Matt said.

"More than that, Mr. Kinler. They don't stop with winning at the ballot box. They launch seek and destroy campaigns against anyone they view as a threat. A friend of mine had become effective at putting initiatives on the ballot that would have limited union power or reduced taxes. Union operatives in and out of government dogged him until they put him in jail on tax charges."

"As complicated as tax laws are, that'd be easy to do," Matt said.

"Lots of stories of how unions destroyed people's lives out there. The unions and their allies will wreck a person financially, file criminal charges or regulate them out of business. A guy told me about a dairy farmer ruined by regulations on his cow poop. And there's another story about a logger who had been bankrupted by lawsuits over muddy water runoff from his logging roads."

"That's one way to staunch criticism—silence the critic," Matt said.

Bauer nodded. "Think about this. Probably ninety-nine percent of public employee union campaign money goes to Democrats—more liberal the better. Over the years a giant money-laundering machine has evolved. The Democrats vote the way the unions want them to vote. Then the money pours into their party's campaign coffers."

"The voters' voice gets drowned out in the shuffle," Matt said.

"Way back in time, FDR opposed public employee unions. He said it would cause the situation we have today. One of the few times he was right."

"You've worked with these union issues. Do you think someone orchestrates the union decisions on who they want to silence?"

"Hard to believe there's no coordination. I have no proof, but I think there is one puppet master for unions in this state. Whoever controls the unions holds any Democrat by the throat."

"Do you have a name for this puppet master?"

"No." Bauer cleared his throat. "I've got a hunch—he or she has a connection with Leach, Philcher and Hannibal."

"The law firm?" Matt waited for confirmation. "Do you work with Marion Walters?"

"No, but we talk. She tries to get the law changed through the ballot box; I try to get the legislature to make the change." Bauer crossed his arms. "You know she's in their crosshairs."

"Figures." Matt shifted in the chair to restore circulation to his numb leg. "Have you heard about Tom Duffy?"

"A shame, real shame." Bauer uncrossed his arms.

"Did you know he had phone threats too?"

"No. No, I didn't."

"My partner has heard your recording and Duffy's. He thinks the same person made the threats."

"Interesting, because I've heard that voice before, but I can't place where or who."

"If you heard Duffy's calls, think you'd remember?"

"Maybe."

"How about I trade a copy of Duffy's calls for a copy of yours."

"Deal."

◆◆◆

The following morning, Matt rocked in the swivel chair beside his rented desk. "Thought about what Bauer told me all the way home last night. Some 'Mr. Big' pulls the strings in this state. Possible, but hard to believe."

Allen tapped the keyboard and studied his desktop monitor. "Leach, Philcher and Hannibal, LLP has been around Oregon a long time. Offices in DC and Chicago. Hannibal's active, Leach is a retired senior partner, and Philcher really retired—deceased." He spun to face Matt. "You know I've done work for the firm—for Faire anyway. Never had a clue that the law firm wielded that kind of power."

"They do a lot of union work, you said." Matt swiveled to use the straight-back chair as a footstool.

"True. Faire told me once—most of his clients were union cases. But he's in the Salem office and they've got a ton of attorneys in Portland. He's never said, but I don't think he's happy with his work situation."

"A huge firm, probably a pool of lawyers to call on when they need expertise in any field of law." Matt gazed through the front picture window and beyond his truck. The midmorning traffic trickled by on the one-way street. "How'd be the best way to find out if they've got a puppet master in their closet?"

"Just like we do on our other cases." Allen left his desk and headed for the washroom. "Snoop, muck around, kick tires—wait for a break." He shut the door.

Matt chuckled at his partner's lowbrow description of detective work. That pretty well nailed it, but how could they stir the pot enough to get "Mr. Big" to pop up? He slid his feet to the floor and moved over to the front window.

Allen had purchased the single-story building before they formed their unofficial partnership. With the service counter removed, this section of the former car repair business served as one office space. "Uninspired" was the word Anna used to describe their décor. One round wall clock, an NRA calendar and two framed private eye licenses adorned the white walls. Gray paint on the concrete floor approximated the color of the furniture purchased from the State's surplus property warehouse.

Adjacent and at a right angle to the office stood another single story building with car repair bays. Old asphalt macadam fronted the line of closed garage doors out to the street. The view wasn't great, but Matt had other things on his mind. He'd spent a few hours with Walters. Not once did she mention a big union law firm or conspiracy theories.

Plumbing sounds followed Allen into the office. "I'm ready to see the old gal anytime."

"Me too. I'd like to get her take on what the lobbyist had to say."

Chapter 12

"Keep going—slow. Go to the end of the block, do a 'u-ee' and park on the other side so we can watch." Matt counted seven demonstrators. With signs and union colors, they marched in an oval on the public sidewalk in front of the WIN office.

Allen managed a U-turn and parked beside an old brown compact, across the street but away from the rabble-rousers.

One of the women carried a bullhorn and the rest hoisted signs above their heads. "Patriotic group," Matt said. "I can make out some words on the signs— 'Freedom' 'God given rights' and 'Respect'— harmless enough."

"There's one not so nice—'Scratch scabs now.' There on the end." Allen handed his compact binoculars to Matt.

"One in every crowd." Matt studied the marchers. "None look too happy."

"Maybe they haven't had their 'Happy Meal.'"

"Very clever, partner. Here." He returned the glasses.

An elderly gentleman with a cane arrived and the group parted for him to use the walk to Walter's office. Five minutes later, the senior citizen left the way he came.

"I'd be bored out of my gourd. They'd need to pay me more than they're getting," Allen said.

A stranger bustled past their car on the sidewalk. A knit cap covered all but her face from eyes to chin. In windbreaker, pants and sneakers, she had the stride and movement of a young woman. She held a manila folder or envelope tucked under her arm like a football.

"She's on a mission," Matt said.

Seconds later, the woman darted across the street straight for Marion's office. "Matt, they're going to confront her—watch."

The slam of the car door put a period on Allen's statement. Matt headed for the demonstrators at a fast pace. The picketers closed ranks to block the woman's path. He couldn't hear the exchange, but someone shoved the woman.

"Stop it!" she screamed as she tripped and fell flat on her back in the grass strip. Papers in her folder spilled. "Stop! Help!"

"Get back!" Matt ordered. He knelt. "Are you hurt, Miss?"

She pushed herself into a sitting position. "You had no right!"

"Wait. I'm not with them. Let me help you up."

Her face froze; with terror in her eyes, she focused behind him.

Matt spun. One demonstrator stomped the papers scattered on the ground. "Enough!" Matt sprang, shoved the man and prepared to fend off the others. No takers.

The woman had regained her folder and crawled about collecting her pages.

Matt joined her. "Do you have a name, Miss?"

She raised her head. "Nancy." Tears trickled down her cheeks.

"I'm Matt. I'll take you inside."

"All my work." She sat back on her heels and wiped at the muddy smudges. "Ruined." Silent as tears continued.

Matt reached for her arm and eased Nancy to her feet. He straightened the collection of papers, but she jerked them away and tucked the papers back under her arm.

Matt escorted her toward Marion's office. A large man in a purple shirt blocked their way. Feet spread, muscled arms crossed, he sneered down at Matt and his new friend.

"No scab lovers here."

"We're not here to make trouble."

"She's made trouble. Assaulted one of my people."

"Not the way I saw it," Matt said. He could feel her tug on his sleeve.

"We all saw her, Bully!" A voice from the demonstrators.

"Liars!" Allen's voice boomed from the side of the confrontation several yards away. "I got pictures." He waved his Smartphone overhead before he tucked it in his pocket.

"Who're you?" Bully growled. "Another scab lover?"

"No. Just don't like union scum," Allen said.

Bully threw his arms out to silence the low grumble from his followers. His eyes narrowed as he glowered at the challenger.

Matt stuck his arm out to protect Nancy and checked his partner, who jockeyed on the sidewalk in a wrestler's stance.

Bully roared as he rushed headlong at Allen.

Allen neutralized the momentum with skilled footwork and arm strength. The giants grappled in a two-man scrum. Taunts and cheers rose as the small mob shuffled closer. Allen blocked and ducked as Bully flailed with unskilled fists. In a sudden move, Allen gripped Bully and lurched backward.

Cheers erupted from the crowd. Matt froze, unsure which combatant took the brunt of the pile-driving force as they slammed onto the sidewalk. The tangled heap lay quiet and still.

Allen shoved and Bully rolled off onto his back, unconscious, face bloodied.

A large woman in a purple t-shirt rushed from the silent group of demonstrators. "You'll pay for this!" Each word she screamed made the big ring on the end of her nose flop.

Matt hadn't noticed her before. Her size, butch cut and nose ring caught his attention. He slipped the cell phone from his pocket.

The woman shouted orders. Some protesters rushed to aid their fallen leader and others remained stunned, still.

As Allen approached, Matt kept his voice low. "Hurt yourself?"

"Nah. An old move I used a lot in the ring." Allen grimaced as he swung his left arm in a windmill motion. "Not getting younger."

Matt glanced back at Bully Boyd on the ground. "He got the worst of it."

A proud smile flashed on Allen's face. "If I didn't like my opponent, he'd get a face plant on the mat. This guy smeared his face on the concrete."

"Knocked him out."

"Yep, but he'll remember. He's not used to dealing with someone who's not afraid of him."

"Better get inside." Matt tugged on Nancy's arm. "Let's go while they're busy."

The door swung open as they approached. Marion Walters waited inside by her chair. Matt said to Darla, "My partner's with us. Let him in."

The freckles didn't hide the worry in her eyes.

"I can't do this anymore, Marion." Nancy plopped her soiled papers on the end of the director's table.

Marion stepped up and held her close. "I understand. You don't have to—you've done enough already."

Nancy pushed the knit cap away from her eyes and placed a hand on her papers. "I had almost a thousand good signatures." Tears puddled in her eyes. "Ruined … all ruined."

Marion covered Nancy's hand with her own. "We'll see what we can salvage. Use my chair. Something to drink?"

"They're horrible people." Nancy wiped at the moisture on her cheeks as she settled in the director's chair.

"They're gone." Darla moved from the entrance to her workspace.

"This is the way it has been, Mr. Kinler," Marion said. "One thing after another. But we're going to make our goal."

"Do you have lots of folks out?" Matt asked.

"Enough. Darla helped me go through those petitions stacked on her table. Sorted by circulator, two-hundred numbered sheets per stack." Marion swept her hand toward the documents.

"Sounds complicated," Matt said.

Marion's eyes narrowed, "They make it complicated to discourage the common folk. Then the unions come along and make things harder."

"They do." Nancy said. "I have friends who won't do this because of the union harassment."

"Union bosses visit the Director of Elections all the time," Darla blurted.

Startled by Darla's statement, Matt noticed her shrunk behind the computer monitor. "Who were the bosses? Do you have names?" Matt asked.

"I don't." She shook her head. "No … I don't. That's what everybody called them."

"Marion, this reminds me of a question," Matt said. "You ever hear anyone talk of some big shot who controls unions, the Democrats—all of state government?"

"No." Marion smirked. "I've heard lots of conspiracy theories in my life. Don't pay much attention."

"From the number of piles, I'd guess you got about ten thousand here," Allen said.

"Nine thousand twenty-seven. But, after we go through Nancy's, there'll be more." Marion slapped a hand on top of the soiled signature sheets.

"How often do you have to turn in the signatures?" Matt asked.

"Monthly because I use some paid gatherers. Since the break-in, I try not to keep many completed signature sheets laying around in here."

"Do you have a safe?" Matt asked.

"No." She nodded toward Darla. "We box 'em up and put them in the trunk of my car. I store all the boxes in a safe place."

"Why not turn them in now?" Matt asked.

"No. Wish I could wait until the end. The union gets all worked up when they find out how close we're getting—do crazy things."

"So you try to limit the number of times they ramp up the harassment of your people."

"Exactly."

Chapter 13

Dread gripped her. She should have said no. *Hey Darla, just wanna know how they're doing. A little extra money and I'll arrange a good job when it's over.* But it didn't stop there.

She had to have a job, for her daughter, her mother. Second thoughts, regrets accompanied her as she drove into the parking garage under the State Capitol mall. Other single mothers found jobs without the risk and guilt she faced.

A rendezvous in the far reaches of the garage stirred no objection from her. She also wished to avoid discovery, but Herb Fish gave her the creeps.

Since State offices had closed for the day, space to park didn't pose a problem. She punched the door lock of her mother's old sedan as she set the brake. The location gave her a view of approaches. In the dim light, a trickle of pedestrians unlocked cars and drove for the distant exit. The garage closed at seven o'clock, but she hoped to be home by then.

Darla scrunched down in the seat, vigilant. She didn't doubt Fish had connections as Chief of Staff for the House Speaker. During her short time at Elections and through errands to the Secretary of State's office she'd had glimpses of influence peddling. This arrangement with Fish opened her eyes.

Nausea welled in her stomach at the sight of the familiar gray sports car. Make, model—it made no difference to her. She'd heard cars like his cost a lot of money, more than she'd ever have. A supposed middle-aged bachelor, he could afford expensive things. That was an assumption, since he'd never mentioned a wife or family.

Before he opened the door, she cleared the passenger side and stuffed her coat and purse in the back.

Briefcase in tow, Fish settled in the seat and shut the door. "Don't have much time. What's your report?" He shoved the briefcase to the floor and straightened his tie.

Darla cleared her throat. "She's got another ten thousand."

"Almost as many as last time. She lose any workers?"

"One might quit … she got roughed up out front." Darla told of the soiled signatures and the big union man injured in a fight.

"Do you know these new guys?" He removed his sunglasses.

"Matt Kinler's the only name I remember."

"Is he the one who hurt Bo—the union guy?"

"No, it was the other one, but I didn't get his name.

"Is she ready to turn in more signatures?"

"Uh-huh … but … ah, she plans to hold all the signatures she collects until the end of the month."

"Why does she wait?" He propped his elbow on the door and cocked his head.

"After somebody broke into the office, she won't keep completed pages with signatures in there anymore. She also wants to keep you from knowing how she's doing." Darla gripped the bottom of the steering wheel.

"Me? She knows about me?"

"No—no." She waved a hand. "I mean the union people." Her blouse, damp with sweat, stuck to her back.

"I see." He grabbed his briefcase. "I don't talk to the unions. As I told you, the Speaker is interested in this initiative." The latches clicked, and he slipped a hand inside and pulled out a plain, white envelope.

"I … ah, Mr. Fish … I don't want to do this anymore." She glanced to her right.

"Can't quit now, girl." He slapped a hand on the case.

"Makes me feel dirty—I can't sleep. Marion's been good to me."

"Look at me!" He locked eyes. "You'll finish what we started or you'll never work for the State again."

She dropped her head and slumped in the seat.

"You understand."

A slight nod.

"If Marion doesn't keep those signature sheets in the office, where are they?"

"I don't know." Darla crossed her arms, refused to raise her head. "She takes 'em somewhere in her car."

Fish slammed the door.

She fingered the bills in the envelope. Five hundred dollars. Tears of betrayal mixed with sobs of remorse. Darla wanted out. She had to find a way.

◆◆◆

Power coursed through his veins. Heinrik Leach thrived on power. From the first day, he'd loved this view. The commanding scene over the Willamette

River and north toward the Columbia River from his top floor office fed his sense of power.

His short, stout build required tailored suits, but he could afford them. Leach sipped from his glass and savored the rare imported Irish whiskey. Not his favorite, but to drink the expensive beverage gave him a rush. Retired senior partner indeed—it was he who called the shots at Leach, Philcher and Hannibal and played kingmaker in this city, in the state.

"Mr. Leach?" It was the voice of his bodyguard.

"What is it?" He kept his eyes fixed on his city.

"Boswell is early for his six o'clock."

"Make him wait—check for wires before you let him in." He trusted no one.

Leach moved to the chair behind his desk; custom-made, leather and real wood. Deep carpet, dark wood furnishings and leather chairs created the ambiance he wanted. He used his office to intimidate the timid and impress the impressionable.

The glass and bottle stashed in a drawer, he settled behind the desk. He plucked a Double Corona from his humidor. He'd wait until his guest left before lighting up because he didn't want to strain the alliance with Boswell. The cigar alone would torment the anti-smoking Nazi. Good.

Bruce Boswell's value came from his strong ties with public employee unions in DC. Leach hoped to exploit those connections and avoid the danger those ties represented. The secret dossier he had developed on Boswell gave him a peek at the man's private side. He'd recruited Herb Fish with Boswell as part of the package.

A soft rap and his bodyguard stepped inside to hold the door for the visitor, who stormed across the thick carpet. "Heinrik, I resent being frisked every time I come here."

Leach remained seated and directed the unlit cigar at a chair. "Please, indulge me the precaution."

The middle-aged man backed into the chair with a slight hop and landed against the backrest. Leach wondered if his feet still touched the floor. He'd never checked. "You said this was important," Leach said. "What's on your mind?"

"Had a call from Herb. They're closer to having enough signatures." He placed his elbows on the leather armrests.

Leach jabbed the unlit cigar at Boswell. "The old gal's like that Eveready Bunny." Fish had already called him, but his guest had no need to know. He received regular reports from Fish, who performed other duties as assigned. Although a couple, Boswell and Fish kept secrets from one another. This had become obvious.

"We've thrown a lot at her. Every time we run a worker off another one pops up." Boswell rubbed a hand over his short, gray hair. "Our latest poll shows, today, their measure would pass by a large margin. We've got to keep it off the ballot. Even our rank and file members favor an opt-out provision."

"With only one Chief Petitioner left…" Leach leaned back and moistened the end of his cigar. "Seems a simple problem, Bruce."

"Under normal circumstances, yes. But I'm running out of people."

"Who now?" Leach aimed the cigar, "You're better off without that fool arsonist. I said accidental fire—not a firebomb."

"Poor—" He cleared his throat. "Poor tasking, misunderstanding."

"By you?"

"No. Boyd. He had a 10K budget. Tried to pocket more by hiring cheap. Said he won't do that again."

"Ha, can't." He leaned back. "Our attorney says your arsonist's going to get serious time." Leach toyed with the cigar. "You said running out of people."

"Yeah, Boyd got banged up at a demonstration—concussion, abrasions."

"Hmm—your go-to-guy."

"Herb's got his hands full with our snitch and Boyd. If I brought in anyone new, my role, your role—our secrets could be at risk."

"How you going to shut the old woman down?"

"I'll have Boyd back soon. But, I need to discuss a new problem—Matt Kinler. He's helping Walters."

"Never heard of the man. Explain."

"Not sure of his role, but one of his goons roughed up Boyd."

His eyebrows shot up. "Must be a big goon."

"Yes." Boswell scooted forward, worked his Smartphone and slid the device across the desk. "You need to see this picture."

Leach examined the screen and returned the phone. "Where'd you get that?"

"One of my sources in the teachers' union. Some middle-school kid took that picture of you and Herb. This Kinler guy paid the kid for an email copy. My source heard the story and sent this." He waved the phone and returned to his chair.

"Why'd he want the picture?"

"No idea. Don't have much on him. The business card he gave the teacher says he's a private investigator. I thought I'd ask if it is time to call Stryker?"

"No!" Leach stiffened. "We don't need more killing. You've had Duffy, the arson—if we have another death, some lawman may try to connect the dots. The press won't because they sympathize with the unions, but cops get curious. We'll handle this in house. If we call the national office, they'll think we can't handle our own problems..."

"I'll have Boyd come up with something," Boswell said.

"Wish you had someone else on your bench. He's too clumsy, heavy handed—you sent him to scare Duffy, not kill him." Leach shook his head and twirled the cigar. "Maybe I'll pull some strings at Revenue. May be time for Marion Walters to have a tax audit. If we can come up with a criminal charge, we'd shut her down."

"Anything. We've got to keep this off the ballot. There's been some bad news coverage on our demonstrations."

"Don't worry about the press. They're no threat to our cause." Moments after he pressed the button under his desk, his bodyguard entered. "Turk, after you show Bruce out come see me."

Leach lit his cigar before Boswell reached the door. Clouds of thick gray smoke drifted over his desk as he poured two fingers of whiskey. Turk returned.

"I need the background on a private investigator, Matt Kinler. If he's got a partner, him too."

Turk, ramrod straight in front of the desk, remained silent.

"We have another one of those situations." He swirled the whiskey and sipped. "You may need to soil your hands again."

Chapter 14

"No doubt in my mind." Anna placed his cell phone on the seat between them.

Matt checked for traffic before he entered the highway's westbound lane. "Like I said last night, I didn't see her until she jumped out to help Boyd. Fit your description to a T. I wasn't sure the pictures would be any good."

"It tickled me when our insurance agent said they'd use your pictures and refuse to settle. No neck brace or crutches sinks her," Anna said.

"Yeah, but everything's on hold until this sting operation is over."

"This'll be fun today. I'm so glad Sophia volunteered to do this. I'd be too nervous to pull it off."

"Oh, she'll be nervous, but she's done this kind of thing a lot in her former life," Matt said.

A short time later, as they passed the golf course, Matt glanced at a foursome in the fairway beside the highway. "They're having fun."

"Nice day for them. Do you miss it?"

"Sometimes, but when would I have time?"

"You'd make time, if you wanted to."

"You know me too well." He reached for her hand. "Sophia told me she never actually did this accident scam. Learned how it worked from other jail inmates and the women in the shelter."

"She'll have plenty of help, won't she?"

"Yep, the NICB investigator works with a federal task force on frauds. Use of mail and wire gives the feds jurisdiction. Think they have postal inspectors, IRS—maybe FBI."

"Do they send someone in with her?"

"No. She'll wear a live transmitter and there'll be a recorder going during the visits. The cover team will be close enough to hear everything on radios." He checked the time. "She's at the attorney's office right now."

"Makes me nervous for her," Anna said.

The truck reached the crest of the hill and a view of Salem on the valley floor.

"How long will she be?" Anna asked.

"Doubt very long. The lawyer and doctor move these things along. Making money not making nice."

"After you explained how this all works, I thought—pretty simple."

"Easier when the task force creates phony insurance policies and accident reports. Sophia holds a hand on her stiff neck, dangles the papers, and dollar signs dance in the lawyer's head—doctor's too."

Anna read a text message. "She's at your office—finished the lawyer visit."

In a turn lane, Matt waited for a green arrow. "We're almost there."

"Do you think they'll still let us go with them when they surveil her doctor's visit?"

"We'll observe, but have to stay out of their way." The truck jostled as Matt drove into the parking lot. "I'm going to paint a great big 'Reserved' in my space." He cranked the wheel and parked in front of one of the closed garage doors.

"Whose car?"

"Insurance investigator, I'd guess."

Matt followed his wife inside. Allen nodded while he worked with their coffeemaker. Matt saw the back of a stranger occupying his desk against the far wall. "Investigator?" Matt mouthed to Allen.

Thumbs up from Allen. Matt joined Anna and Sophia beside Allen's desk. "How'd it go?" he asked.

"No problems." Sophia sat in their only straight back chair. Hair in a ponytail, she wore a red windbreaker over a gray sweatshirt and blue jeans. "Kinda like going through an assembly line. He had the routine down."

"Heard he's done it before." Matt glanced at the investigator who had a cell phone stuck to his ear.

"You dressed down today." Anna settled into Allen's swivel chair.

Sophia smiled as she opened her jacket. "Had to look the part."

"You wear that too?" Matt asked.

"Yes." She tapped the neck brace on Allen's desk. "Really uncomfortable."

"He ask any questions?—suspicious at all?" Anna asked.

"Not really. I handed him the phony accident report and insurance policy." She stuck out her hand to accept coffee from Allen. "After he looked it over, he told me he'd handle my case. I'd get three percent of any settlement and he'd cover the medical." She sipped and placed the cup beside the brace. "I said okay and he called the doctor and made an appointment."

"They do have the routine down," Anna said. "Hope they toss the whole bunch in jail—especially Hazel."

"You must be Matt." The agent shook hands. "Good to meet face-to-face."

"My wife, Anna." Matt stepped aside. "Agent Houser."

"I'm glad you're doing this," Anna said. "It really upset me when our insurance company wanted to settle with that woman—Humphries."

Houser's chest swelled to rival the middle-age bulge at his waist. "Things don't always work out, but Matt here—" He nodded. "—called in the middle of this sting operation."

"How many other undercover accident victims have you run through?" Matt asked.

"She makes four." Houser fixed on Sophia. "You're good. Got a fulltime job if you want."

"Oh no. Stirs up too many bad memories. Besides, I don't want to run into old friends."

"Did you check the recording on her visit yet?" Allen perched on his desk behind Anna.

"Yeah," Houser said. "The tech guys checked. Picked up everything—perfect."

"What'll happen if the doctor examines me?"

"You won't wear the transmitter or mic. We'll hide them in your purse. But the doc didn't do much on the other patients we sent."

"I've worked soft tissue injury cases before," Allen said. "Tough to prove one way or the other."

"You're right," Houser said, "but we've had success with this undercover approach."

"Since you're going federal, it's a one-party consent on recording, right?" Allen asked.

Houser nodded.

"What's that mean?" Anna asked.

"Only one person in a conversation needs to consent to use the recording as evidence in court," Allen said.

"You still okay with us tagging along this time?" Matt asked.

"Sure, I'll give you a handheld and you can monitor. There's plenty of cover in the strip mall across the four-lane."

"Matt, I don't need to go," Allen said. "I'll stay here and track down info on that Smith guy in Bend—the driving under the influence arrest."

"Almost forgot about him," Matt said. "You have the contact number for my Yamhill deputy friend, right?"

"Got it," Allen said.

"Since Anna started all this," Matt said, "I'd love for her to get in on some of the action."

"Hazel Humphries." Allen made eye contact with Houser. "In your case, have you developed any information on her that you can share with us?"

Houser knit his brow. "Yes, but I'm not sure I have it with me." He moved over to Matt's desk, grabbed a leather folder and leafed through some pages, "Here. Unemployed, white, female, thirty-seven years old, divorced, three felony convictions, shoplifting, forgery, false identity. Altogether, about forty months in jail."

Allen finished his notes. "Do you have any of her aliases?"

"Let me see." He flipped more pages. "Two divorces. Humphries the last, Snyder the first, and she's been using Boyd lately. She used a last name, C-R-U-M, on her first arrest for shoplifting. Umm … Crum might be her maiden name, but we didn't need to go back that far."

Matt exchanged surprised expressions with Allen.

"Did you turn up any family members, like Gerard Crum?" Allen asked.

"Don't have any family background for her."

"Hey partner, something else to work on while we're gone," Matt said.

◆◆◆

"You're sure?" Anna leaned forward to study the building. "It can't be a doctor's office."

"It is." Matt had parked across the busy street from the office. A shade tree hung overhead and a row of spindly bushes hid the front of the truck. The single-story fifty's style family dwelling had white lap siding and a hip roof. The front yard had been paved, and painted stripes marked four parking spaces and one handicap access. A badly worn brown compact occupied the handicap spot.

"Matt," Anna whispered. "That's Hazel's car."

"She can't hear you." Matt touched her hand and smiled. "You sure?"

"I'm sure. What if she recognizes Sophia?"

"I'm not cleared to use this—supposed to just listen." He studied the radio and pressed the push/talk button. "Matt here, Hazel's car in front. May recognize your party."

"Package on foot. En route." Matt recognized Houser's voice.

"Matt," she whispered. "What are you going to do?"

"Be patient." He scanned the sidewalk. "They know. Sometimes these things require a little creativity."

"I hope Sophia avoids her." Anna kept her voice low. "What kind of doctor is this guy Boiko?"

"Houser said he's from Eastern Europe, maybe Ukraine. He didn't know of any connection but the lawyer also came from over there."

"What's his name?

"Gurka." Matt tensed. "There's Sophia." He offered the binoculars to her.

"The neck brace holds her chin funny," Anna said.

"Oh, oh. Hazel," Matt said.

The big woman equipped with crutches and a neck brace made an awkward descent from the porch. She jerked the door open and tangled the crutches with the headrest and seatbelt. Matt chuckled as she untangled her props, but stopped when Hazel stared across the roof of her car. "She's checking Sophia out."

Anna swung the glasses to Hazel.

"Atta girl." Matt had trained his eyes on Sophia. She had stopped, faced away from Hazel and grabbed a pair of large sunglasses from her bag.

"Where'd she get those?" Anna said. "Bigger than her face."

"Nobody'd recognize her now."

Hazel lost interest, climbed in behind the wheel and drove off.

Matt fiddled with knobs on the radio to switch channels and increased the volume until they could hear the swish of clothing and footsteps. "That's from the transmitter."

Minutes later, they heard the sounds of Sophia's entry and a woman's accented voice. "Judith Benson? Please have a seat. My husband will be with you in a moment."

"I forgot Sophia used a different name," Anna said.

"Hard to understand with the thick accent."

"Dr. Boiko will see you." The swishing sounds of clothing and footsteps played from the speaker. The woman said. "Remove your jacket and top. Undergarments leave. Use this gown. I'll tell Doctor you're here."

"I've been trying to spot the surveillance. You see any?" Anna asked.

"Half a block down." He raised his hand to their left. "The service van across the road by the utility pole." He waved to the right. "The surveyor with the tripod."

"I'd probably pick 'em out next time."

"Might, but they do different things. With this scam they may have a house or apartment rented around here, but they'll have mobile units for a quick response."

Voices on the radio interrupted. Matt grabbed the radio, increased volume and leaned sideways to share the speaker with his wife.

"So—about the accident, tell me." The doctor also had a thick East European accent.

"Not very loud, hard to follow him," Anna whispered.

"The transmitter in her purse muffles sound." He kept his voice low and his words clipped.

They listened. Sophia described how after her car was struck from behind she had suffered from a stiff neck, back pain and recurring headaches.

"What's he doing?" Anna asked.

"Sounds like he's checking where she hurts—not much talk."

"Hope they get a decent recording," Anna said.

"Should. The recorder is in her purse and a backup recording is made off the transmitter. Tech guys will enhance the audio later."

"Do I need an x-ray?" Sophia asked.

"Yah, sure. I order for you," the doctor said. "Report and bill I send to attorney—Gurka."

There was the sound of a door and Sophia whispered close to the mic, "Whew."

"Now she has to get out of there," Matt said.

Chapter 15

Matt and his wife had rejoined Allen in the office. Anna, at the rented desk, spoke with Sophia on her cell phone while Matt briefed Allen on the surveillance at the doctor's office.

"Oooh—yuckee." Anna tossed the phone in her purse. "Gives me the willies hearing about the doctor visit."

"What do you mean?" Matt asked.

"You know, doctor running hands over you when there's nothing wrong."

"He didn't get fresh with her, did he?"

"No. Just the idea of going through an exam like that—creepy."

"Good thing Sophia volunteered." Matt smiled.

"I agree." Anna rode the swivel chair over to Matt and Allen. "She's at the lab for the x-rays."

"If they do her like all the others, Houser says she'll have one more trip to the attorney to sign the settlement papers. Then wait for the check to arrive in the mail."

"When are they going to arrest these guys?" Anna asked.

"Here's the way it'll work." Matt said. "After Sophia's claim is settled, the feds will search the offices and seize the fake claim files from the lawyer and the doctor. Then the case goes to the Federal Grand Jury. Any charges and arrest warrants will happen after that."

"I won't be happy until they arrest Hazel. Gets me mad every time I think about what she tried to pull," Anna said.

"Allen, what'd you find out about Hazel and her family?" Matt asked.

Allen dug through papers scattered on his desk. "Didn't find any parents—deceased maybe. Hazel's the oldest sibling, has two brothers, Richard and Gerard. Except for Gerard, the Crum offspring have arrest records and jail time—nothing violent. I told you Richard used the Smith alias in Deschutes County. Your deputy buddy updated the aliases on the APB."

"Richard must be hunkered down somewhere," Matt said. "A motor home towing a runabout listed in an all-points bulletin would've been spotted by now."

"You'd think," Allen said.

"Find any current addresses?"

"Last known for Hazel and Gerard, some RV park near Turner. Called the manager, moved, no forwarding. Richard had the Dundee farmer's address listed."

Matt leaned forward with elbows on his knees in the straight-backed chair beside Allen's desk. "Easiest thing would be to wait. Richard will get popped. They'll bust Hazel on the insurance fraud. Then talk to them."

"Patience hasn't been one of your strong points." Anna patted him on the shoulder.

"Might be best to wait," Allen said. "Hard to imagine Richard has much information on Duffy's death. Maybe Hazel, but Gerard's the one we need to squeeze. He's the one who lured Duffy out that night."

"Any ideas on how to find the slippery weasel?" Matt straightened in the chair and crossed his legs.

"He's got Hershel's truck. Maybe Hershel has an idea where to look."

"If he'd talk," Matt said.

"I got him figured out—he'll talk to us."

"I'll get hold of Trudeau. Maybe he'll arrange an attorney room for us." Matt left the chair and moved to the front window.

Early rush hour traffic passed. Nothing in his view registered. His mind wrestled with all the bits and pieces of information. They had to find the common denominator. What was the connection between Duffy's death, Boyd, Crums—and the firebombs? He didn't buy coincidence. Could this all be about union opposition to the right-to-work movement? Was Baxter right about a puppet master? He closed his eyes as he pinched the bridge of his nose.

"Earth to Matt." Anna approached from behind and wrapped her arms around his waist. "Take me home."

"Let me call Pasqual, then we'll go."

"I can't do it myself. You gotta help me." Gerard Crum slouched on the foot of the queen-sized bed and peered into the square hole cut in the floor. In the darkness, a beam of light played on wires strung along the edge of the hole. The younger, Gerard's facial features resembled his brother's. Both stood less than six feet tall. More muscular, Richard had always been his protector.

"I don't gotta do nothing. I'm done doing for Sis and her friends." The muffled voice of Richard Crum rumbled in the compartment under the motor home's floor. Fingers, screwdriver and wire cutter had turns in the light as he fixed wires in place. "Hey, hand me the tape."

Gerard used the toe on his good leg to nudge the roll of black tape near the edge for his brother. "She's eighty something. I could do it myself—if wasn't for this bum leg." He ran a hand over the locked knee. "If things go bad, she might get away or I might get caught."

"Hey, Bro." Richard emerged to stand waist deep in the storage compartment under the floor. "You can do it." He switched the headlamp off. "Tell me again, what they want you to do."

"Rob an old woman."

"How much does she have?" Richard resumed work with the wires.

"Not money—" He cleared his throat. "Papers."

"Papers!" He shot a glance at Gerard. "You're joking, right?"

"No." He rubbed his hands back and forth on his thighs. "Guess this broad has stacks of paper where people signed their names. Hazel says Boyd wants 'em all to disappear."

"There." Richard slapped a screwdriver on the floor and stuck his fingertip under the edge of the hole. The click of a switch sounded. "What's he paying?"

"A grand."

A light flashed inside the hole. "Hey, it works, Bro." Richard squatted out of sight for a moment and popped back. "You take the risk, give him the stuff and get petty cash."

"Burn—I'm supposed to burn 'em."

"Hey, either way—piddly cash." He placed his palms on the floor. "This is why I won't run their little errands anymore. If I do a job, it's going to be for big money. Hey, I scored big off that old farmer." Richard grinned as he threw his hands overhead.

"Why you gonna blow this rig up?"

"Don't plan to, but if the law or anybody comes after me—I'll hit this switch, slip outside through here and seconds later—boom." He clapped his hands.

"Nobody'll find you out here. I got off I-5 at Ankeny like you said, but I still got lost. Good thing you answered your phone."

"Great location. The third foreclosure I checked out. Secluded, tree cover, and they haven't unhooked the electricity."

"How long can you stay?"

Richard flashed a broad grin. "Until somebody runs me off—little something I learned in jail along with blowing things up."

"Hope I'm not here if somebody comes for you—I couldn't get through there with my stiff leg."

"Might surprise yourself." Richard hoisted himself up to sit on the floor, his legs dangling in the hole. "Think about this nothing heist they want you to do, Bro. Hazel's been doing this measly stuff all her life and what's she got? Jail time and flat broke. From now on, when I score—I want a big payday."

Gerard wrung his hands. "You're right. But I need this job. I'm broke."

"Better get paid up front. Hershel's sitting in his cell, hasn't been paid—hasn't heard squat from Boyd."

"I'll ask, but—"

"Hey, Bro. How 'bout this? Rip off this old broad and sell the papers to the highest bidder. Union's got a ton of money—maybe the old lady does too."

"I'd never be able to pull that off."

Richard cocked his head and studied Gerard. "Little brother, we may have fallen into one of those big paydays. I got an idea."

◆◆◆

Back in their canyon home, Matt left Anna with the mail piled on the dining table while he strolled outside to monitor the dogs from the front porch. Sam and Eddy acted out their excitement over being released from house arrest. His phone vibrated with an incoming call: WIN.

"Hi, Marion."

"Matt, we've had a bomb threat."

"Call the police?"

"Yes, they've been here and didn't find anything. I wondered if you have any ideas on better security at my office."

"Oh. Well let's think this through. What needs protection there? You, Darla and the signatures you have collected. Anything else can be replaced, right?"

"Yes, I think so. Well, we're about to close up and go home. I'll just take the signatures home with me."

"I understood you've been doing that."

"Yeah, ever since the burglary. Tomorrow, I do my monthly turn in. Best month yet, almost twenty-five thousand."

"Put on a full-court press, did you?" Matt followed the dogs into the house.

"Sooner I reach our goal, sooner I can close this office and get away from all this harassment."

"Do you need help tomorrow, Marion?" He winked at Anna.

"No. Darla's going to meet me at the office. We can do it."

"Only security measures I'd recommend are for you to be aware of your surroundings. Each time you open the office check for anything out of place. Don't be afraid to call the cops. Let them check things out."

Matt ended the call and dropped the phone on the table. "They had a bomb threat. Just more harassment."

"Oh, my. I hope so."

"Me too." He rummaged through the mail. "Anything important?"

"A few bills and a notice from the vet. Eddy needs his rabies renewed. They're both due annual check-ups."

"I sure hope Hershel opens up tomorrow."

Chapter 16

"Big day tomorrow." Marion Walters counted the stacks of signature sheets one last time. Darla had verified the initials on each page and the number of pages in each stack. "After tomorrow, we will have turned in well over half of the required signatures."

"We still have two months before the deadline." Darla tapped the date on their wall calendar.

"Let's load these in the boxes and you can help carry them to my car," Marion said.

"Want me to follow you home?" Darla asked.

"Oh no, I'll be alright. Besides I live way out in the country. You need to be home with your little daughter."

"I ... I'm worried about you. The threats, all the problems ... feel like I, ah..."

Marion stepped over and hugged Darla. "I'll be fine. There's nothing you did to cause this and there's nothing you can do to change it."

Darla opened her mouth to speak, but stopped. She blinked her moist eyes, pressed her lips and nodded.

"No need to worry about me." Marion surveyed the stacks. "Let's get these in my trunk and lock up."

Marion visited the deli section of the supermarket on the way home. Southbound on I-5 she headed for the Jefferson exit. The pace and stress of recent days had taken a toll. She was weary and unsure how long she could keep her brave face. Sleepless nights, too much junk food or skipped meals; she couldn't remember the last time she'd taken her beta-blocker.

Tonight she purchased a balanced meal and resolved to eat well, sleep and follow the doctor's orders. She couldn't count the number of times she had turned over that new leaf in her eighty-plus years.

◆◆◆

Two men in an old Dodge truck parked on the shoulder of a rural road. Behind the wheel, Gerard studied the gate across the entrance. "How was I supposed to know she'd have a fancy security gate?"

"Hey, Bro. You gotta do your research or you'll always run into surprises—complications." Richard jumped out of the truck and trotted across the road to the gate.

Gerard waited. He'd never be as smart as his brother. Neither Boyd nor Hazel told him about the gate. They probably didn't know either. They weren't so smart.

Back in the cab, Richard said, "There's an automatic opener, but no alarm. Being miles from Scio, who'd respond anyway?"

"What're we going to do?"

"I'll grab the tow chain from the back of the truck. After I disable the gate, I'll hide in the bushes and ambush her when she gets out to check."

"What about me?"

"We don't want her to see your gimpy leg. Too easy to identify you. Go park down the road and I'll flash her lights when it's clear."

◆◆◆

Dusk accompanied Marion through Scio. She turned on the headlights. A widow for seven years, she never enjoyed being alone, but the responsibilities of the petition drive didn't allow time for loneliness.

One quarter-mile from her driveway, she passed an old truck parked on the shoulder of her road. The truck didn't belong to a local. She stole a glance at the cab—no one inside.

She pressed the remote and waited in the entrance for the gate to open. The gate jerked with a clang, but remained closed. In the headlights, she spotted chain wrapped near the gate latch. Matt's words flashed in her mind. *Anything out of place, call the cops.*

Marion grabbed the shift lever. Before she found reverse, the side window exploded as a large rock plummeted onto her lap. Her reflexes drove her sideways until her head bumped the stack of deli food beside her. Instinct warned of an attacker; she grabbed the container of broccoli salad and rebounded to smash the container into the face of her hooded assailant.

A man's hand grabbed her blouse and jerked her toward the shattered window as his other hand searched for the inside door handle. She struggled to free herself as he grappled with the handle.

Her fingers searched under her blazer for the butt of the gun. A paralyzing pain struck in her chest; she couldn't breathe. The gun—she jerked with her last ounce of energy as the attacker ripped the door open. She fired until she couldn't. The man screamed, and smashed his fist in her face. Marion slumped motionless in the car.

♦♦♦

Richard grimaced as he collapsed on the ground behind the car. Curses spewed through clenched teeth as he pressed a hand to the wound on his thigh. He ripped the pillowcase hood from his head. With his pocketknife, he cut and tore ragged strips from the fabric.

The truck skidded to a stop behind Richard. Gerard jumped out. "Heard shooting. What happened?" Wide-eyed and frantic he hobbled back and forth to survey the damage, and the old woman. "Oh. Geeze. What are we going to do?"

"Calm down. Get these tied around my leg, tight."

Gerard settled beside his brother and worked on the bandage. "She dead?"

"Beats me. Didn't have time to check."

"Here, press on this so I can finish the knot," Gerard said. "There."

"Did you know she was armed?" Richard cursed.

"No. You need a doctor?"

"No way—didn't hit an artery—no broken bone. Think it went clear through. I'll need to stop infection."

"What're we going to do now?"

"Here, help me up. We'll finish what we came for."

Richard pulled the small, motionless woman from the front and slung her in the back seat. He tucked her gun in his waistband, moved the car to the side of the entrance and opened the trunk. "Here we are. Put these boxes in the truck and pull up to the gate."

While Gerard positioned the truck, Richard limped to the gate, untangled the chain and found two remotes in the car. He punched a button on each until the gate swung open.

Gerard sped up the driveway through a stand of trees. Richard stuck the other remote out and, moments later, one of the garage doors crawled up the track. "Okay, you go make a quick check for more of those same boxes."

Gerard set the brake and hobbled into the garage. "Wow-ee!" In the dim light, he grinned at his brother from the entrance. "Two more, right here!" he shouted.

"Get 'em and let's go." Richard let his head fall back against the rest. *Something went right tonight.*

The old Dodge rumbled along the rural road. "Way things are going, maybe we better just burn them and settle for the thousand," Gerard said.

Richard sat bolt upright. "No way. Not now."

"What if the old woman's dead? We don't need a murder rap."

Richard laid his head back. "What old woman? We found these boxes in a ditch, officer." He rolled his head and forced a smile.

"You're better at storying than me."

"Stick around, you'll learn." He used both hands to reposition his injured leg. "You're going to have to take on more, now that I'm crippled up."

"What do you mean?" Gerard slowed and moved to the shoulder as an oncoming ambulance passed, lights flashing and siren screaming.

"I'd guess they found the old woman alive," Richard said.

"How do you know?"

"If she was dead, there'd be no ambulance."

Gerard slowed for the Scio speed zone. "Want me to buy first aid stuff here?"

"No. Too close. We'll stash the boxes at my place and I'll give you a shopping list."

"Bandages—what else?"

"Throwaway phones. You'll need those to start the bidding war."

"Richard—I can't. Not smart like you. Why don't you do it?"

"We have to be careful." He shifted to face his brother. "New rule. From now on, don't use any cell phone around my motor home. Don't even have one on."

"Why?"

"The law can pick up pings to give them a rough idea where your phone is. I'll keep mine off until I get out to I-5. You do the same."

Gerard squirmed as he fished a phone from his pocket and pressed the off button. "There." He shot hurried glances through the side windows and in the rearview mirrors.

With an amused expression, Richard said, "They're not after you yet."

"You're scaring me. Maybe we better burn this stuff and get our money."

"Hey Bro, we're not taking the easy way on this. Gotta work hard for the big bucks."

"I'm telling you—I'll mess us up."

"I'll write everything out for you. Step by step."

Gerard sighed. "I'll try."

"Drop me off at my place. Stash the boxes in the motor home. Then you go into Salem for bandages and phones, six to start."

"I told you—I'm broke."

"I got plenty left from what I ripped off the old man. Also stashed a nice boat in storage. When I get low I'll convert it to cash."

"What kind of phones?"

"Cheap, prepaid ones, but only buy two at a time—different places. Don't want anybody asking questions."

"Do I call Bully Boy first?"

"We'll start there, but he's too low on the totem pole to negotiate. You haven't told Hazel where I am?"

"No."

"Good. Don't. We'll have to lay low for a few days. Wait until we can read the newspapers on our excursion and check messages. Then we'll have a better idea on what steps to take next."

Chapter 17

"How long do they keep them there?" Matt asked.

Allen signaled for the southbound ramp to I-5. "Depends. With twenty years, they'll probably ship him to a prison in the eastern part of the state."

"Not what I expected. You described him, but he's glummer, more sullen."

"I told you he's slow. Never showed much emotion, but he's angry. The look in his eyes."

"No doubt he thinks Boyd abandoned him. I picked up the vibes when I asked if he'd heard from Bully." Matt viewed the glassy surface of the Willamette River as they crossed the bridge south of Wilsonville.

"Crum brothers stay in touch," Allen said, "but he still gave up Richard as the bomb maker."

"So proud of what he'd learned, I don't think he realized he gave us his teacher's name," Matt said.

"It's a shame the inmates don't learn wholesome things."

"Boyd made a mistake by not paying Hershel," Matt said. "I'm not sure I'm buying that Gerard Crum didn't help, but I can see Boyd, the recruiter."

"As long as the Crum brothers stay in touch and keep money on his account, he won't rat on 'em." Allen smiled. "On purpose."

"Got to be someone behind Boyd. Can't picture him as the brains behind all the union mischief."

"Maybe we should tail him for a few days. Might lead us to somebody important."

"Let's keep the idea on a back burner—a last resort. Oh, I forgot we had to stash these." Matt opened the glove box and grabbed their cell phones. "Want me to turn yours on too?"

"Sure." Allen reached for his phone. "I'm not used to being in blackout mode."

"We got trouble." Matt studied the screen on his phone. "Marion's in the hospital—intensive care. Anna's on her way to Salem." He checked the time. "Probably there."

Thirty minutes later, Allen dropped him off at the hospital's main entrance. Matt hustled inside and got directions to Marion Walters' room. After an elevator ride to ICU, he found Anna in the waiting area. They embraced.

He placed his hands on her shoulders and looked into her eyes. "You've been crying." He wiped moisture from her cheeks with his thumbs.

She laid her face on his chest, hugged and stepped back. "I'd never met Marion. Just what you told me. When I got here they had her curtain open. Her face is swollen, there're bandages, she's hooked to machines—it's just awful. She's in a coma, Matt. They're trying to find next of kin."

"Who called you?"

"Darla, the lady in Marion's office. She called an hour or so after you left. I'd just let the dogs out. She told me she came in early to help turn in the signatures, but no Marion. She called Marion's house and a detective answered. Wouldn't tell her what happened—told her to check with this hospital."

"Nurse or doctor tell you anything?"

"I begged, but didn't learn much … head injuries and heart attack."

"She told me about her bad ticker." Matt twisted his lips as he thought. "Since the cops answered—probably more than a bad fall."

Allen arrived and received a whispered update.

Matt slipped his phone out and scrolled for Trudeau's number. After he gave the sparse details, he asked Trudeau to find out what happened to Marion.

"Will he help?" Anna asked.

"For this—yes." Matt tucked his phone away.

"I'll get some coffee after I check with the nurse for news." She grabbed her purse and disappeared down the hall.

"Took you a while to find us—get lost?" Matt asked.

"Nah." Allen shrugged. "I had to call Beth."

"You been seeing a lot of her. Serious?"

"I'm not sure what serious is like." Allen squirmed in the chair. "I've dated some, but never had a lady who showed much interest in hanging out with me."

"Guess I probably don't either, but if you can't wait for her next call or if you can't wait to see her again—it's close to serious." Amused by his large friend, Matt asked, "Is her daughter okay with mom dating?"

"Yeah." Allen smiled. "We still laugh about how we met at her safe house—knocked me flat on the ground. Julie Ann plans to work in her mom's shop after she's finished school."

Matt pawed for his phone; it was Trudeau. He listened to the brief report and ended the call. "They're not releasing much."

"Accident or criminal?"

"Criminal—anything from assault to homicide." He nodded toward ICU. "Depends."

"Where'd they find her?"

"Beaten and stuffed in the backseat of her car—out by her gate."

"Robbery? Did they break into the house?"

"They haven't discovered anything missing." Matt jumped out of his chair. "Darla!"

"How is she? Can I see her?"

"Not yet. She's in a coma." He motioned to a chair. "My wife went to check with the nurse."

Darla plopped down in a self-hug. Her freckled face held a sad, pensive expression. "Is she going to die?"

"Let's hope not. She could use our prayers. Anna told me you called the house," Matt said.

"Yes," She gripped the arms on her chair. "I don't know what to do. We were going to turn in the signatures—a whole month's worth."

"Could I help with that?" Matt asked.

"Marion had all the signatures in boxes at her house. I don't have them."

"Where'd she keep them?"

"I'm not sure. She hauled them in her car, but I don't know where she kept them."

"Someone new." Anna arrived and passed out cups of coffee. "Let me guess—Darla?"

Darla nodded.

"How about you?"

"No, not your last one," Darla said.

"I can get more." Anna placed the cup beside Darla. "Black, nothing in it."

"Get any news for us?" Matt asked.

"Nurse said they haven't found next of kin yet. We've become buddies." She crossed her fingers and smiled as she slid into a chair. "Marion's EEG shows brain activity and they may take her off the machine to let her breathe on her own. Good signs."

"May be here a while." Matt leaned toward Darla. "Are we talking a lot of boxes?"

"Not many, three or four, book-box size." She reached for the covered cup.

"Honey, do you want to stay here? I think Allen and I'll hop down to Marion's—check on those boxes."

"If I had them, I think I could turn the signatures in." Darla sipped through the hole in the lid.

"What if the crime scene's roped off?" Allen asked.

"I'll call Trudeau. He'll grease the skids."

"Go ahead." Anna said. "I'll stay here with Darla."

"I can't stay long. Nobody's in the office."

◆◆◆

Forty minutes later, Allen stopped behind the unmarked car parked along a farm road. Matt jumped out to approach a woman dressed in slacks and a blazer as she wrote in a notebook on the car's hood.

"Deputy Saunders? Matt Kinler. I'm a friend of Trudeau's."

"A lot of people say that." She cracked a smile. "At least he vouched for you." She brushed bangs of dark brown hair away from her eyes.

"Don't want to take a lot of your time. What can you tell us?"

"What happened ain't complicated." She stuck her thumb back over her shoulder toward the gate. "Vic's car stopped there. Perp bashed in the window, punched the vic, tossed her in the back. Must've moved the car to the side. Popped the trunk. At some point, perp drove a different vehicle up to the house."

"Trunk empty?" Matt asked.

"Yep."

"Sexual?"

"No. We found shell casings in the car and on the ground, but no gun. The vic wore a shoulder holster, empty."

"Was she shot?"

Deputy Saunders shook her head. "Doc says no. Blunt force to the face, like a fist. She suffered a heart attack at some point."

"Who found her?"

"A couple—neighbors. Vic unconscious and the perp gone."

"Motive?"

"Unknown at this point. Vic's purse didn't appear to be missing anything—don't think it'd been touched. House seemed in order—not ransacked."

"Well, we learned of something that might be missing. Marion had three to four book boxes with papers. She kept them in the trunk of her car or at the house."

"Papers? Any value?"

Matt condensed his explanation of the initiative petition and the signature collection, and the history of union harassment. He tossed in the arson in Salem and Duffy's suspicious death. "Someone broke into Marion's office before and messed with the sheets with signatures. Possible they came here for the same reason."

"I told you the trunk's empty." She closed the notebook, "You guys ride with me. We'll check the house."

Trampled grass and weeds along the side of the driveway entrance marked where Marion's car had been found. "Recover much evidence?"

"Besides the shell casings on the ground, we found blood and fingerprints in the car and on the rear bumper. We impounded the car for a good going over."

The single story ranch style home appeared in an opening surrounded by a mixture of old fir and oak trees. Yellow crime scene tape stretched across the garage doors and front entrance. A sheriff's office van had been backed up to the one open garage door.

"They're still processing inside. Stay here while I check for the boxes. Then we won't have to log you into the crime scene and do all the admin stuff." She left them in the car and marched into the garage.

"I'd guess we have missing boxes," Matt said.

"That'd be my hunch," Allen said from the back seat.

◆◆◆

Southbound on I-5, Gerard signaled for the rest area exit near the Santiam River. Beyond the restrooms, he found a spot to park near the water. The back of his shirt stuck to his skin. He wiped sweaty palms on his trousers. He grabbed a cell phone from the bag on the seat and hopped out of the truck and landed on his stiff leg.

Phone activated, Gerard worked his way toward the river. Rounded river rock covered the shoreline. He found a place to sit and checked to ensure there'd be no eavesdroppers. A few people explored the river's edge, but they weren't close.

He unfolded Richard's script. *Boyd's gonna kill us for this*. Nausea welled deep in his gut. He didn't want to do this, but Richard couldn't travel yet. *Why'd he have to get shot?* After one more practice, he entered the number.

The call went to voice mail. Gerard sighed to calm himself as he waited to read at the sound of the beep. "We have the signatures." He fought to keep a monotone as his brother instructed. "If you want them, the cost is fifty thousand cash. We'll call with instructions in a few days. If you refuse, we'll return them to the owner."

He went limp as he pushed the end button. Chills rippled through his upper back and neck.

After a moment, Gerard unfolded the script for the old woman. They had no idea who might answer. Didn't matter. After a practice read, he tapped out the number for the old gal's office. He felt calmer as he waited; there was no killer on the other end.

A soft female voice answered. "WIN office, may I help you?"

"Shut up and listen. We have the boxes. Cost you fifty thousand to get them back. In a few days, we'll call with instructions. No cops."

Gerard ended the call and smashed the phone on a rock. In one piece, he flung the trashed phone out into the river. During the stiff-legged walk to his truck, Gerard ignored the maintenance worker who eyed him. He didn't need witnesses. On the other hand, nobody had any idea what he and Richard had going.

Chapter 18

"Matt, where are you?"

He pressed the phone to his ear. "We're in the parking garage. On the way to ICU—aren't you there?"

"Yes." Anna lowered her voice. "Darla's here—we've got a problem."

"Marion?"

"Just hurry."

Seated close, Anna and Darla paused their conversation as Matt arrived with Allen. His wife slapped the chair beside her.

Matt balanced on the front of the seat and leaned in. "What's up?"

Darla lowered her moist, reddened eyes.

"Someone stole the signatures they had ready to turn in," Anna said.

"I know."

"How'd you—never mind. They want fifty thousand dollars to get them back." Anna placed a hand on Darla's arm. "She got the call."

"At the office?"

Darla nodded.

"You tell anyone else?" Matt asked. Her freckled face appeared as pale and fragile as a China doll.

"No."

Matt beckoned to his partner. "Scoot your chair over here." He met Darla's eyes. "Tell us about the call—take your time."

She cleared her throat. "I got back to the office. Maybe an hour later the phone rang." Darla told them what she remembered about the demand for a payment before the caller would return the signatures.

"Did you record the call?" Allen asked.

"No." She leaned into the huddle. "I—I didn't think, it happened too fast."

"I wouldn't have either." Anna touched Darla's arm. "Don't lose sleep over it."

"How about caller ID?" Allen asked.

Darla shook her head.

"So you're to wait for more instructions—that it?" Matt asked.

"Yes, but—I don't—I can't … Marion needs…" Darla hid her face in her hands.

"We'll help with this." Matt waited for Darla to drop her hands. "You're not alone."

Darla forced a smile. "Thank you, but I feel responsible."

"You're not," Anna said. "You couldn't be."

"Do you think we should call the cops?" Allen asked.

"Not yet," Matt said. "I'll talk to the deputy who works Marion's case. Need to hook a recorder to their phone." He gauged Darla's reaction. "We'll show you which button to push when they call."

Darla hugged herself and stared at the floor. "All my fault." When she raised her head tears had streaked her cheeks. "Marion's been so good to me—she didn't deserve this." Darla lowered her eyes.

"Wh—" Matt and Anna in unison.

"Sorry, honey," Matt said. "Go ahead."

"Darla, why is this your fault?" Anna touched her shoulder.

Darla's fingers fidgeted in her lap. She wouldn't raise her head.

"Tell us. We'll walk with you in this. You won't be alone," Anna said.

"I … I've been sp ... spying." Moist brown eyes glanced at Anna. "Herb Fish, he asked me."

Anna raised her hand to silence Allen. "Who is he?"

"He's Chief of Staff for the House Speaker." Darla squirmed in the chair. "He promised me a good job." She kept her head down as she wiped her eyes and cheeks.

Matt leaned back and marveled at his wife's patience as she drew the details from Darla. He exchanged a knowing glance with Allen.

"He deceived you." Anna scooted forward and clasped Darla's hands to make eye contact. "He started with a harmless request to report how Marion was doing and then he had you—forced you—to do more."

"I wanted to quit—tried..." She broke eye contact.

"I'm sure you did." Anna released her grip.

"I wish I could talk to Marion—tell her how sorry I am."

"Maybe they'll let us visit her."

Matt leaned forward. "Honey, we need to run over to the office. Allen has to get on his computer. I'll come back in my truck.

◆◆◆

"She's breathing on her own," the nurse whispered and waved her forefinger at a screen with wiggly horizontal lines. "Brain activity—a good sign. Whatever happened, her whole body kinda went into shock. We hope she'll wake up soon." As she moved to the door, she said, "Just a few minutes, now."

Beside the bed, Darla grabbed Anna's hand. "I didn't think anybody'd get hurt … all my fault." She snuggled closer as Anna placed an arm across her back.

"No. It's their fault. They'll pay for this—someday."

Struck by the extent of the injuries, a pit formed in Darla's stomach. She studied the bandaged nose, the bruising around the eyes and the swollen, scabbed lips. Marion had tubes and wires attached everywhere, or so it seemed. So still, so small, her form made only a slight ridge in the blanket down the center of the bed.

As Anna scrolled her phone, Darla pushed away and moved closer to the side of the bed. The safety rail had been raised. She gripped the top bar.

"I need to make a call," Anna whispered as she touched Darla's shoulder. "Be right back."

The monitor on a stand across the bed showed lines and numbers in greens and blue. Marion's chest rose and fell with an easy, regular rhythm. Darla couldn't make sense of the display.

On the blanket, Marion's arm laid along the side rail. A bag of clear liquid, suspended above the side of the bed, dripped into a tube attached to the back of her hand. Darla slid her hand under Marion's to avoid the needle and gripped with light pressure. The warm fingers and the contact caused tears to well in her eyes and trickle down her cheeks. She hadn't meant to betray her friend. Prayer wasn't a part of her life. Nobody had ever taught her any magic words, but she needed to try. This was her fault.

"God, if you hear me," she whispered, "Marion's always saying how you care for her. Well, she needs help now and she can't ask." Darla leaned down, closed her eyes and gently placed the side of her face below her friend's chest.

In a soft voice, she said, "Please wake her up." Darla's shoulders quaked as she wept. "Marion, you have to wake up. I betrayed your trust—your friendship." Punctuated with soft sobs and sniffles, she told Marion how she spied for Herb Fish. Finished, she laid still.

"Please wake up, Marion. I need to ask your forgiveness." She felt a hand stroke her hair. Startled, she jumped back.

Darla spun to see who had intruded on her private moment. Nobody. Marion remained as before except for the imprint left by Darla on the blanket. Back at the side rail, she straightened the blanket. Her mind must've tricked her.

"Oh!" A hand on her shoulder made her jump. "It's you."

Anna placed her arm around Darla's waist. "Sorry. Didn't mean to scare you."

"I guess I'm just a little jumpy."

"Something happen? Everything okay?"

"Nothing's changed."

"How long has she had her eyes open?"

"What!" Darla covered her mouth to smother the shriek. "Marion—you're awake." She grabbed

Marion's hand and leaned close to study the swollen eyes.

Marion coughed and fought to clear her throat. "Wa … wa … water." Her voice was weak and raspy.

Anna grabbed the controller, raised the head of the bed and punched the call button.

Darla gripped Marion's hand. "I'm so happy you're back. I have so much to tell you."

"I know." Marion struggled with a catch in her throat.

Darla grabbed a cup of ice and offered chips on a spoon to her friend. "Marion, I did something very wrong." Tears returned to her eyes. "I need you to forgive me."

"I did."

"How could—?" She stepped back and cocked her head. "Did I wake you up?"

"You and that lady." Marion eyed Anna.

♦♦♦

"Matt, she's conscious," Anna pressed the phone to her ear as she paced in the waiting area.

"Great news. How is she doing?"

"They paged the doctor, but my nurse buddy thinks she'll be okay—after she heals."

"She talk much about what happened?"

"No, too many nurses and aides in and out of the room."

"I'd guess they have a standing order to call the detectives when she's conscious. Be good to find out what she remembers before they muzzle her."

"Can they do that?"

"Might try, I'm on my way. If you get a chance, ask her what happened."

Anna stuffed the phone in her pocket. In the room, she joined Darla off to one side as the nursing staff tended to Marion.

"They've had her in and out of the bed already," Darla whispered.

Anna widened her eyes and raised her eyebrows. "Good sign. Has the doctor been in?"

Darla shook her head.

"We'll have to ask you to leave," a nurse said. "We expect the doctor any moment."

Anna led out into the hall and passed several rooms before she pulled Darla to the side. "Far enough." She faced Darla, but kept an eye on Marion's entrance. "Pretend we're talking," she whispered. "I'll try to catch a glimpse of the doctor."

"Then what?"

"If things calm down in there, I want to talk to her."

Darla's eyes focused down the hall beyond Anna. "All of a sudden I'm tired. Too much stress with that phone call and Marion—I hope she's going to be okay."

"Me too." Anna grabbed Darla in a hug as Marion's nurses rushed past. "I think she's alone. Let's go."

Eyes closed, Marion reclined at a forty-five degree angle. Anna moved to her side and Darla stopped at the foot of the bed. Tubes and wires remained in place.

"Who are you?" Marion strained to speak as she studied Anna for a moment and shut her eyes.

"This is Matt's wife, Marion." Darla joined Anna. "You remember him. This is Anna."

Eyes opened and closed on her discolored face, scabbed and puffy.

"Matt told me of the harassment and now, this." Anna touched the old woman's hand. "We want to help."

"Water," she croaked.

Anna grabbed the cup of ice and offered a few chips to Marion. "Do you remember what happened?"

Marion focused on Darla. "Turn in our signatures?"

"No. I couldn't—you had them."

"Marion," Anna interrupted. "Whoever did this to you stole the signatures."

She gasped and her eyes squeezed shut. "No, ooh, we're finished." She sank deeper into the bed.

"We could buy them back," Darla said

Puzzled eyes opened.

"The thieves have asked for money to return the papers," Anna said.

"Not sure Elections would take them—if we're late."

"Oh, I forgot," Darla said. "We had a lot of signatures from paid gatherers. Those have to be turned in monthly and there's a deadline."

"Surely, they'd make an exception—under the circumstances."

Marion managed a scoff.

"They've been pretty by-the-book with her," Darla said.

"Can't let them beat us." Anna gripped Marion's fingers. "We'll help you. Do you remember what happened to you?"

She gathered herself, "Not much—water."

Anna spooned a few ice chips into the old woman's mouth. Marion struggled to talk. In a raspy, weak voice she told how she arrived at her gate, but the remote opener failed. She recalled a large rock crash through her window and land in her lap and a hooded man ripped open the door. She told how she pulled her gun and in the struggle fired several times. She remembered the man yell in pain.

"You shot him." Anna said.

"Think so."

"Just one man?"

"Uh-huh. Wait!" Her eyes came alive. "Back seat—I heard a truck sound. Last thing I remember, maybe two." Her eyes closed. "…a strange truck down the road."

"Ladies!" It was Anna's nurse buddy. "You're not to be in here. Outside—please."

Anna led Darla out into the hall and passed a man and woman dressed in business casual. The badges clipped on their belts left no doubt.

In the empty waiting room, they had their choice of tables. Anna sat close to a window and said, "I'm encouraged by how she's doing."

"Me too," Darla said. "Still looks pretty beat up."

"Wait here," Anna said. "I'm going to use the little conference room to call Matt." She scrolled for his number as she moved past the restrooms and into the room. As she briefed Matt, Anna had a view of the ICU entrance through the door glass. Fifteen minutes into her conversation the detectives, followed by her nurse friend, left the floor. Anna finished and rejoined Darla.

"Your friend stopped by while you were in there," Darla whispered.

"The nurse?"

"She's headed home, but she told me they're moving Marion."

"Where?"

"Across the street to a regular room. There's been a bad traffic accident and they need her room for somebody worse off."

"My. She must be doing a lot better."

"A temporary shortage of ICU beds, she said. But they'll give her special attention over there. I got the new room number."

"I'm starved," Anna said. "While they move her, let's find something to eat."

"Maybe we could find a vending machine somewhere," Darla said.

"Let's go to the snack bar on the first floor. It'll be on our way." Anna headed for the elevators.

"I need to get back to the office and relieve Nancy."

"My husband and Allen are still there. They've got visitors." She stuck her phone out for Darla. "Just got his text."

"I'll need to check on things. Nancy gathered signatures—never ran the office."

"Oh, I recognize the name. Nancy's the one Matt rescued."

A short time later, Anna led Darla off the crowded elevator with hands full of snack bar fare. Other visitors filled the waiting area nearest Marion's room. Anna pivoted and said, "Let's find a quiet place."

Several doors down, Anna ducked into an unused patient's room. "Shut the door," she whispered.

"Won't we get in trouble?" Darla glanced back at the door.

"They'll just ask us to leave. Relax, we won't hurt anything." Anna slid onto the upholstered window seat and left room for her companion. "Let's catch the afternoon news." She punched the power button on the remote.

Anna tore the wrapper and removed half of her tuna salad sandwich from the package. "Oh, too loud." She adjusted the volume and selected a channel with local news. She chased the first bite with a swig of cold cranberry juice. "Have you thought about how you're going to tell the Chief of Staff you quit?"

"No … I haven't." Darla set her orange juice on the counter to her left and picked a potato chip from their shared bag. "Hope I don't chicken out."

"You won't. If you want Matt to help you— I'll ask."

"It's Nancy!" Darla stared at the screen. "They're talking about Marion."

"Listen, they're interviewing her," Anna said.

A reporter stuck the microphone in Nancy's face. "Are you accusing the public employees' union of assaulting your director?"

Nancy's eyes narrowed, boring in on the camera. "That's not what I'm saying. What I said— the police will find a union goon responsible for this despicable act. I, myself, have been harassed and assaulted by union thugs.

"An eighty year old woman nearly died because of them. They stole a month's worth of signatures. Our effort to put this right-to-work issue before the voters is in jeopardy."

"So, there won't be enough signatures to get the measure on the ballot?" The reporter waggled the microphone from her lips to Nancy's.

"We're going to do everything possible to get this measure on the ballot. I'm calling on citizens from every corner of this state to join me. Everyone must rise up against corrupt union leaders who want to crush our efforts and trample on those who wish to petition their government." Nancy spun and rushed into the WIN office.

"There's Matt." Anna aimed the remote at the screen. "In the doorway."

"She's good with reporters." Darla took a drink of juice, "I couldn't … wouldn't know what to say."

"Might surprise yourself." Anna pressed the off button. "Do you think she'll be able to round up enough signatures in time?"

"Maybe." Darla shrugged.

Chapter 19

Buffoons, all buffoons. Leach drew on his Double Corona and blew a plume of thick smoke against the window glass. Once political enemies, now he found them useful, ideological idiots. He sipped from the extravagant, amber liquid in his tumbler. After an unsuccessful run for governor, he'd realized the liberals had the deck stacked against him—the press, judiciary, academia, legislature, bureaucrats—all co-opted.

Pragmatism compelled him to switch sides before he could seize the power he deserved. The wealth inherited from his father and grandfather made it possible for him to wield influence and control.

He hoisted the glass to toast the northern horizon and drank the last drop. Liberals skeptical of his shift in political allegiance dropped to their knees at the sight of dollars for their foolish causes. Concealed in family trusts and entities with meaningless names, his inherited wealth had come from fossil fuels and timber. Probably didn't matter, but he'd never tell.

Years ago disdain for public employee unions had motivated him to oppose the firm's generous offer to provide legal services to the unions. Fortunately, his partners prevailed and the lucre flowed into the firm's coffers. Leach moved from the window and tapped the cigar on the ashtray before he settled behind the desk. He hit the call button with his knee.

Turk appeared at the door, silent, arms crossed.

"He's waited long enough." Leach puffed clouds of smoke out into the room. The headlines troubled him. Union bosses in DC read the papers and he didn't need their oversight.

"Disgusting." Boswell fanned the smoke from his face with a hand as he bustled into the office. "That'll make me sick."

"You'll be more than sick if you don't rein in your stooge."

Boswell jerked out a handkerchief to cover his nose and hopped into the chair in front of the desk.

"Have you read the papers—watched the news?" Leach glared as he aimed his cigar at the visitor.

"Unfortunate the old gal got roughed up, but they scooped up her signatures." The cloth and hand over his nose muffled his voice.

"How many did they get?"

"Don't know."

"Did they destroy them?"

"Don't know."

"Who has them?"

"One of Boyd's helpers."

"Mr. Boswell—" Leach rose and leaned forward with his fists on the desk. "I expect answers to simple questions on your operation." He plucked the cigar from the edge of the ashtray and enlivened the ember on the end. Smoke hung over the desk as he leaned back in his chair. "I could arrange for you and your boyfriend to lose those jobs just as easy as I found them for you."

"Understood, but Boyd gave the job to one of his errand boys and..." Boswell squirmed in the chair "...he kind of messed things up."

Leach's eyes focused on the stream of smoke from the end of the cigar in his hand as he spoke. "You better get your husband or whatever you call him to straighten things out. I told him myself, after the first death, to keep a lid on this thing and to stop the initiative. He said he had the old gal's organization stalled. Now, after this stunt, they've got news coverage and revved up a statewide campaign."

"They've only got one Chief Petitioner left. She's in ICU. If she doesn't make it, the initiative dies too."

"Fool!" He grabbed Boswell with his glare. "We don't need more people dying. Probably time to dump this Boyd. Too clumsy—short on smarts—fits the union thug stereotype."

"I can't, not yet." Boswell tugged at his collar behind the bowtie. "I need him to find the Crum brothers. They're the ones who got the signatures from the old lady." He cleared his throat. "They want fifty thousand or they'll return them to the old gal."

"What?" Leach sprang forward, forearms on the desk. "How long have you known this?"

"Couple of days."

"Why wasn't I told?"

"I—ah, Herb—ah, we thought he could handle it quietly." He pled with his hands. "But the Crums disappeared and their sister doesn't know where they went."

"What's the sister got to do with this? It's dangerous to have too many players."

"Hazel's her name. Boyd's girlfriend."

"Offer them the money—have Boyd silence them." He aimed the cigar at Boswell. "Then I suggest you dispose of excess witnesses."

"Thought you wanted to avoid more people dying."

"Yes. The ones involved with Walters' initiative petition." He leaned back in his chair. "Boyd—these Crums—" His eyes darted to Boswell. "—You—no connection."

"Yeah—but." He fidgeted in the chair. "I'm not a killer, Mr. Leach."

"You're not?" He raised his eyebrows and then narrowed his eyes. "One man dead, another almost burned in his home, an old woman in critical condition and you're not a killer?"

"But I didn't—"

Leach cut him off with a wave of his hand, "Spare me the denial. You're as responsible as Herb or any of your minions. May be time to soil your hands."

"We'll figure something out." He scooted forward in the chair. "Does Boyd need to finish the lobbyist before—ah, before?"

"No, better leave him alone for now. His bill is dead this session and if we took another run the cops might decide your first imbecile didn't act alone."

Turk returned after he ushered Boswell out of the office.

"Using outsiders to handle our dirt had worked before, but these two—I may come to regret." Leach hoisted his whisky bottle out of the drawer and set another tumbler on the desk beside his. "Boswell and his boy are the only two who can link me to their royal mess." Two fingers each and he shoved one toward Turk. "Keep an eye on them."

Turk drained his glass in one gulp. "Matt Kinler."

"What'd you learn?"

"Retired FBI and works as a private eye with a guy named Allen Mann. Mann does work for Faire in your Salem office."

"How'd Kinler get hooked up with Marion Walters?"

"A question I can't answer yet."

"May need to figure a way to neutralize him." Leach swirled the liquid in his glass. "See what else you can develop. I'll be out of town for a few days. The wife has a judicial conference. Use the time to follow what our boys do to destroy those signatures." He downed his drink. "If you get a chance, you might check in on Ms. Walters. No one else needs to know of my concern." He fixed his eyes on Turk's. "Be a shame if something happened to her."

◆◆◆

"Should've brought the truck." Gerard shifted in the passenger seat. "My bad leg don't fit so good in little cars."

"Sorry, Bro, didn't think about that. Got the cheapest rental they had. Soon as we drop these instructions we'll get something different." Richard squinted into the setting sun as he studied the office entrance. "You're sure this is where the old woman worked?"

"Yeah," Gerard said. "I dropped Sis off for a rally once. Right up where that truck and car are parked."

"Hard to tell from here if anyone's in the office. Either the car or truck must belong to someone inside."

"Could drive by to get closer."

"Be patient, Bro, don't want to be too close in case our sister or Boyd come by to harass them again. That's why we didn't bring the truck."

"Hey, if they did, we could give 'em theirs too." Gerard chuckled.

"That'd be dumb."

"Just a joke." He squirmed in the seat. "Wish they'd hurry up."

"Here we go." Richard scrunched down and peered over the steering wheel.

A man and woman appeared in the entrance. The woman pulled the door shut and worked her hands near the lock. The two spoke at the curb before she entered the car and the man climbed into the brown pickup.

"Okay, soon as they're gone drop the envelope in the mail slot." Richard grabbed his brother's arm. "Wait. Remember, gloves before you handle it."

Fifteen minutes later in the northeast part of town, Richard drove the rental car along a quiet residential street. "I'll go by the end of his street. Check and see if their cars are there."

Gerard scanned right to catch a glimpse of Boyd's driveway in the cul-de-sac. "Nope, nobody's home."

"Better not try to make a drop. We'd be had if we were in there when Boyd or Hazel showed."

"They're probably at their favorite watering hole," Gerard said.

"Be a good guess—let's kill some time and come back."

"Ah, I'd like to get out of this car."

"Could you stretch out in the back seat? Hershel gave me the address for Kinler, the private eye who'd asked about me."

◆◆◆

"You've been a busy boy." Matt leaned back in the swivel chair and plopped his feet on the desk. "All this came from Facebook and LinkedIn?"

"News stories, blogs and a few websites for unions."

Matt skimmed the information on the printed pages his partner had prepared. "This is why I don't do the social media thing. The whole world can get this." He waved the papers at Allen.

"Can't stop it. I'm sure there's a lot out there on both of us."

"No doubt." Matt peered over his glasses. "So this Fish guy came from the East Coast to be the Speaker's Chief of Staff?"

"DC. From a lobbying firm, specialized in government employment issues—unions."

"Odd career path, and this Boswell moved at the same time?"

"They're close friends on Facebook stuff. Boswell had a manager position in the DC office of some public employee union and transferred to be a diversity consultant in the union's office out here."

"Whatever that is."

"Social media shows they're both into the LGBT movement."

"So, Fish pressured Darla for his union buddy. I suspect they're more than buddies."

"Same Portland address."

"Quite a cast. Then we got Leach here," Matt said.

"Yeah. I started out on the law firm and ended up with him. Philcher's dead and Hannibal heads the firm's maritime and international law stuff. Leach has ties to unions. Besides, from his picture I'd guess he's the one you saw at the Capitol."

"I didn't think the kid's picture was that good."

"Wasn't," Allen said, "but the plate number on the black Mercedes listed him as the owner. Those S63 AMGs are a nice ride."

"Guess that cinches it."

"Somewhere I read he's a retired senior partner, but he keeps office hours," Allen said, "Surprised me to learn he ran for governor on the Republican ticket. It was a good number of years back, but he took a royal whipping."

"What surprised you—the run for governor or the whipping?"

"Republican. He's registered to lobby for public employee unions and is listed as a board member for one of them."

"I take your point."

"Hope you don't mind, but I called your Lake Oswego buddy, the lobbyist. We discussed Leach, but he didn't have much. About an hour later he called back with scuttlebutt he'd picked up from friends. Leach has free access to the Democrat leadership and meets with their caucus. Lots of rumors about how he holds control over the union's political money. Apparently, candidates get no money unless blessed by Leach. Which means they march to his tune."

"Makes him a definite power broker. Fits with the little drama I observed on the Capitol steps."

"His family ties also might interest you. The current and third wife happens to be a Justice on the Oregon Supreme Court. She didn't take his name. I think a stepdaughter serves on the Oregon Investment Council, but she doesn't use Leach either."

"What's her investment council do?"

"They decide how and where all Oregon State funds are invested. The State Treasurer and the director for the retirement system also sit on the council."

"You sure these two women are family?"

"Ninety-nine percent. Checked my databases and all of them had listed his address as theirs. The wife currently and the stepdaughter some years back."

"I'll be in the doghouse if I don't get myself home." Matt tossed the papers on his desk. "A lot more pieces for us to fit together."

"Tomorrow." Allen stood. "I'm tired and hungry."

◆◆◆

"There's the pickup we just saw over at that office." Richard drove past and looped around the block to park where they could watch. "Looks more like an auto shop than a private detective business."

"Don't make sense, asking about you and hanging around the old woman's office. What kinda private eye is he?" Gerard asked.

"Shh. Two guys're coming out," Richard said.

"Wish it wasn't so dark." Gerard strained to study the two men from the backseat. "Hey, I remember now—those are the two guys who asked me about Duffy at Marion Forks." He slumped into the back. "Didn't recognize 'em before, but the big guy—think he sat by Hershel at the trial."

"Don't explain why he's asking about me." Richard stayed low behind the steering wheel. "After they're gone we'll have to break in over there."

"How? Both of us got bad legs."

"Hey Bro, do what we have to do."

Chapter 20

"You burned the bottom again." Anna used her fingernail to peek at the underside of the pastry on his plate.

"I prefer the term crispy." Matt tilted the fry pan over his plate to dump scrambled eggs beside the butterhorn. "Want this? I can fix more."

"Not for me." She wrinkled her nose. "If I ate junk like that I'd lose my school girl figure."

"You'd still be my school girl." He wrapped his free arm around her and they kissed. "Did you sleep well?"

"I did." She tugged her robe closed and tightened the sash. "What time did you get up?"

"Around five." He hooked a coffee mug from the cupboard and offered to pour.

Anna yawned as she nodded. "How's the run?" She headed past the bar divider for the dining table.

"Got my heart pumping." Table set, Matt joined her with his plate.

"If you didn't exercise, that stuff'd clog your arteries." She gave him a soft smile over the mug between her hands.

"My grandpa always warmed butterhorns in a fry pan and scrambled eggs when I stayed the night. I stole his recipe."

"I heard you on the phone down here." She sipped coffee.

"Allen—we got burgled last night."

"You're kidding, right?" She thumped the mug on the table.

"No." He wiped a napkin across his lips. "Didn't take anything. Nothing there, but I'll check when I get in."

"Kids." She wiped at the puddle of coffee around her mug.

"Probably." He loaded the fork with eggs and pastry. "I forgot to ask last night. You get a report on Marion?"

"Doctor said her heart's damaged, but it works about seventy percent now."

"Huh." He studied his wife. "How'd she react to the news?"

"'Just one more trial,' she said."

"God bless her," Matt said. "Life would be pretty futile apart from His promise to rescue us in the end."

"She's jazzed up after Nancy reported how things took off."

"I've seen the news coverage." He drank from his mug. "Is there more to it?"

"Yeah, a firestorm." Anna used her fingers to pick a piece of leftover roll off his plate. "Nancy's got the Midas touch. Marion's story swept the state. There's a caravan of motor homes on the coast and one through the high desert—maybe more. She's cranked up publicity and they've collected signatures by the bushel basket. Darla said she's up to her ears in volunteers." Anna washed the bite down with a swig of coffee.

"Maybe the bad guys lose this time."

Anna fluffed her hair with her fingers. "Beth said she'd do my hair and add a little tint."

"What's wrong with dark and curly?"

"Haven't you noticed the gray?"

He squinted and studied her hair. "You sure?"

"I'm sure."

"Well, just don't come home with some weird do. You'd scare the dogs."

"If you didn't notice the gray, you won't notice my new tint." Anna cleared the dishes and carried them to the sink. Across the bar divider she said, "I got a call from Sophia. She had her last visit with the lawyer."

"Oh, good, how'd she do?"

"Fine, but she did have a little scare."

Matt raised his brows, "The lawyer suspicious?"

"No, she almost ran into Hazel again. She'd finished and as she opened the door to leave, her old jailhouse friend pulled up in front. So she ducked back inside and asked to use the girls' room. She hid there until they called Hazel into the attorney's office. Then Sophia snuck out."

"The attorney has them close together on the assembly line."

"She said all she does now is wait for the check from the attorney."

"Yeah, whatever's left after the lawyer and doctor skim their share."

Anna returned to the table with the coffee pot and poured refills. "Matt, you ever talk to Allen about Beth?" She slid the empty pot to the side as she sat.

"A little, why?"

"She thinks he likes her, but he never says much about his feelings."

"Hard for him. You know how he grew up. The other day he told me he'd never had a meaningful relationship with a female." Matt drank from his mug.

"I think he sees Beth as someone he'd like to have a relationship with, don't you?" Anna asked.

"Plain as day—that's the problem. He's afraid she'll say no."

"I think she's—ah, well she'd like to know if he's serious."

"I asked him once. Didn't know what serious looked like."

"Oh, you men."

"Me?"

"Yes—you tell Allen to tell her how he feels."

"I can't twist his arm—too big."

"Matt—when you get a chance tell him."

"I will."

"You going to be in town all day?" Anna asked.

"Don't think so." His phone vibrated on the granite counter in the kitchen. "After I solve the burglary of my office I plan to come home." He grabbed the phone to check the screen. "Darla. I better take this."

"Hope Marion didn't take a turn for the worse," Anna said.

"Darla, Matt Kinler." He motioned a need to take notes as he listened. "No, don't call her—don't call anybody else. Did you open it? Okay. Try not to touch it anymore. Nobody touch it. Use a pencil or a pen, anything but fingers. Can you read it to me?"

Anna slid a tablet and pencil beside his hand.

Moments later he said, "Yeah, no, sit tight. I'll be in about nine-thirty. Don't worry, I'll take care of this." He exhaled tension as he ended the call. Their eyes locked. "She found payoff instructions in the mail slot this morning."

"When's the payoff?"

"Week from now, Wallace Marine Park. I didn't write all the details down. Doesn't matter right now."

"If Nancy gets enough signatures, will it matter?"

"The sheriff will want to catch the guy who whacked Marion. If he shows, they'd nab him."

"So much for a short day in town. I'd go with you but I want to do lunch with Sophia and drop in on Marion."

"Between retirement and a business, I don't get much time off."

"Hobby—a business makes money."

"You're so down to earth. That's why I love you." He kissed her.

◆◆◆

"Boyd's a stupid, stupid man." Richard shifted in the driver's seat to relieve the pain in his wounded leg. "He was so angry and drunk, he gave me the time and place over the phone and then he leads us to the spot." He glanced at his brother in the back seat.

"I should've put him on speaker. He knew it was me. He said, 'I can't get that kinda money, Richard.' So I said, 'You know people who can.' He blew up, threatened to kill us."

"I can't see his truck." Gerard had his back against a door with his stiff leg on the seat.

"Don't matter. Supposed to meet over near the tunnel entrance." He aimed his finger straight ahead. "We'll see 'em."

A couple rows of separation in the dim light of the underground parking garage provided a perfect vantage point. Richard smirked as he recalled Boyd's angry reaction over the phone. If his sister ever talked to him again, he planned to ask her how "Bully Boy" acted. That is, if she wasn't too drunk to remember. One hitch in the plan had been how to get his demand to the moneyman. Boyd, the slow thinker, had resolved the problem. Angry and panicked, he'd decided to hand carry the instructions and had blurted out the location. Easy to follow a man with a hangover.

"Is the clock right?" Gerard asked. "They're late."

"I set it, Bro." Richard tapped the digital display in the dash. He often wondered if he'd been adopted, but their parents died before he'd thought to ask. Hazel and his brother weren't too bright, but he considered himself a genius. Someday he'd have to take a test. "Remember—we're in the Capitol's underground parking lot where two state employees have an appointment."

"I'm stiff and tired from being in this car all night."

"I hear you, Bro." He waved several pages of paper above his shoulder. "We need to figure what all this stuff from the PI means."

"The names didn't mean anything to me. I 'member Sis has friends who've talked about those letters, L-G-T or something."

"L-G-B-T." He read from one page. "Fish and Boswell—the other page on this Leach doesn't have any gay stuff."

"I don't get it."

"Those letters mean—gay people."

"Oh—I didn't—you're smarter than me."

"This Leach must be a lawyer." He tossed the papers on the seat. "Wish we could've broken the private eye's password. Can't figure why he'd ask about me when he's working on people I got nothing to do with."

Tall and barrel-chested, Boyd ambled into view and approached the pedestrian tunnel. After a peek inside, he stationed himself near the entrance against the wall and fished his phone from a pocket on his purple windbreaker. He punched the pad to make a call.

"His face—somebody worked him over," Richard said. "The money man's late."

The squeak of tires and the sound of a revved engine broke the quiet. A silver gray Porsche sped from the entrance and screeched to a halt in the no parking zone close to Boyd. A slender man jumped out and marched up to Boyd. He was six feet tall and wore dark glasses, a coat and a tie.

"Never seen Boyd act 'fraid like that." Gerard peered over the front headrest.

"Think he just handed him our instructions," Richard said.

A shiny, black Mercedes sedan glided into the crosswalk behind the sports car. Tinted windows concealed any occupants. The driver; head shaved, muscled, and black leather blazer, strode over to join Boyd. The other man continued to read from the piece of paper.

The suit slapped the paper to the chest of the new arrival and waggled his finger in Boyd's battered face.

Richard grinned as he punched a number on his phone. "This'll be cool."

Boyd stepped back, glanced at his phone and said something before he slapped the phone to his ear.

"Hey, Bully Boy. Deliver my message?" Richard asked.

"I'm meeting now," Boyd said.

"How lucky for you. Big goons aren't good middlemen. Put your boss on."

Boyd jerked the phone from his ear to press it against his body as he spoke to the others.

The man in leather spoke and returned the paper to the suited man.

"Can't tell what they're saying—but I sure got Boyd going." Richard studied the distant scene through the windshield.

"He's gonna kill us for this," Gerard said.

"Don't worry, Bro. He's not clever enough."

The suited man grabbed Boyd's phone.

"Whoa," Richard said. "You don't need my name. Yes, you will pay."

"Look smart guy, turn those signatures over to us or you're history," the man said.

"What—are you, stupid? Follow those instructions in your hand."

The suit jerked his head around to scan the parking lot.

Richard slapped the phone against his chest and scrunched down behind the wheel. "Keep your head down," he whispered as he peeked over the dash. All three men, standing abreast, studied the sea of parked cars. "I messed up," Richard whispered. "Glad we got a rental."

"Okay, wise guy, you're a dead man," the suit said.

"You touch me and those signatures go back to the old woman. Pay up and all this goes away."

An enforcement officer stopped his mountain bike behind the fancy cars. He began to write in his citation book. The suit shoved the phone into Boyd's stomach and joined the leather-clad man in front of the officer.

"We'll be there. You better hold up your end." Boyd kept his voice low as he spoke into the phone.

"You got it." Richard smirked at the scene. Boyd slipped out of sight.

"I hear Boyd's truck," Gerard said. "He's got that noisy muffler."

"Stay down, I think he's patrolling the lot to find us." Richard snagged the stolen Browning pistol from the glove box and slid down on the floor. Pain shot through his thigh.

The throb of the truck's engine signaled Boyd's location as he worked each row. Richard picked safe moments to check on the ticket scene. Before long, he heard the sounds of the Porsche and the truck leaving the underground parking lot. Richard eased off the floor and checked for danger. The leather clad driver, arms crossed, leaned with his back against the Mercedes as the officer finished and tore the citation from his book.

"Hey Bro, let's see where this guy goes."

"Aww, yer gonna get us caught."

"No I won't." He wriggled up behind the wheel. "Better to find out who these guys are. We'll start with him."

"You said we'd practice with the drones today."

"We will, but with all your crashes—I need to buy more rotors."

Chapter 21

Matt parked in front of an old car bay. The office front door had been removed and placed flat on sawhorses in his reserved space. The glass company van blocked his path to the entrance. He obeyed signs, but others had no reluctance to use a spot clearly marked "reserved." No more delay, he'd paint bigger, brighter letters. Matt paused to inspect the deadbolt and doorknob on the door.

"No damage there, just the glass." The repairman sat in the side entrance of the van with his feet on the pavement. "I'll be done pretty soon."

"No hurry." Matt waved as he avoided a broom beside a pile of broken glass in the entrance.

"About time." Allen studied the monitor on his desk. "I called the insurance guy and he wants a police report."

"Wants to make sure you're not tricking him." Matt surveyed the room. "Nothing missing, huh?"

"The bottom drawer was open." He motioned toward the file cabinet. "Everything seems to be there." Allen leaned back in his swivel chair. "I found your top drawer pulled out. Better see if they took anything."

Matt slid his laptop bag onto the desk and did a visual inventory. "As far as I can tell, all here."

"They tried to open up my computer, but I don't think they got in." Allen moved over to the copy machine. "I left these where I found them." He grabbed several pages from the copier tray and passed them to Matt. "It's like they ran these through for copies and left the originals."

"Your research on Fish and Leach—not where we left them." Matt tossed the papers beside his bag. "They were right there when we left."

"Hard to imagine who'd break in just for those." Allen returned to his desk. "Wouldn't be kids."

"Nope." Matt swiveled toward the sound of voices. "Cops are here. Can you handle them? I need to call my old buddy, Trudeau."

Allen met the officers out front as Matt dialed.

"What's up, Matt?" Trudeau asked.

"Nothing much, just curious whether you had a chance to check the recordings on Hershel's calls. No big deal, just wondered."

"As a matter of fact, let me find my notes."

Matt smiled as he pictured the detective sorting through notes on what had to be a messy desk.

"Here. Only caller has been David Smith," Trudeau said.

"Hmm—thought some union rep would call."

"Negative. Not many calls, but I listened to one conversation they had right after you guys went up there. Hershel told Smith a Matt Kinler had been asking about him. He gave Smith everything on your business card."

"Suppose that explains why we just got burgled?"

"Doubt it, you're in the phone book."

"Good point."

"What'd you lose?"

"Nothing, as far as we can tell."

The squeak of Allen's chair told him his partner had returned. Matt ended the call and spun the chair. "What're you doing?"

"I'm sending my crime scene photos to the officer for his report."

"You make their job easy. This one of a string in this area?"

"Kidding, right?" Allen studied Matt before returning to the screen. "First report they've had around here in months."

"What I half expected." He glanced at the repairman who checked the fit and operation of the door. "When he's done we need to get over to see the mail Darla found."

Allen beckoned Matt with a jerk of his head.

Matt rode his chair across the floor.

"I had an interesting call today." Allen hunkered toward Matt and kept his voice down. "Remember Faire, Hershel's lawyer? He fired me."

"Wh—?" Matt lowered his voice. "Why?"

"Not real clear, but he said he was following orders from the managing partners. Nothing personal, he said. The bosses thought my associations created a conflict of interest when it came to their union clients."

"So, I got you fired."

"I got me fired. Faire said if he ever opens his own office he'd keep my name handy."

"You got enough work?"

Allen reared back to wave at the repairman. "Just leave the slip by the door. We'll send you a check." The door closed and he crossed his arms. "Plenty of work. Faire also arranged a buyout of our agreement." He rubbed his thumb across his fingertips.

Matt smiled as he propelled his chair back to his desk. "Let's go check what Darla has. We'll take my rig."

"Okay, but I've got dinner with Beth. Don't make me late."

"We'll be done." Matt glanced at the clock. "Figure out if you're serious yet?"

"I have." Allen logged off his desktop.

"Told her yet?" Matt opened the door.

"Tonight. If I don't chicken out."

Minutes later, Matt stopped at the curb near the WIN office. Three listless demonstrators huddled on the sidewalk, placards piled in the grass. "They need a kick start. Wonder where their mighty leader is," Matt said.

"We don't need his action today," Allen said.

Curtains were drawn and cardboard remained over the glass of the locked door. Matt rapped with his ring.

Darla peeked through the raggedy hole before she opened for them. "I've been a nervous wreck." Her eyes searched the street before she secured the door. "I called Nancy to keep me company. Hope it's okay for her to be here." She brushed past Matt and Allen.

Stacks of forms lined the table beside her workstation. Matt patted one pile. "Quite a few signatures."

"Oh, yes." Her freckled face brightened. "They've been pouring in. Nancy's helped a lot."

"Did you put the payoff instructions somewhere safe?"

Darla batted red hair away from her eyes as she headed for Marion's desk. "Under this." She tapped the wire in-basket.

Matt tugged latex gloves from his jacket. A plain, white business envelope, no address, contained one sheet with typewritten text. In his gloved hands, he read the instructions and set the paper down for his partner. "Did you remember the plastic folders? I plum forgot."

Allen bent over the note. "In my notebook."

"You ever been to Wallace Marine Park?"

"Once or twice. I remember the first parking lot. There're soccer fields and ball diamonds all over." Allen slid two clear plastic folders beside Matt's arm.

"Fire up my laptop. Let's Google this place and get a satellite shot." Matt slipped the one page note into one folder and the envelope into the other. "There." He ripped the gloves off and tossed them in the wastebasket.

"You're not alone!" Nancy rushed to Darla's side from the back entrance. "I dropped in on Marion." She plopped an armload of forms on the table and adjusted her glasses.

"They're here about some mail I got. Mr. Kinler, can I tell her?"

Matt peered over his glasses. "The guys who hurt Marion and stole the signatures want to sell the papers back for fifty thousand." He raised the letter encased in the plastic folder. "They sent instructions."

Nancy frowned as she slipped out of her windbreaker. "We may not need them anymore." She hung her jacket on the back of a folding chair. "I've got a caravan of seniors working their way down the

Gorge. If their signatures check out, I think we'll be over the top."

"Do you have time to help me do a final count on what we have here?" Darla asked.

"Love to. We'd all like to know where we stand," Nancy said. "Marion cheered up when I told her how we're doing."

"How long before she gets to go home?" Matt asked.

"She thought any day now." Nancy pushed her sweatshirt sleeves up her arms. "If I'm right about the count, it'll be good. Marion doubts Elections would accept the stolen signatures if we did get them back—too old and probably messed up."

"Doubt the bad guys thought about that," Matt said.

"We don't have that kind of money," Darla said. "Marion told me she'd have to borrow on her house."

Allen worked the keyboard on Matt's laptop. "Should we put the payoff on hold?" He positioned the screen for Matt, who waited beside him.

"No." Matt leaned sideways to study the layout of the park. "Deputy Saunders will want to nab these guys. I'll give her a call after we've figured this out."

"The main road and this parking lot divide the park into two sections." Allen used his pen as a pointer. "The north end is ball diamonds and soccer fields. The south has only soccer."

"Been a long time since I've been in there." Matt used the mouse pad to move the image. "The south is where we drop the cash?"

"Here." Allen tapped his pen. "Just off the main road—there'll be orange flagging tied to something."

"Odd how they want two business size envelopes with twenty-five one thousand dollar bills in each," Matt said.

"I've racked my brain to figure out what'll happen."

"Says here," Matt read. "They'll provide a cell phone with more instructions."

"Two possibilities, a phone near the marker or one'll be delivered."

"Just use redial and they'll talk to us." Matt returned to the screen. "Hard to figure—have to be prepared for anything."

"Whoever makes the drop will probably be robbed, kidnapped or sent somewhere else." Allen said.

"Man." Matt leaned back in the chair and stared at the ceiling. "Eleven in the morning—broad daylight."

Commotion at the counting table grabbed Matt's attention. "What's with the high-fiving?"

"Mr. Kinler, we're over the top," Darla said. Sparkle and color had replaced the sad, doe eyes and pale skin. "That is, if Elections agrees with our count."

"I forgot about all the single signature petitions we had pour in from the Internet." Nancy bonked her forehead with a hand. "Every time we had a news story on what happened to Marion the Internet kicked out signatures."

"Which means, every signature your old folks' caravan delivers will be insurance for when the

Secretary of State starts disqualifying other signatures," Matt said.

"Exactly!" Nancy said.

He searched for his phone, swiped and tapped until he had the new text on his screen. "Partner, Anna needs me at the hospital an hour ago. I can drop you off or you can come with me."

"I told you, I have something to do tonight— better take me to the office."

"I'll get hold of Detective Saunders," Matt said.

"What do we do about that note?" Worry had returned to Darla's face.

"Nothing," Matt said. "We'll handle it. For the next few days let your calls go to the answer machine—in case they call again. By the way, Darla, when things calm down I'll go meet with Mr. Fish and tell him your deal is off."

♦♦♦

"Finally." Richard fell in behind the taxi on the exit from I-5. "Hope we can handle Portland." Screened by the cabbie, he checked the taillights on the Mercedes for a turn signal. They didn't need a repeat of the near failure at the Salem Hospital. Stuck in traffic on Mission, he had lost track of the black car as it entered the hospital complex. If the leather-clad driver's visit to the hospital had been short, Richard wouldn't have had time to tour the lots and locate the car. The freeway from Salem had been easy, now came another dicey time.

"Don't get too close." Gerard peeked around the front headrest.

"Gotta stay close in the city or I'll hit a red light and lose him." He punched the gas to close the distance from the taxi. After five blocks, his target turned, the taxi didn't, and Richard followed the luxury sedan one block to a red light. "Keep your head down."

Tires screeched as the fancy car sped into a right turn with the traffic. Richard stopped at the light, but a city bus lumbered after the Mercedes and blocked his view. Now behind the bus, he signaled, hit the gas and entered the middle lane to scan for his target. Left, one block ahead, the luxury car signaled and disappeared under a tall office building. Stopped for another red light, he had time to plan.

Richard circled the block twice before he drove into the entrance of the underground parking. He whistled at the hourly rate, jerked the ticket and drove through the gate.

"How we gonna find him?" Gerard asked. "Might be a doctor."

"We'll follow the arrows and see what happens." Richard coasted on the gentle slope as he scanned for the fancy car. The lane circled the first level and as they looped back toward the front he spotted the Mercedes, parked in a section of reserved spaces near the building's elevators.

Richard cranked the wheel and stopped in a handicap space. "Wait."

"You'll get a ticket." Gerard said.

"Chill, Bro." He limped over to the reserved section. Each space had a placard mounted on the wall to mark the assignments. The black car occupied a space marked for "Leach." The same name as in the private eye's papers. Richard memorized the plate number and circled back to his car.

Behind the wheel he said, "He's the lawyer." He scribbled notes of the name and license number then slapped the car into reverse. He paid at the booth and glanced in the rearview mirror as he waited for the gate arm to lift. The man in the leather jacket stood near the elevator entrance, eyes fixed on them. A chill rippled down his spine. "How long has he been there?"

"Who?" Gerard followed his brother's eyes, glanced back and ducked down. "Oh no."

"Shut up." Richard stomped the gas.

Chapter 22

Matt rounded the corner. Anna, in the hall, shook her finger at a patient's room as she spoke to a woman in a business suit. He spotted a nameplate on the woman's lapel as he approached his wife from behind. The woman's eyes telegraphed his presence.

Anna glanced back and spun to greet him with a hug. "About time."

"I came right away. You didn't tell me they moved her."

"Sorry, everything happened so fast." Anna moved to his side. "My husband."

The woman smiled. "Staff" was etched on the shiny silver plate. She said, "As I told your wife, we take the safety of our patients very seriously."

"Thank you," Anna said. "I apologize if I sounded angry. I'm not—this whole thing scared me."

"I'll leave instructions with the staff on this floor and alert security." She left them in front of the doorway.

"I feel like I arrived in the middle of a movie," Matt said.

"Wait." Anna poked her head in the room and returned. "Let's move. She's asleep, but I don't want her to hear this."

In the hall, several feet from Marion's room, he said, "What's going on?" Matt kept his voice low.

"Someone tried to kill her," Anna whispered.

"You call the police?"

"No. I told the nurses. You got here on the tail end of the hospital's response. I couldn't prove what the guy was up to—but I'm not dumb."

"No you're not." He glanced up and down the hall. "Tell me."

"They'd moved Marion out of ICU over to here. She's a lot better." Anna jabbed her thumb back over her shoulder. "After they had quit fussing with her, Marion fell asleep. I'd walked Nancy to the elevator and found some coffee. When I got back somebody'd shut the door. I poked my head in and there's this guy bent over her. All I could see was his back, but he had his hands up around her head. She was fighting with her arms and legs. I yelled—don't remember what."

"What'd he do?"

"He jumped back, face all red—looked right through me. Slammed me into the wall—spilled my coffee. Might've burned his hand from the way he cursed. Something in his other hand caught on the door handle as he ran out." She fished a ragged piece of thin plastic material from her pocket. "Here."

Matt examined the plastic. "Like the stuff they use at a dry cleaners—put over the clean clothes."

"My thought exactly—he tried to suffocate her."

"What'd he look like?"

"Your height—a little shorter ... strong, husky. Thing I remember most is he wore a black leather coat—almost like a sport jacket. Oh—had a shaved head."

"Reminds me of a guy I've seen before—when I met Marion the first time."

"I don't think she's safe here, Matt."

"Maybe they'll move her to a different room. Let me try to talk to her."

The monitor remained beside the bed above Marion's shoulder. One bag of fluid hung from a stand beside her bed with a tube connected to her arm. There were bandages on her nose and colorful bruises around her eyes, but she forced a smile.

"Anna says you've had some excitement."

"Yes." Her voice weak, her diction muddled. "Didn't know him."

"Did he hurt you?" Matt sensed her fear.

She shook her head. "Tried to smother me with this." She stuck her free hand under the blanket and yanked out a strip of thin plastic. "This tore off when I tried to stop him. Anna saved me."

He compared her material with what Anna found. The plastic appeared to be the same. "Same guy who put you in here?"

"No—don't think so."

"Remember the guy who chased those school kids?"

"I was on the bench, couldn't see much."

"Think you'd recognize this guy if we caught him?"

"I doubt it."

"Did the doctor say when you can go home?"

"Day or two."

"If we find a safe place for you, are you ready to get out of here?"

A slight smile formed on her injured face.

Anna rushed in. "Matt, I got the doctor's emergency number."

Matt grabbed his phone and moved near the window to call. He left a message.

"What if this were a real emergency—life and death?" Anna frowned.

"Probably has another number for those." Matt placed his arm across Anna's shoulders as they faced Marion. "Would you mind company tonight? I don't think you should be alone."

"No … but—"

Anna cut her off, "Good. We'll stay."

"What'll we do about the dogs?" Matt asked.

"I'll call Beth."

"Got a text from the deputy down south. I'll be right back." Matt stepped out into the hall and found an empty room.

"Deputy Saunders, Matt. Take it you got my fax."

"Yes," Saunders said. "I understand why the victim doesn't want to pay for signatures she ain't going to need. Since we've got an unsolved murder attempt, my DA wants us to set up a payoff and scoop these guys up."

"Figured that."

"Trudeau said he'd help us with the stakeout. He's familiar with the park. Also suggested you would be a good victim—deliver our play money."

"Ha. Some friend he is."

"You're not interested?"

"I'm on board. I'd do anything to help you snag the guys who hurt Marion. I've worked extortion payoffs."

"Good. We've got several days to get lined up. Trudeau checked the site. Someone had already tied the orange flagging to a tree. We'd planned to catch 'em doing that, but too late."

"Hmm. Maybe more clever than I thought," Matt said. "Can't figure how they plan to deliver a cell phone. I'm supposed to punch redial when I get it."

"We can't figure that either," Saunders said. "We'll have to be ready for anything—car, bike or someone on foot."

"Yeah. Something else. Someone just tried to kill the old lady in her hospital bed."

"What? You're kidding, right?"

"No. We told the hospital someone suspicious came to her room, but they didn't call the cops. I wanted you to know first."

"Same guy?"

"Marion says no. I have a hunch I've seen the guy before. Doesn't make sense, but I have a plate number for you. If I come up with anything else I'll get it to you."

"Was she hurt?"

"No. My wife chased him off."

"Somebody up there needs to know about this. I'll call Trudeau and find out who to call."

"Okay, but I'll babysit her until we can move her somewhere safe."

"I hated God." Allen drank the last of his iced tea and returned the glass to the patio table. The memory of lying on his Grandpa's grave was vivid in his mind. He stared out across the pasture behind the house.

"How long did you stay?" Beth poured a refill and pushed the plate with cookies closer.

The glass wind chimes tinkled under the eaves. "I don't remember." He plucked a cookie and shrugged. "I'm ashamed of how I acted. The social worker had to drag me to her car."

"Don't be." She scooted her chair and wrapped her arm under his. "It's difficult to be all alone at eight years old."

"I hated everybody—a real brat."

"When my husband drowned, Julie Ann wasn't much older. She blamed me." Beth dabbed each eye with the napkin in her free hand. "She wouldn't talk … ran away."

"Maybe we better change the subject." Allen lifted her hand to his lips.

"No, I'm okay. Besides, after what you've said, you need to know what you're getting into."

Allen blushed. "I do, but we both have pasts to share."

"And futures." She snuggled his shoulder. The setting sun angled under the umbrella and cast their shadows on the table.

Tires crackled on the gravel road and a car door slammed on the other side of the house.

"Julie Ann?" Allen asked.

"Probably." She untangled her arm and grabbed the iced tea pitcher to refill her glass. "There's something I need to ask before she gets here. Anna said you haven't been a believer very long. What happened?"

Allen described how he had received a journal with news clippings from his old wrestling coach. "He'd written what he planned to tell me while he was alive … didn't happen." Allen stared at the sunlit tea in his glass.

"What'd he write?"

"Listen up!" He smiled. "What he always said to us kids when he coached. He wrote, 'God is! Stop acting like you're eight years old.' He'd clipped and pasted Bible verses in the journal. I guess he'd planned to read them to me."

"What a great story. You read the journal and gave your heart to God?"

"Not so simple. Matt had always teased me about being agnostic. 'Nothing more than a fence sitter,' he said, 'afraid of the truth because to know would require you to change.' The message from my old coach challenged me to figure things out for myself.

"I shut myself up every night for several weeks with the Bible and a pile of books." He jutted his chin and fixed his eyes on her. "Coach was right. There is one true God. By grace I'm saved through His Son. I'm certain God will keep His promise when my life ends."

"I found you guys." Julie Ann closed the sliding door. She slid into a chair across the table. She was in her early twenties, with dark hair tinged red.

"We didn't leave much." Beth shoved the cookies toward her daughter.

"I've eaten, but I'll have a cookie." She selected a broken half.

"We've got something to tell you." Beth wrapped his hand with hers.

"Don't—" Julie Ann waggled one hand at her mother and covered her mouth with the other to swallow. "You're getting married." She rushed around the table with a hug for her mother.

"No, wait, we're just—"

"—Going steady." Allen placed his arm across Beth's shoulders. "Something I've never done."

"Oh, pooh." Julie Ann returned to her chair. "You're so old fashioned."

"I wasn't sure how you'd take the news," Beth said.

"Mom! I'm so happy for both of you."

Beth's phone sounded. She checked the screen. "Anna needs me to get the dogs. She and Matt won't be home tonight."

"Not like them." Allen thumbed his phone and waited for Matt to answer. After the call, he said, "They think someone tried to kill the old lady in the hospital. They won't leave her there alone."

"How awful—who'd do such a thing?" Beth said.

"Same ones who put her there in the first place." Allen gathered dishes. "I'll help you pick up and then take you over to get the dogs."

"Are you going to the hospital?"

"I better."

Chapter 23

"This wasn't built for those boxy rigs," Matt said as he drove onto the narrow, covered bridge behind the medical transport.

"How much farther?" Anna asked.

"Not sure. Nancy gave me a rough idea, east valley—other side of Crabtree. With her in the lead, we won't get lost."

"I'm worried about Marion."

"She'll be fine. The nurse popped up in the back window a couple of times—doing her job."

"I'm glad Nancy knew a registered nurse."

"Private too. Doctor told the cops he wouldn't sign off if we didn't have a nurse."

"Did Saunders say if the police identified the guy I chased off?"

"No. When they had me watch the video from the hospital's surveillance cameras I could tell they hadn't."

"You said they didn't find one picture of him."

"Several pictures of him—none useful." Matt slowed to fall farther behind the transport as it jostled along the narrow and uneven rural road. "Guy's a pro—he arrived with a hat and kept his head behind one of those balloon bouquets. Then when he left, he carried a big harp wrapped with a cover over his shoulder."

"They should've let me see the pictures."

"Not much to see. I told them the guy was probably the one I saw in front of the Capitol building. Similar build, leather jacket. I gave them the license plate number."

"Where'd he get a harp?"

"Stole it from a hospice group. The musician had set the thing in the hall while he used the men's room. Comes out—no harp."

"I sure hope they catch him."

"Don't hold your breath. Security found the harp down in the parking garage."

The small caravan slowed. Nancy's compact entered a lane as an automated gate opened. Matt followed the transport through the entrance. A black iron picket gate swung closed behind them. The gravel drive led more than one hundred yards up to the right end of the house. In the headlights, only white wooden fence and pasture showed until they reached the single-story house atop the knoll.

In the lights of the lead car, Matt counted three garage doors on an underground floor of the house. One door rose as Nancy parked off to the side. "Did I tell you Saunders got some palm prints and DNA samples from the crime scene at Marion's?"

"Can they tell who left them?"

"Not yet. No matches in the national databases."

"Seems like we always strike out."

The transport turned around and backed up to the open garage. "Be patient. When they pick up our extortionist we'll probably be able to put him in Marion's car with her."

"I hope so—the payoff is the day after tomorrow, right?"

"Two days after."

Matt killed the engine. "Let's get Marion settled and check this place out."

A smile formed on Marion's bruised, colorful face. She stuck a thumb up as Matt approached. Beside the gurney inside the garage, two transport attendants waited for the nurse.

"Long ride, bet you're ready to get some rest," Matt said.

Marion nodded.

"This way." Nancy brushed the sweatshirt hood off her head and hurried up the stairs.

"It's cooled down, glad I brought my jacket." Anna crossed her arms to keep the jacket closed.

"Bet the heat's been off since her uncle left for Palm Springs." Matt waited with Anna while the nurse followed the attendants who carried Marion up the stairs on the gurney. "Nice of him to let us use this place."

"Yes, but what is it—some kind of farm?" Anna asked. "It's so dark I couldn't tell."

"Her uncle raised horses. That's why there're wooden fences everywhere."

"I thought the building in back looked like a stable, but I wasn't sure."

Matt followed his wife up the stairs into a hall.

"Sounds like they're getting her settled back there." Anna glanced down the hall to the left.

"Nancy said all the bedrooms are over the garage," Matt said. "Let's go this way." To the right, the hall emptied into the other half of the house.

There was a raised ceiling over a large open area with a kitchen and a sizable living area. "Oh, look, Matt." Anna rushed past the kitchen into the big room with three windowed walls.

"Should have a nice view in the daylight." Matt had detoured into the kitchen and smiled across the island built to separate the two rooms. "If we had this, you could cook and do clean up with a view."

"Who could?"

The sound of voices spilled out of the hallway as the nurse barked orders. Nancy pumped her fist as she rushed into the kitchen. "I escaped."

"From what?" Matt asked.

"The drill sergeant." Nancy jabbed a thumb back over her shoulder.

"She does take her job quite seriously." Anna had moved over to the bar across from Matt and Nancy. "Lovely home," Anna said. "Your uncle probably has a great view during the day."

"He loves to plant himself down there." Nancy waved a hand toward two recliners faced toward the windows in the east wall. "Every morning he watches the sun come up from behind the mountains."

"From what I could see, the front is all pasture. What's in the back? Trees?" Matt asked.

Nancy used her fingers to comb dark hair mussed by the hooded sweatshirt. "Just more horse pasture." She moved through the kitchen into the large room. "He has acres of pasture all around the house and stables." From a stool beside Anna, Nancy faced Matt across the bar.

"My partner will be here at first light," Matt said. "We'll assess the security, but I'd guess nobody'll be able to sneak up on us here."

"I hope not." Nancy pushed her glasses in place. "We could make some coffee."

"Maybe later," Anna said. "After they get Marion settled."

"When's your uncle due back?" Matt asked.

"Oh." She brightened. "He's not leaving Palm Springs until we're done here. When I told him what's going on he jumped to help. I got his signature too."

The haggard medical attendants emerged from the back bedroom.

"Let me show Mr. Kinler how to operate all the doors and gate and we can go," Nancy said.

Ten minutes later, Matt faced windows on the north side of the great room. The lights of the transport and Nancy's car eased down the lane and through the gate. She hadn't told him of the soft sound of a chime when the gate opened and closed.

Anna wrapped her arm around his waist as he placed an arm across her shoulders. "How's Marion?" he asked.

"She's asleep. So is the sergeant."

"Same room?"

"No, across the hall."

"After our short night last night and a long day, you better get some rest," Matt said. "Use the couch and I'll stay up."

"Matt, I'm worried. What if they find us?"

He embraced her. "We'll be safe here." They kissed.

"Think the dogs are okay?" She pressed her face to his chest.

"Beth's got them. They'll be fine." Her hair brushed his chin as he enjoyed her fragrance.

Hours later, Matt lay in a recliner, admiring the dark silhouette of the Cascade Mountain Range against the early morning sky. Because of the quick move with no glitches, they had time to tighten security before Leach could mount another run at Marion. He glanced to the side at his wife sprawled on the couch. Anna, Marion and the nurse hadn't stirred all night. He yawned as he eased out of the chair, stretched and snuck into the kitchen.

He poured all-night coffee and used milk to dilute the burnt flavor. The taste and smell wrinkled his nose. Fresh would be better, but the noise and smell might wake Anna.

The cell phone vibrated on the counter. He snatched it and whispered, "Standby. I'll hit the opener." Matt poured the putrid coffee in the sink and found the button for the gate.

The chime sounded. He grimaced and glanced at Anna. She stirred but remained stretched out. With a noiseless exit, Matt eased down the stairs to open the garage door.

Allen climbed out from behind the wheel and met Matt in the entrance.

"Everybody's asleep." Matt kept his voice low. "Thought we'd talk here and check the perimeter first."

"Interesting place," Allen said. "Dug out the top of this knoll. The roofline blends with the slope. Two story?"

"No. Single, but he's got this garage under the bedrooms on this end." Matt headed for the stables. "These buildings and this end make our only blind spot. The other three sides—" He stuck his thumb back over his shoulder. "—are open pasture for more than a hundred yards."

"I woke my friend up—Victor. Borrowed a trunk full of security stuff."

"Have I met him?"

"Nope. I've only seen him a few times since we took computer classes together. He's into security systems for businesses."

At the back of the stable, Matt scanned the expanse of pasture lined with white fence. "Just like the front."

"I think you're right," Allen said. "This would be the approach I'd use to sneak up. The stable, outbuildings and corral block any view from the house."

"How do we do this? Should I hire some guards?"

"No. You'd need a small army for around the clock coverage. I've got wireless cameras, motion sensors and some mics. They come with a nifty laptop so we can monitor everything from the house—just the two of us."

Matt led Allen into the garage and up the stairs. Anna had moved from the couch to the recliner. The sun had climbed above the distant peaks. "Saw you guys tramping around out there." She sipped from her cup.

"You made fresh?" Matt raised his eyebrows.

"Yeah, after I scrubbed the pot. You left it empty on the burner."

"Sorry. Can I blame sleep deprivation?"

"Blame what you want. Next time you clean the pot."

Matt headed for the kitchen.

"Did you have trouble finding this place?" Anna asked.

"Not after I used Matt's directions." Allen snickered. "Started out with my phone's GPS. It kept sending me down graveled roads. I didn't remember Matt saying anything about gravel. I pulled out my notes and found the paved route."

"I've run into that, too." Matt gave Allen a cup. "Those GPS routes do get you off the beaten track sometimes. Shorter maybe, but not beaten."

"How long do you think we'll need to keep her safe?" Allen asked.

"Don't know. Until we're sure Marion's out of danger," Matt said.

"At least until after the deputies arrest the bad guys at the park," Allen said.

"I'm not sure the attempt to kill her had anything to do with the shakedown," Matt said.

Allen cocked his head. "Run that by me."

Matt moved over to the windows and gazed north toward a distant hill across the road. "Whoever tried to kill her wants to stop the petition drive. She's the last Chief Petitioner. Eliminate her, the measure doesn't make the ballot. Doesn't make sense they'd return more signatures." He drank from his cup.

"Didn't you tell me—maybe Darla? They've got enough signatures now." Allen settled on a couch near Matt. "If we turned them in, Marion's job's done. She'd be safe."

"They either have enough or real close," Anna said. "But I think Marion wants to be present when the final batch is turned in. She'll need some time to get back on her feet."

"Did you talk to her?" Matt asked.

"No, but Nancy says she's got her mind set." Anna pushed out of the recliner. "Probably helps her recovery to have a goal. I'll go check on her."

"Partner." Matt studied the hill across the road. "If someone were to spy on us—I think the high ground out there'd be their first choice"

Allen rose to join Matt. "Be a good spot."

"This makes no sense. Leach wants her dead. I'd bet anything the guy Anna chased off is his driver. If Marion hadn't snagged some plastic like the piece Anna found there'd be scant evidence she had a visitor."

"You're right about two different things going on. Otherwise, they'd have killed her instead of grabbing papers."

Matt continued his study of the distant hill. "I'll never understand a guy like Leach. Acts like he has a right to kill."

"Anyone who gets in his way," Allen added.

Voices from the bedrooms interrupted his thoughts. "Anna stirred things up back there," Matt said.

"Might work." Allen jutted his chin at the hill to the north. "A long way for the signal to reach, but we'd have line-of-sight. I could try a motion sensor and a mic out there."

"Let's try."

"Check this out," Anna said.

Marion scooted the walker into the kitchen flanked by Anna and the nurse.

"I'm hungry." There was a slight smile under the bandaged nose. Determined eyes on her discolored face surveyed the room.

Matt rushed to the table on the other side of the kitchen and pulled out a chair. "You must be feeling better."

"Better or not, I've been laid up too long." Her voice was stronger. She backed up and plopped into the chair steadied by Matt.

Anna and the nurse were busy in the kitchen. Matt settled across the table. "You feeling good enough to handle a question?"

Marion folded her hands on the table and waited.

"I heard you've asked Nancy to wait on the final turn in. If she's got enough signatures, why not do it now and end this?"

Her eyes hardened. "I've been through this. There're folks all over this state who rallied behind me. We'll wait for all of their signatures to get here. I want each one to count." She accepted a glass of water from Anna and drank. "Besides, I want to march in there to let whoever's behind this to know— I've whipped 'em."

Chapter 24

"Like I said, Officer. I was out of town with my wife. My car was parked in the garage." Leach pressed the phone to his ear to catch the response. "You're welcome. Call anytime if you have any more questions." Furious, he restrained the urge to smash the phone in the cradle. He struck the call button under the desk with his fist.

Turk arrived, silent, without expression.

"You told me nobody'd put you at the hospital." He narrowed his eyes.

"I'm positive I wasn't made—by anybody important."

"What do you mean, important?" He checked the gold Rolex on his wrist. Seldom did he engage in vices before eleven. Today called for an exception. He reached for the drawer and grabbed the bottle.

"I picked up a tail. Not sure where, but I spotted them on the freeway after I left Salem."

Leach sipped. "How do you know they weren't cops?"

"I just know. The driver had a passenger in the back—cheap compact. I got the license number when I spotted the driver in our garage. He had a gimpy leg."

"If you're right—" He slapped his hand on the phone. "Why'd this cop just ask me why my car was in the hospital parking garage?"

Turk remained ramrod straight. "Bluffing. If someone spotted me at the hospital, the coppers wouldn't make a phone call—they'd be here in person."

"I suppose you're right." Leach picked a Churchill from his humidor and grabbed the cutter. "Any idea who tailed you?"

"Three possibilities. I'd eliminate the cops or the PI, so that leaves Boyd's crew—maybe the ones who stole the papers. I'd met with Fish and Boyd about paying for the stolen signatures. They were watching us—could've picked up the tail there."

"You went to the hospital before or after you met with Fish?" The lighting ritual complete, billows of smoke drifted above the desk.

"After."

"Then they followed you to visit the old lady."

"I don't think so. I'm certain they weren't on foot, I'd have noticed the guy with the limp."

"The cop had my license plate number!" Leach jabbed the cigar toward the phone.

"Don't know how he got it, but like I said, if it was tied to the old gal, there'd be no phone call."

Leach studied the smoke spiral from the burning ember. "I won't be tied to your missteps."

"Understand."

"Can you find out who owns the compact your tail drove?" Leach swiveled the chair and rose to survey his favorite view.

"Ran it. Belongs to a rental company in Salem—only two outlets. I'll see if they've returned the car."

"Find out what they're up to."

"I plan to. You remember Fish's got the buyback coming up."

"I do, but I don't want to get tangled in that mess." He sipped from his tumbler. "Keep an eye on how they pull that off. Doubt I'll get a straight story if they foul up."

"Back to the old lady—they've moved her. Don't know where."

Leach swirled the puddle of amber in his glass and returned to his chair. "Let's think this through." He aimed his cigar at the chair in front of the desk. "Have a seat."

Turk said, "I called and asked for her room. 'Checked out' the receptionist said. Then she put me on hold. When she came back on line she asked my name. I hung up. They didn't ask the first time."

"Hope you didn't use my phone." Leach dribbled another measure into his glass and offered some to his man.

Turk refused with a wave of his hand. "I'd dropped in on Boswell. He was gone—his phone was free."

Leach nodded, amused. Boswell had become such a disappointment. A little trouble from a prank couldn't hurt.

"I called Faire, one of your attorneys in Salem."

Leach raised his eyebrows. "Why?"

"Wanted his PI to find where they moved the old woman. Probably down the hall, different name, but I didn't think I should loiter around the hospital. Faire's assistant said they'd fired the guy."

"Interesting." Leach sent a cloud of smoke toward the ceiling. "Boswell says the signature count is close. They've been waiting until the end of each month to submit the signature pages."

"End of the month's about ten days away." Turk studied his watch.

"If they have enough to make the ballot, our internal polling still shows it will pass." He gulped the last. "Boswell has filled the union newsletter with doom and gloom if right-to-work passes, but the rank and file support the measure."

"Not much time. I'll find her."

"Not you." Leach stuck his glass and bottle in the drawer. "I'll call Stryker—don't need our fingerprints on this. Not with the cops sniffing around my office."

"Have you ever seen him?"

"No, just a voice on the phone. Never met the man. Don't want to."

"You got it, Bro! You got it!" Richard slapped his brother's back. "Oh. You're soaked." He rushed over to inspect the drone.

"Afraid I'd crash again." Seated on the ground with the control unit between his legs, Gerard wiped his hands on the front of his shirt. "I'm not sure I can do this."

"Hey, Bro. You just did three for three on the hardest part. Piece of cake." Richard held the drone between his hands. "All in one piece each time."

"My hands won't quit shaking. Look!" He stuck his hands out.

"Ah, you'll do fine." He positioned the drone several feet from Gerard's controller and grabbed a couple of sodas from the ice chest. "Take a break and we'll do a dress rehearsal."

"Rather have a beer." Gerard popped the tab.

"If you thought you had trouble before…" Richard drank. "Don't need to be messed up on beer or any of your weed."

Gerard drained the can, tossed it aside and flopped on his back, eyes shut.

"You hear me, Bro? Nothing else."

"I heard you."

Richard finished his drink, picked up the discarded can and dropped both empties in the trash bag beside their rental van. He collected his controller from inside. There would be no more team efforts with his worthless brother, or sister. Regret settled in the pit of his stomach. *Never should've agreed to this.* The controller positioned, he grabbed his drone and prepared for the rehearsal.

Gerard rolled over and pushed to his feet. "I gotta go before we do this." He hobbled behind a bush.

The plastic mixing bowls worked. The rounded bottom, with a puddle of hardened plaster inside ensured they landed top up every time. The clothespin to clip the envelopes had been his brother's idea. The hook under the drone easily caught the wire handle he'd installed. Designed with Gerard in mind—foolproof.

"Okay, I'm ready." Gerard hitched his pants.

Richard arranged both sets of equipment in rows ten feet apart—controllers, drones and his fabricated bowls with a cell phone placed in each bowl. He'd calculated the weight of the money, phone and bowl. The combined components were well under the maximum payload for the drones.

"Remember, timing's important. These have a one-mile range and the batteries give us twenty minutes flight time. Plenty for us. Now, let's do this like the real thing. We'll pretend the trees, and we won't fly out as far to the drop."

"Whose gonna take the phones when we land out there?"

"We'll pretend that too. I want us to fly with weight close to the real thing. Now, tell me what you're supposed to do."

"What do you mean? I drop the phone, they call, put the money in the bowl, I fly the thing back. Then I skedaddle."

"I mean, tell me how you are going to do all that, step by step. Get your phone set up hands free. Check the controller and drone—the bowl. Lift off at the exact time, hook the bowl—you finish."

"Ah, Richard." Gerard hung his head.

"Tell me. You talked me into this. I don't want mistakes."

"Okay." He shifted on his stiff leg. "I fly straight up two hundred feet and use the camera to check for the drop site."

"Why so high?"

"You told me to," Gerard said.

"But, why?" Richard closed his eyes and pinched the bridge of his nose.

"You mean so I won't hit trees?"

"Go on." He sighed as the knot in his stomach tightened.

As he talked, Gerard raised his arm to trace his imagined flight path. "I fly straight over the trees and parking lot and stop over the soccer field."

"Before the net," Richard interrupted. "The guy should be out there."

"Yeah. I hover and check the camera for the guy with the money. Then I fly straight down, leave the bowl on the ground where he can see it, fly straight up fifty feet and hover."

"If there's wind, you'll need to keep the drone over the bowl," Richard said. "Okay. He grabs our phone and calls. You tell him to clip the envelopes in the bowl with the clothespin. Go on."

"Yeah, I say stand by for the papers, drop down, hook the bowl and hover fifty feet high. Tell him the boxes are stacked at midfield by the parking lot. Then I climb to two hundred feet, hit auto-return and wait for the money. Oh, yeah. Any sign of danger—cops, don't wait."

"Good," Richard said. "Remember you've got to start right on time. Timing, Bro. Timing." He grinned, clapped and rubbed his hands together. "Oh, man this is too cool. Double payoff two hundred yards apart for the same worthless boxes. I'll be doing the same thing at the other end of the field. Timing—we need to be done before they realize what happened." Richard took up his controller. "Let's do this one last time. No mistakes."

Side by side, the brothers rehearsed their missions. The flights flawless, they gathered the equipment to load in the van.

"Richard? What if one of these guys spots both drones?"

"Good. You're thinking, Bro. That's why we got the camo models. If we get the timing right, we'll be in and out before they realize they've been had. Get it, Bro? That's the beauty of my plan. We'll go down in history."

"I just don't want to go to jail."

"Hurry, close the door," Richard said. "We don't need anyone seeing this stuff."

Gerard slammed the doors as an old man in a pickup drove into the refuge viewing area and stopped.

"Get in." Richard climbed in behind the wheel. "That guy would probably remember drones if he caught a glimpse."

He drove out of the lot and headed for his temporary home. A sense of regret troubled him. If he'd told Gerard no, he'd be with his next mark, a rich, elderly widow who needed help on her alpaca ranch. The minimum wage she offered had no appeal, but she struck him as rattle brained and feeble. *Of course you can park your motor home here. Low hanging fruit to be sure.* Richard smiled as he considered his next score.

"Tomorrow, at eleven?" Gerard asked.

"Perfect time. Kids in school, before lunch, shouldn't be too busy in there."

"If I use this van, what do you drive?"

"I think I'll get another white van. Easier to hide our drones. Besides, we'll blend in with deliverymen or guys stopped to repair something."

"Did you figure out where we'd meet after we get the money? We won't come out here until things have cooled down. Right?"

"Right." Richard signaled for the loop road that led to the foreclosure and his motor home. "In case you or I pick up a tail, we'll need to stay away from each other for an hour or so."

"Not too long. I'll be jumpy as a cat."

"No, Bro. After you get the money drive out to the main road and take a right. Go to the old folks' golf course. You know it?"

"Yeah." Gerard wrung his hands.

"I'll head straight for Monmouth. I'll call you from there and give my location. By then it'll be safe for you to join me."

"That'll be almost two hours, Richard." He showed his hands. "Look, I'm shaking just talking about it."

"Bro, you can do it. You've never seen a hundred grand before. We pull this off, it'll be worth it."

Gerard shifted in the passenger seat. "I'll be glad when this is over."

"You and me both, Bro. You and me both." He stopped the van between Hershel's truck and the motor home. "Let's hook the chargers to our drones. Then we'll run into town, get some dinner and rent another van."

Chapter 25

Perfect. He scanned above the roofline on the row of storage units between his rented space and the park. Blue sky, scattered cumulus and calm treetops fueled his excitement. Chills rippled across his back.

Preparations made, and after a good rehearsal, Richard Crum started the new day early to put his plan into action. The great unknown: whether his stupid brother could carry out his role. If not, Richard would lose half the take. Uncertainty required him to keep his brother in the dark on parts of the plan. Today, Gerard didn't need to know his whereabouts.

He examined his latex gloves for holes. Last night when he rented the van, he told the lady a skin condition required him to keep his hands covered. She bought it. The fine ridges on his fingertips and palms happened to be the dreaded condition, but he didn't tell her. He knelt to check the drone and controller one more time before he grabbed the strap on the overhead door and yanked down.

The exit from the storage business sloped down to the road from West Salem into the park. Richard drove to the right and into the park basin. A few cars, pedestrians, dogs, joggers and bikes met his expectations; it was a normal early morning. He passed the main parking lot on his left, and on his right the orange flagging hung from a tree along the edge of the soccer field. Most people wouldn't notice, but he had to check.

The road curved to the right into a stand of tall leafy trees along the soccer fields. Several empty cars were parked in the strip of graveled dirt close to the edge of the playing surface. Richard calculated the mid-point for the field and backed the van to the barrier. He sorted through his shoulder bag to find his red plastic tape. Outside, he went to the back doors and made an "X" with tape. He moved back to examine it, not too small, not too big, just right. *Clever*. The mark could be handy if Plan A hit a snag. He locked the white van, removed the gloves and strode back toward the park entrance.

A taxi picked him up at the West Salem Library and dropped him off at a car rental business he hadn't used. During the short ride across the river into Salem, he decided this had to be his last use of the Delbert Hines credit card from the Las Vegas bank. With most of his take transferred out of the account, he'd need to develop another name to use in future capers. Hines' card would become radioactive when the cops discovered the fraudulent account. Richard pulled out a fresh pair of latex gloves and headed for the entrance. After a problem free transaction, he drove a white compact from the lot to find an old friend. After he'd read white was the most popular color for vehicles, he stuck with the white. His schemes required him to avoid notice. *Seen one, you've seen them all*.

Forty minutes later, he spotted his friend's car behind the third vacant warehouse he'd checked. He parked behind the old Ford Galaxy with its raggedy black vinyl top, oxidized yellow body and fogged windows. Personal belongings stuffed the back seat. Bones, his tall frame curled in a fetal position, filled the front seat.

Richard tapped his key on the window.

"Yeah. Okay, I'm leaving," a muffled, morning voice yelled.

"Bones. It's Richard."

A hand cleared a spot in the condensation and the bearded face of the unkempt man peered out. He squinted, blinked and gathered himself.

Richard paced outside as he waited for the man, all seven feet of him. Drug use had ruined Bones' collegiate basketball career before Richard had met him in jail. A loan at a time of need gained gratitude from the gentle soul, who Richard found easy to exploit.

"Thought you were the watchman." Bones swung his bare feet out onto the ground and rose to full height. Hands rubbed his face into a smile. "What's up this time?" Fingers ran through tangled hair.

"Came to see how you're doing, Bro."

"I got no money—nothing, man." He stretched his long arms out and away from his sides and rolled his head.

"Need you to run an errand."

"What's it pay?"

"A hundred bucks and a cell phone with prepaid minutes you can keep. All yours, if you'll move a van for me this morning."

"I haven't had breakfast."

"Put your shoes on—we'll talk while you eat." He'd need to keep the windows open.

"You're buying." Bones tamed his hair with a knit cap, locked his car and followed Richard.

During the drive across town, his passenger devoured two fast food meals. Richard parked at a curb near the Gilbert House. "You understand what you have to do?"

"Yup."

"Tell me so I can be sure."

"You're always so particular."

"Humor me, Bones. This is important."

"Okay." He sucked coffee from the hole in the lid. "Ahhh—hot." He nodded toward the park. "About ten-thirty, I walk across the old railroad bridge, turn right and go down toward the river. Go through the parking lot along the soccer fields to a white van with a red X on the back. Hey, I need the key."

Richard fished a wadded latex glove from his pocket and slapped it on the center console.

"What's with the gloves? Should I have some?"

"Nah. I'll need them later and didn't want to forget. This one just got tangled with the key in my pocket."

"I don't believe you." Bones' eyes narrowed. "Am I gonna get busted for this?"

"No way, Bro. I borrowed the rig from a guy named Hines. The rental contract's over the visor."

"You stole it?"

"No. Just move the thing, leave it behind the warehouse and you're done. Now, tell me what you do when you find the van."

Bones removed the key from the glove. "Unlock the door and wait for you to call." He grabbed the phone from his pocket and pressed the on button. "Almost forgot."

"Okay, that's when I'll tell you to remove the boxes and stack them out on the edge of the field."

"Then I drive away."

"You got it. I left your money above the visor with the contract." A black motorcycle cruised down the street near the park. It had caught his attention the first two times. Maybe he'd get himself one of those after his next big payday. The man wore all black leather and a helmet with a dark face shield to match. "I got things to do. Finish your coffee in the park while you wait."

"Can you tell me what this is all about?"

"Better you don't know, Bones. Don't forget the charger for the phone."

The tall man unfolded himself from the compact car and ambled into the park. Richard followed him with his eyes. Bones had trusted him, but maybe not after today. He sighed as he drove from the curb and headed for the Marion Street Bridge. The black motorcycle passed and roared into West Salem ahead of him.

He checked the time. Several blocks later, he circled into a neighborhood near the edge of the park. Glimpses of the north parking lot and softball fields appeared through the trees as he eased along a residential street. The familiar white van had been parked in the driveway of the vacant house. A for sale sign stood in the yard. Richard smiled as he pictured his brother in the backyard, nervous and fidgety. He passed, looped south toward his end of the park and entered the gated entrance to the storage business. In front of his unit, Richard dialed the rental company. When they answered, he reported their van had been stolen. Yes, he'd drop by and file a report, as soon as he could. Police? Certainly.

◆◆◆

"I didn't push it. She wants to keep the number of cover units down. Preferred to have her own people—avoids a lot of confusion." Matt had his ankles crossed on the desk.

"Don't need that," Allen said. "I'll hang around here—got plenty of my own work to do."

"Guess I have tied you up lately." Matt grinned across the office at his partner.

"I don't mind. More interesting than my stuff—more important too."

"Hey. Give me a ride over to the cop shop. Then you can pick me up after I'm through."

"How will I find you?"

Matt jumped up. "Better idea—get the satellite shot of the park."

The keyboard clattered and Allen angled the screen for both to view the picture.

"I'll be there." Matt jabbed his finger at the spot. "On the end of the field along the main road." He slid his finger across the field to the old railroad bridge at the south end of the grass field. "If you park across the river it won't give Saunders any heartburn. Come across the bridge with all the other walkers and joggers. You can play sidewalk superintendent."

"Right. But I won't be able to hear—or talk to you."

"We have our phones."

"You'll have your hands full."

"True."

"Well, guess I could pick a place." Allen tapped the end of the bridge. "I'd be high enough to see what's happening, but you'll be a long ways away."

"What would it be—a football field?"

"More like two. I'll stick those little binoculars in my pocket."

"You'll have a better idea of what's going on than I will. I'll be wired up with the funny money—a sitting duck."

"How do you think they'll come for the money?"

"Not sure." Matt returned to his desk. "Anything but a car—dirt bike maybe. They can't be tied to the road." He swiped the screen on his phone. "Saunders said they lined up a patrol boat in case the bad guys try to get to the river."

"Still got those boxes of signatures. Those have to be in the mix."

"Yeah, but once these guys show themselves Saunders will snatch them up—papers or not."

"That's one advantage. Those goofballs don't know the signatures don't mean anything to us."

"I have to remember. In their eyes, I'm a pigeon out there with fifty grand."

Chapter 26

After a deep drag from the doobie, he held the pungent smoke in his lungs for a moment before he exhaled a column shaped cloud skyward. Gerard chuckled softly. *Richard saw this, he'd kill me.* The silent chuckle continued. Hunkered on the patio of the vacant house, he gazed at the drone and controller arranged on the back lawn. With the phone and bowl positioned, he waited. Last night, Richard had laughed when Gerard showed his shakes. His brother may be smarter, but he didn't understand.

Gerard took another hit. Sounds from a lawnmower or blower erupted somewhere in the neighborhood. *Good. Nobody will hear my drone.* He giggled as he raised steady hands. *Timing, Bro. Timing.* The words had stuck in his mind. Before he had lit up, he set the alarm on his watch so he'd lift off on time. Relaxed and mellow, Gerard scooted over to use the patio roof support as a backrest. He pinched the ember from the end, slipped the remnant in his pocket and closed his eyes.

He trusted no one. Richard sat on the stool he'd commandeered several days ago. The loaded pickup, unattended in front of another storage unit, invited him to help himself. He made one more check of the controller, drone and bowl as he laid them out on the floor. The beauty of his plan was he had sole control of his share of the take. He taught his brother how to capture the other half, but the odds for Gerard's success rode at fifty-fifty.

Hazel had accused him of being dishonest with her and Gerard. *The queen of liars, Ha.* Self-preservation required him to keep them in the dark on his plans. If his brother snagged the money, he'd head to Monmouth to rendezvous as he was told. *Sorry, Bro.* Richard planned to get his motor home and move out to the alpaca ranch. After the commotion settled down and if his little brother remained free and clear, he'd reach out. *Probably wheedle more money from the deal.*

Won't be long now. Richard checked the time. Before launch he planned to move the drone outside behind his car.

◆◆◆

Dressed in leather to match the black motorcycle, he idled into the parking lot near the Carousel in Riverfront Park. The driver of a silver gray Porsche waited behind the wheel at the far end of the lot. Turk dismounted and approached the open window. "All clear over there. Didn't see any coppers. The stake with the orange tape's right where they said." He held the helmet in the crook of his arm.

"See the little stiff-legged rat?" Herb Fish asked.

"No. Problem is—I don't think I've seen either him or his brother up close, but I'd sure notice the walk."

"Plenty of time." Herb checked his watch. "I'll move up near the end of the railroad bridge on Union

Street and park on this side. I don't want to get trapped in the park—only one way in and out."

"You've seen the map. You'll find the stake down to the right as you come off the railroad bridge."

"Where you going to be?" Herb peered over his dark glasses.

"I'll be over near you." Turk stuck a thumb back at his bike. "Nobody's going to trap me in there. Besides, I need to track the money once you hand it over." He exposed the top of a Smartphone in his side pocket.

"I've got Boswell on standby in West Salem," Herb said.

"Good." Turk bent over to window height. "Remember, no matter what they say or do, you give up those envelopes. Once they've got the bait I'll be able to find them." He patted his side pocket.

Allen sauntered onto the Union Street Bridge to cross from Salem to the park across the river. The old railroad bridge had been converted for use by pedestrians and other non-motorized traffic.

"Excuse me." A pregnant jogger approached behind a stroller loaded with toddler.

He moved to the side and gazed up at the old bridge's superstructure. He checked behind before he resumed his trek. An elderly gent on a three-wheeled bicycle waved as he passed.

Amused, Allen moved up to the midpoint of the span. Below, the silent, dark green water of the Willamette River churned and rolled on a relentless journey to the sea.

High above the shoreline, through the trees, the bridge continued over a roadway and connected with a walk along the rim of the park bowl.

Two hound-like mutts huffed and puffed as they pulled a dog walker. Allen stepped to the side to avoid being trampled. He remained at the rail where he had a northerly view of the large park complex. Tall, mature trees lined the riverbank and blocked easy access or view of the river. A light breeze rustled the leaves. The sound of a vehicle drew his attention as a truck towed a boat under the bridge. Allen moved to the south side handrail as the truck and boat continued on into the parking lot near the boat launch ramp.

Back on the north side, Allen studied the large oval of parkland. The businesses and dwellings of West Salem bordered the park's western rim. From the entrance, the tree lined road and parking lot divided the grassy basin to create two open areas. He had the perfect spot to observe the smaller area where Matt and the deputies planned to operate. As he judged the distance to be about two hundred yards, he tapped his pocket to check for his compact binoculars. From his research he had discovered that beyond the parking lot, the larger section on the north was a pie-shaped complex of softball fields.

Below him the grass ended at a small dirt lot. The mutts had towed the walker down to the field and busied themselves with the marking ritual. *Who's walking who?* A slight smile formed as the dogs jerked on the leashes to roam in the grass. The black and white lifted a leg on a three-foot stake driven in the ground. The tan copied. Orange flagging on the stake caught his attention. *Hmm, orange flagging like Matt's supposed to look for.* Dog walker tugged the companions out onto the field.

Allen slid his phone out and thumbed a call. Several sets of soccer nets had been positioned to allow simultaneous matches in the field. As he waited for Matt to answer, he pictured vanloads of screaming kids playing soccer on weekends.

"Matt—me, can you talk?"

"Sure. We're killing time. Where're you?"

"In the treetops—on the bridge, the place we spotted on the map. Glad I wore my jacket. Shady here and the breeze has started to rustle the leaves."

"Warm here. I'm in front of a market with Saunders in the undercover car."

"You have all the fun. Listen, you said you'd be on the north end of this field, right?"

"Correct. Across the road from the middle parking lot."

"You're supposed to find some orange flagging, right?"

"Yep."

"Well I'm near the other end of your field and there's some orange tape on a stake right below me."

"Well, the directions we have are pretty clear. Doesn't say stake and we've got some orange tape wrapped on a tree where we're set to go."

"Thought I'd better tell you." Allen glanced over his shoulder at the back of a tall, smelly, unkempt man. "Somebody needs a bath," he whispered.

"What?"

"A guy smelling like a Bigfoot just walked past—homeless type."

"The detectives say there's a lot of homeless hang out in the brush around the park."

"He just turned down into the field headed for the brush—he's one tall dude."

"Talked to Anna. Guess Marion didn't feel up to a trip into Elections today."

"Oh, they still have time before the deadline." Allen said.

"Yeah, but I told her the sooner she closed this out, the sooner she'd be safe."

"You guys going to stay out there?"

"Plan on it. Your tech guy, Victor, he's been great, but we'll stay the duration."

"I thought Beth told me Anna had something coming up."

"Vet appointment for the dogs. Hard to get in and she didn't want to miss again."

"Count on me if you need to be spelled."

"Sorry I couldn't get you a radio to at least listen in on this."

"I got my phone if you need me. Besides, I've got a great view of where you're going to be. I think I've picked out a couple of your people pretending to be groundskeepers."

"Not too obvious—I hope."

"Nope."

"Hey, when I'm through come over and pick me up. I don't want to go back to the cop shop."

Allen dialed Beth after Matt signed off. "How's my favorite hairdresser?"

"Oh, I'll bet you say that to all the girls."

"Only my favorites."

"I can't talk long. I've got a lady under the dryer, and she'll be through in a little while. What's up?"

"Not much. I'm waiting to watch Matt do the payoff, but I just wanted to say how much I miss you."

"That's sweet of you. Miss you too. See you for dinner?"

Allen's gaze had drifted to the parking lot in the trees along the side of the field. "Now, this is interesting." The tall man had opened and closed the back doors on a van.

"What? Dinner?"

"There's a homeless guy. Trees are in my way, but I think he just climbed into a fairly new white van."

"Might be his new home?" She chuckled.

"No." He snickered. "Don't believe he has the means." Allen moved toward the end of the bridge to study the van. "Guess he could be one of the deputies in undercover garb, but nobody would smell that way on purpose."

"Do you always go around smelling people?" She laughed. "What kind of private eye are you?"

"Couldn't help it. He walked by and I was downwind." He moved back onto the bridge to gain cover from the trees. "You like motorcycles?"

"Too dangerous for me. Why?"

"A guy just came in the park on a nice black one. Guess it's a guy. Two hundred yards away makes it hard to tell."

"I'd rather ride a horse."

"That's the second time you've mentioned a horse."

"To you maybe—that's the reason we bought the farm, to raise a couple of horses."

"Then you lost your husband—"

"On top of that Julie Ann ran away. Life wasn't so fun, but I clung to God—kept me from losing my mind. Sad and content at the same time. Does that make sense?"

"I think so. You believed He had things all worked out for you."

"I do."

"You know—I've never been around horses, maybe I should help you get one."

"Oh, I don't know. We can talk about it."

"Hey, you'd like the place where Matt's hiding the old lady. They used to raise horses—big empty stable, now."

"Sounds interesting, I've got to get this poor lady out of the cooker. See you for dinner?"

The line dead, Allen stared at the phone. *Why is it so hard to say, I love you?*

The sound of hard leather soles marched behind him. He leaned on the rail and glanced at the man's back. A business suit and briefcase made an odd sight, but there'd been several odd sights during his short stay. A short distance into the park, the man stopped in the walk and faced the playing field. Through sunglasses, the man studied Allen for a moment before scanning the grassy basin.

Allen faced away and moved several paces toward the river as he scrolled to Matt's number. Dumped into voice mail, he ended the call.

Chapter 27

Something's going on down here, Matt. Allen cupped the compact binoculars in his hands as he pressed them to his eyes. *If only you could read my mind.* At the far end of the field, Matt stood on the grass shielding his eyes with a hand.

The suited man had moved off the path, down the bank and onto the field near the stake with orange flagging. From the bridge above, Allen had a clear view of the man's back and of Matt, who remained still beside a distant tree at the other end of the field. The suit had placed the briefcase on the grass and waited several feet from the stake. Allen set his jaw and kept the binoculars clamped in his hands. He fought the urge to shout, to wave his arms, to warn Matt.

The man on the black motorcycle parked below Allen's position on the bridge. Less than one hundred feet behind the suit, the rider leaned with a hand on the cycle's instrument cluster.

Allen lowered the glasses and checked the time, eleven o'clock. Two men positioned at the same time by orange flagging, but at opposite ends of the field. *What is going on? More than coincidence.*

A faint sound grabbed his attention. Allen searched the sky above West Salem's commercial buildings on the edge of the park to identify the source of the unusual noise. A voice below drew his attention to the motorcycle rider, who motioned toward the park rim. The suit twisted his head skyward.

The sound grew louder. Allen spotted the source, a drone above the trees. Suspended from the craft hung a rounded, bucket like object. He studied the strange object with his binoculars. At one hundred feet, the drone hovered above the suit and rotated a full three-sixty. He'd read and studied pictures of these new innovations. This one had a camera. The drone's pilot was hidden, nowhere in sight.

Allen scoped Matt, who remained statue like. The drone dropped to fifty feet and resumed hover. Then the craft dropped to above the grass surface, left the bowl, and rose to thirty feet above the drop site. Near eye level, Allen studied the drone. Matt remained still. Allen thumbed Matt's number and got voice mail.

Below, the suit snatched something from the bowl on the ground. Allen focused his binoculars on the man. The suited man poked a finger at a cell phone and waited to connect.

This mirrors what Matt's supposed to do. I can't call him—9-1-1 would keep me tied down on the phone. I'll have to improvise. The suit waved his free hand as he talked. The rider in black leather with the helmet hung from his hand joined the suit. Allen noticed the rider's shaved head and build.

Matt remained near the tree but had turned with his back to Allen, the suit, and the drone. *What is going on?* Allen lowered his glasses, swiped a hand over his eyes and caught movement at the white van. With the binoculars, he observed the tall stranger remove boxes from the van and stack them on the edge of the field. Bigfoot jumped in the van and headed out of the park.

Allen swung the glasses back as the motorcycle rider grabbed something from the suit and tossed it in the bowl on the ground. The drone eased down after the men stood back. Allen studied the carrier and recognized envelopes similar to those Matt had prepared. *Really odd. Is Matt victim of a big prank, while the real deal is right here—in front of me? Did the bad guys spot the cops?* He focused back on Matt.

Another one? Above Matt, a drone hovered, tilted, flew erratic, and careened into the tree; parts tumbled to the ground. Several men dressed as groundskeepers ran to the crash site, and a dark sedan with red and blue strobes flashing stopped for Matt. The screech of tires followed the unmarked car with Matt out of the park as sirens howled in the distance.

Below Allen, the drone rose with the bowl. The suit flayed his arms in a panicked state as he talked with the rider. Allen couldn't understand the conversation, but several words rang clear from the raised voices: "Police." "Boxes." "Arrest."

The leather-clad rider strapped the helmet on and strode to the bike. The suit snatched his briefcase and headed for the bridge. After he slipped and stumbled up the bank, the suit fumbled with his phone to place a call. The sounds of the motorcycle moved toward the boat launch area, not the park entrance. From maps, Allen had learned of other routes in and out of the park. He tried another call to Matt. With a glance he caught a glimpse of the drone before it disappeared behind the treetops. He'd better stick with the suit.

"Bruce, we've got a problem." Suit's voice was low as he pressed the phone to his ear, but Allen heard as he kept pace behind him.

"No, no, no. You've got to get the boxes. I can't be here. Crawling with cops."

"I told you where."

"Send Boyd." The man glanced back over his shoulder at Allen and did a double take. The second glance telegraphed the fear and panic behind the dark lenses.

"Wait." Allen's call kicked in the man's afterburners.

Allen tried to keep pace, but he'd never been a sprinter. Across the river, the suit darted right at the end of the bridge and out of Allen's sight. Down the side street he chugged and spotted the suit crouched gasping behind a parked car.

"Hey." Allen waved his arm. "Wait a minute."

The suit sprang from behind the car and veered toward Commercial Street and the skateboard park. But he didn't look as he sprinted into the path of a large pickup and trailer. The truck skidded to a stop, but only after the suit had been knocked to the pavement and flattened.

Allen arrived as the driver and three workers jabbered in Spanish. The limp body sprawled in the road behind the truck and trailer loaded with yard maintenance equipment. The sunglasses were gone from a face with lifeless eyes. Sounds of sirens approached as the driver and workers fled. In front of the truck, Allen spotted a homeless man grab the briefcase from the gutter and hustle away from the scene.

Here we go again. Allen trotted and closed the gap until the homeless man noticed. A burst of speed ended the short footrace when Allen found the discarded briefcase in an alley, unopened.

◆◆◆

Over in West Salem, the man whimpered, face down, cuffed behind his back in the fenced backyard of a vacant house near Wallace Marine Park.

"Gerard Crum? I know who he is," Matt said.

"Stoned." Deputy Saunders nudged a marijuana roach on the patio with the toe of her shoe.

"I followed the surveillance on the radio." Matt tapped the earpiece attached by wire to a receiver hidden under his clothing. "Couldn't picture how you found him."

"We got lucky," Saunders said. "My rover happened down this street and spotted the drone fly up out of the backyard. Didn't think too much about it at the time, but the thing zigzagged so much he kept an eye on it. Then when the drone headed for the park my guy gave us a heads up.

"I heard it first, then spotted it from the parking lot behind you," Saunders said. "When it hovered above your tree, I told them to grab anybody in the backyard."

"When I heard you say that—I ducked." Matt showed how he covered himself with his arms. "I figured if they grabbed the pilot there'd be a crash. Sure enough."

"If I'm remembering, ain't this guy a suspect or accessory in your murder?"

"Uh huh. Has he said much?"

"We haven't tried yet. So dopy dumb I didn't think he'd be much help."

"Mind if I try?"

"Let's move him out to my car," Saunders said. "I'll put you in the back with him."

Matt helped roll Gerard and hoist him to his feet. Together he and the deputy ushered the prisoner around to the front driveway and stuffed him in the back seat.

Outside the car, Saunders said, "I'll interview him. When I nod, that'll be your cue."

Matt opened the door opposite the prisoner, who had his stiff leg across the front of the seat. "Make some room for me," Matt said. Gerard shifted to make a space.

Gerard rolled his head back. "My brother's going to kill me." He sniffed and rocked forward with his chin on his chest. "So nervous—got blasted." A side glance at Matt. "Didn't hear my alarm." He sighed. "Ohh … I ruined his big payday. Crime of the century he called it."

Saunders talked Gerard though his rights then re-cuffed his hands in front so he could sign a waiver. After he gave permission to record their conversation, the deputy asked, "What's your brother's name?"

Matt resisted the urge to answer for the dullard.

Gerard raised his chin off his chest and tried to focus on Saunders. "Richard."

"Where is he?" The deputy asked.

"Waiting for me in Monmouth." He mumbled and shut his eyes. "Gonna kill me. I messed up—always messing up."

"Where in Monmouth?"

"Don't know. He's going to call when he gets there."

"The big payday—was that the money you tried to pick up with the drone?"

His reddened eyes opened wide. "No. Half. Richard's smartest. Down at the other end of the field—his drone picked up the other half." He searched the faces of his inquisitors. "Did he do it? Did he?"

"We ask the questions, Gerard," Saunders said.

"Hot diggity." He slapped his bum leg. "He did." Gerard smiled as he shook his head.

"Who was he supposed to rip off?" Saunders asked.

"Union big shots. Boyd's bosses."

The story developed for Matt in dribbles and drabbles. Matt's phone vibrated. Allen needed to talk. He sent a standby message to his partner.

Gerard described how they planned and carried out the assault on the old woman, the theft and the attempted double extortion. After he drew a map to locate Richard's motor home, Saunders nodded.

"Gerard, have you ever killed anyone?" Matt asked.

"No." He studied Matt's eyes. "I'm not too smart, but I can't hurt anybody."

"I believe you." He paused. "Who killed Duffy?"

A blink. "Boyd." He shook his head. "Didn't see him do it, but had to be him."

Gerard recounted his role in Tom Duffy's death and implicated Boyd as the one who planned to cause the accident, which turned fatal.

Outside the car, Saunders said, "Ain't real sophisticated. Think we'll put together a good case and pick up his brother Richard."

"The smartest ever." Matt smiled. "We're going to have to see what happened at the other end of the field. I saw a couple of guys down there, but didn't pay a lot of attention."

"We did have other things on our mind."

"My partner's been trying to reach me. He was down there, somewhere." Matt fished the phone from his pocket and punched the number.

"About time," Allen said.

"We're tied up with Gerard. Picked him up for the extortion, and they'll get a warrant for the brother."

"I figured you got someone, but you missed the other half."

"How much did you see of the other payoff?"

"Everything. But I didn't know the Crum brothers were the pilots."

"Where are you?"

"Across the river, about a block from the Gilbert House. I'm behind the wheel of a nice Porsche Carrera."

"Whose?"

"Herb Fish, Speaker's Chief of Staff."

"He with you?"

"No, he ran into the grill of a truck. They hauled him off to the morgue. I recovered his stolen brief case. Found his keys, wallet and a bunch of papers authorities may find interesting."

Matt spotted Saunders with several officers at the curb. He cupped his hand and kept his voice low. "Lock the car. Take the briefcase over to our office and copy everything. I'll stall as long as I can before I bring Saunders by to pick the stuff up."

"Something else," Allen said. "Did they pick up the guy in the white van or the boxes he left?"

"Don't think we know about that. Here comes Saunders. I'll put her on the phone and you can tell her."

Chapter 28

Sirens screamed. A dark sedan streaked past, colored strobe lights flashing. In the gateway, Richard stomped the brake, frozen at the wheel. An alarm bell clanged because he blocked the automated gate. Nerves churned in his gut as he eased off the brake and drove out of the storage lot.

With his head on a swivel, stuck at a red light, Richard fought panic. The signal turned green. He regained control as the traffic moved. Over the bridge, into Salem's business district he circled blocks and drove through a parking garage to check for pursuers. An accident snarled traffic. Cars blocked his view as he passed the scene around a stalled truck and trailer. Near the incident he caught a glimpsed of a large man who struck him as familiar.

Clear of danger, he headed out of the city, feeling haunted. Haunted by concern for Gerard. Stupid, clumsy, but his blood nonetheless. Richard had drilled Gerard, but he had to let him succeed or fail on his own. Before he completed his flight operation, he'd pivoted the drone's camera to the other end of the field. Gerard had been late.

Maybe dumb luck rescued him. He congratulated himself on the precautions taken because of his brother's tendency to fail. If arrested,

Gerard would give up the locations for their rendezvous and his motor home. He hoped a stakeout in Monmouth would delay the cops long enough for him to hit the road in his motor home. Time to move onto his next score anyway.

It was a tight fit for the white rental car between the house and Hershel's truck, but he needed room to drive away in the motor home. The rips in his gloves required him to wipe the rental down to remove his fingerprints. He grabbed his gear bag. Alert for unusual activity or sounds in the rural neighborhood, he made preparations to leave. Inside, he dropped the bag and removed the windshield curtain. After he retracted the levelers, his attempt to reach Gerard on the phone confirmed his suspicions. Neither the voice nor the manner matched his brother's.

Richard snatched the bag from the floor. He needed a moment to admire his take. From inside, he grabbed the stolen gun and stuffed the cold steel inside his waistband. The two business sized envelopes made him smile. He bent down to peek out the window as a motorcycle passed the foreclosed property. *Same bike and rider when I was with Bones—has to be.* He fingered the butt of the gun.

The two envelopes appeared the same, but the one in his left hand had more heft. Richard dropped the lighter one back in the bag. He ripped open the heavier envelope and found a thin rectangular box sandwiched in the one thousand dollar bills. *Tracking me—not the cops—union guys.* He snatched the plastic device from the bundle, hurled it to the floor and smashed the tattletale device with his heel.

Again, the motorcycle passed. Alerted, Richard held his breath as he followed the sound. The foliage that concealed the motor home also blocked a clear view of the road. The rumble from the engine quit.

Convinced the motorcycle rider remained near, but out of his sight, Richard prepared for the worst. He tucked the rest of the money in his bag and grabbed the backpack he had prepared for such an occasion. Raising the hatch lid, he dropped his bags into the lower storage compartment and felt a flood of regret as he prepared for the fiery destruction of his home. Richard took a position to watch for the intruder.

The man shoved the gate open and strode up the driveway toward the motor home. He showed no caution, only purpose. The black leather outfit and shaved head fit the arrogance of his approach. Richard recognized the man from his visit to the Portland parking garage.

He snuck to the front and locked the door. *Too easy might make him suspicious.* He hurried back to the bedroom and slipped down into the compartment with his bags. A deep breath and a slow exhale calmed him. He swiped at the sweat on his forehead.

He hunkered down, listening to the metal on metal sounds of a forced entry. The door banged open as the intruder succeeded. *Quiet.* Richard felt the motor home rock with the weight of the man's entrance. He raised his hand and hooked his finger on the trigger for his bomb. The sound of the plastic crumbs under a hard sole signaled the moment. He yanked the cord to slam the lid as he tripped the timer switch.

Rushing out the side hatch with his gear, Richard dove into the bushes toward the road to gain as much distance as he could in seven seconds. The shock wave, heat and sound blew through the brush and knocked him to the ground.

Richard shook his head to stop the ringing in his ears. Over his shoulder, a ball of fire consumed the motor home and anything near. Bags in hand to shield his face from the intense heat, he stumbled toward the house to find his rental. The side of Hershel's truck was scorched and smoke billowed from the tires. He hoped the car had survived.

The intense heat had discolored the roof. He started the engine, drove through the open gate and sped past a few neighbors who gawked at the spectacle. He'd need to get out of sight and dump this car.

Thirty minutes later, Richard found anonymity in the large parking lot near a WinCo store. Surrounded by cars of all shapes, sizes and conditions, his disfigured rental fit unnoticed. A newsbreak on a local radio station headlined a house fire fought by firefighters from Turner and Jefferson. There were early reports of one dead. *Good. You made a run at me, Mr. Leach. You'll hear from me soon.*

After sundown, Richard backed out of his hiding place and drove out of the lot. The back streets slowed his travel, but they had fewer snoopy eyes. He needed several passes of Hazel's cul-de-sac to confirm Bully Boyd's absence. He entered the neighborhood and stopped against the rear bumper of Hazel's wreck.

"How could you?" She cursed him.

"Now, Sis—wait," He stiff-armed his way in and shut the door. "Hear me out."

"Nothing you say—" she sputtered, "Nothing can fix what you've done." She stormed about the room in a hysterical rant, cursing.

"Calm down." He waved his arms like a choir director. She was a mess, reddened eyes, tearstained cheeks, nose ring flopping, short hair in every direction. "We're family. I need your help."

"You're not family. I disowned you." She slumped on a battered, threadbare couch. "If Mom and Dad were still alive they'd do the same." The waterworks flowed.

"After all I've done to help you over the years." He pled from the center of the room. "You show no appreciation."

"Yeah, you sure helped me now. Boyd paid my bills. Because of you he's been arrested for murder and Gerard's in jail for extortion and for trying to kill some old woman."

"I had nothing to do with any murder. What? You need money?" As long as he could remember, the mere mention of money played to her weakness.

"I hate you, Richard." She wiped her face with the sleeve of her purple t-shirt. "Boyd paid for my phone and the cable hook up. I gotta have those."

He opened his wallet and handed her five hundred dollars. "Hazel, I need a place to spend the night."

She glared, the money clenched in her fist. "One night—that's all."

"Anything to eat?"

"I ain't your cook." She cranked up the TV volume and crossed her arms. "Call for a pizza."

A shower later, Richard ate pizza at the table. "Hey, Sis, I can't eat all this. Won't you have some? You always liked the pineapple before. C'mon."

Hazel shoved herself from the couch, shuffled over and opened the refrigerator. Two beers in hand she joined him at the table. With the remote, she selected local news.

He gave a nod and a grin as he twisted the top. "To old times."

"Ha, no thanks, Brother." The nose ring swung as she shook her head. "You're out of here tomorrow. You only look after yourself—no one else—not even family." She grabbed a wedge of pizza.

He drank and leaned back in the kitchen chair. News stories rolled by without notice until one jarred his attention. "Turn it up."

A reporter fired questions as she stuck a microphone in the woman's face. The building in the background he recognized. He stared at the man in the doorway behind the woman featured in the report— the private eye. Anger surged. His face flushed. He swiped at beads of sweat on his forehead.

The reporter said, "The police have not revealed the identity of the man arrested. Do you have any comment?"

"Yes. Union leaders tried to bully Marion Walters to stop her right-to-work measure from being placed on the ballot. The man arrested and his accomplice nearly killed a gentle lady. They can rot in jail."

"She talking 'bout Gerard?" Hazel asked.

Richard waved for silence.

"Are you suggesting the union leaders are behind the violence?" the reporter asked.

"If the shoe fits," the woman said. "Within a few days, Marion Walters will march in with the last of the signatures required for the ballot measure."

"A serious charge, do you have proof union leadership is behind the violence?"

"She doesn't have to prove anything."

Richard flung the bottle at the private investigator on the screen, but missed.

"You break it, you'll buy me a new one," Hazel yelled.

"And who are you?" the reporter asked.

"I'm a private investigator. I've worked with the leaders of this petition drive." The name, Matt Kinler, displayed on the screen. "If your station wants proof, I can point you in the right direction. We've had people killed, assaulted and burned out of their homes. Responsibility can be factually placed at the feet of union leaders. I challenge you—any news organization—to look into this."

"Do you have your Internet connection up?" Richard asked.

"Yeah—Boyd's."

He jumped over to the laptop on the end table beside the couch. With the browser up he queried Matt Kinler, private investigator. As the information displayed, he grabbed a note pad and pen with matching union logos. Richard jotted notes as he viewed the search results.

"What're you going to do?"

"Payback. You don't need to know anything else." A little pressure and she'd give him up just like his little brother. Weak. He stuffed notes in his pants pocket and hooked the pen in his shirt pocket. "Hope you don't mind."

"No. Plenty of union pens around here."

"Sis, I need to dump my car—it's too hot."

"I don't want to get arrested for helping you. You'll be gone tomorrow, right?"

"Yes, but I want to get rid of that car, now." He stomped in the middle of the room.

"I won't ride in no hot car." Hazel grabbed another piece of pizza. "You can follow me over to the state employee parking. I need to get Boyd's truck. You leave your car there and drive mine back here."

"Deal."

◆◆◆

Twice he'd brought police to my door. He'd outlived his usefulness. Leach surveyed his favorite city. Dusk. The pungent smoke swirled up and against the window. First the Salem detective called about his car at the hospital. Now, some sheriff's detective had found Turk's body and black motorcycle near a house fire. *No. I have no idea. Haven't seen him for several days.*

He returned to the desk and measured two more fingers of whiskey. Swirl, a taste, he drew on his Corona. *Next of kin? Sorry, detective, can't help you.* Accidental death or by the hand of another, it gave him a sad pause. Heartless, he wasn't. Turk had been loyal and effective. He gave a toast before he tapped a number on his desk phone. Message left, he'd wait for Stryker to return the call.

Boswell called earlier in the day. Fish had been killed after the payoff. Turk had the tracker, but he and the money were gone. Worse, Boswell heard the old woman had enough signatures and planned to turn them in soon. Recent polls continued to show the measure would pass. *Can't let that happen.*

The light for incoming blinked. "Leach." He jabbed the button for speaker and replaced the handset.

"What can I do for you?" the caller said.

"The problem we discussed several days ago. Need it resolved—without delay."

"Immediate action doesn't allow proper time to prepare. I've found the location as you asked, nothing more. I've no confirmation the target is there."

"You've got the only description I have and my source is no longer available."

"These extraordinary circumstances require an extraordinary fee."

"Without objection."

Chapter 29

Whoa. Richard's stomach flipped and flopped before the car landed on the plank surface of the old bridge. He braked for the sharp pitch off the wooden span. The brown beater sputtered as he punched the accelerator to climb another hill. For an hour he'd pressed his luck on the back roads from Salem. South, across the county line, through forest and farmland, he headed for his new hideout.

He'd paid one thousand for the battered subcompact with over three hundred thousand miles on the odometer. Not a good deal, but he gained ground with Hazel. She smiled when he slapped the money on the table. *May need her again someday.*

Open fields of spring grass along the narrow road alerted him to slow for the Webster farm. He ignored the "Keep Out" signs on the open gate and drove up the graveled lane to the old two-story house. A gray cat streaked uphill for a shed beyond the house and disappeared. The old gal waited on the covered front porch. Straw hat, light blue housedress, white apron and black rubber knee boots. She held a double-barrel shotgun in the crook of her arm.

In the dirt yard at the bottom of the steps, Richard eased out of the car and raised his hands. "Ms. Grace? It's me, Toby. Don't you remember?" Her memory was the reason he'd selected this opportunity.

She squinted to study the visitor. "What you want?"

"I'm here to start work. Help with your alpacas."

Grace clomped down the steps. "I don't have my glasses." Again she squinted and said, "You the one with the motor home?" She tapped the fender of his car with the barrel.

"You remembered. It's in the shop for repairs."

"Thought you were going to hook up by the barn. Can't stay in my house." She raised the gun. "Don't want anybody in my house."

"I'd be glad to use your old workshop. Just temporary."

Grace sucked air through her clenched dentures. "I haven't done much with it since I cleaned out the chickens."

"I'd pay rent."

"Well, I suppose you can." She smiled. "You'll have to deal with the barn cat; he's staked a claim in there. None too friendly—good mouser."

The balance of the morning and afternoon he spent in the workshop. The old prune-faced woman loaned him an ancient canvas army cot left behind by her husband. She didn't want him in the house. *What's she hiding in there*? He'd need access to formulate a plan to separate her from her money.

When she called him for chores he had the old shed whipped into a barebones man cave, with electricity, cot, woodstove and workbench. The overstuffed chair, claimed by Cat, he'd shoved in a back corner. The dark gray, sullen creature used a two by three foot opening in the back wall to come and go. Outside, the board ramp from the opening reminded him of the kind used on chicken coops, but when he swept he didn't find feathers.

At the sound of her voice, he glanced out the only window. She waited downhill between the house and the barn with a lunch box.

"All tidied up." Richard met her at the barn door.

"Fixed you some supper." She swung the metal box out for him.

Stacks of baled hay filled the front half of the barn. The back half had been built as a three-sided shelter. As they dropped hay in the trough, alpaca paraded inside to dine.

"Do you make a lot from their fur?" he asked.

"Fleece." She slapped the end of a hose to his chest. "Fill their water. I'll turn on the faucet."

"Do you get much from the fleece?" He counted seventeen animals.

"No. All my alpaca are culls—behavior problems or flawed. Nobody wants them for their fleece, breeding or show. I don't need the income anymore so I save these rejects from the slaughterhouse. Every once in a while I'll sell one as a pet or donate their fleece to a 4-H club for them to practice making yarn."

"Like an animal rescue—a charity."

"Might say that."

After chores, Richard tucked supper under his arm and headed for the shed. The dry tuna sandwich, apple and pear didn't cut it. Mr. Cat glared at the intruder. A weak cell signal under the metal roof made his Smartphone erratic. He tossed the phone on the cot, glared back at the feral beast and moved to the window. The sun had set. Scattered and sparse lights dotted the valley below. *She doesn't need the income?*

Preoccupied with revenge, he had no interest in panoramic views or lights in the dark. Before he'd left Hazel's, he'd found an address for a Matt Kinler in the Santiam Canyon. Rather than the man's office, he wanted to hit where it'd hurt most, the home.

Richard grabbed the old soldering iron under the workbench. If the thing worked, he had the parts in his bag to assemble the detonator and trigger. The other ingredients he'd purchase on a trip into Albany before the stores closed. A smell and the thin curl of smoke from the iron spurred him into action. His plans didn't include tomorrow morning's chores. If the old woman remembers she had an employee, she'd be angry. But it wasn't a concern; he'd schmooze his way around her.

As he fitted parts together, he thought of supplies for a shopping list. A piece of paper had been rolled and stuck with a pen in an old canning jar on the bench. He plucked the ballpoint and paper from the jar. Printed on the barrel of the pen, he read "Webster 4 Alpacas." A tip protector remained, as the pen hadn't been used. Richard unrolled the paper, which was a two-year-old invoice for the purchase of gold coins. His mind churned with possibilities as he read twenty thousand dollars. *A pile of gold—is that why you don't want me in your house?* Through the window he studied the farmhouse.

The Webster ballpoint worked better than the one he'd taken from Hazel. He finished his work and tucked the pen in his pocket with the list of supplies.

Richard carried his handiwork to the car and placed the parts in the trunk beside a can of motor oil.

Hazel told him the engine burned oil. Hood up, he checked and had to use the last can. He added oil to his list on the back of the invoice. With the flashlight he bent down to shine the light under his engine. A dark patch on the ground confirmed his suspicion, but he'd be rid of the car before long.

◆◆◆

Rouge killer. Lone wolf. Psychopath. Labels entered into the record of his court martial and etched in his mind. Trained as a sniper by the US Army, commanders in the First Gulf War called Stryker one of the best. Best, that is, until the time he returned to base from a mission at three in the morning. His spotter and driver dropped him near his tent. Passage of time hadn't dimmed memories of that night. Vivid in his mind were the heat and the child's screams above the din of a base operating around the clock.

Stryker adjusted the head harness for the night vision goggles. The grass field allowed a straight line approach up to the back of the knoll. After he had scaled several fences and tromped over a mile through grass on uneven ground, his knees and ankles ached. He adjusted the sniper rifle slung on his shoulder. *Retirement sounds better and better.* In his day, to pack his rifle and gear mile after mile posed no challenge. But not today; he had to accept the toll of aging. Eyesight, hearing, stamina—all diminished.

He hadn't understood the language of the child, but the frantic pleas for help in any language would've compelled him to act. When he yanked the flap of the tent aside a naked Arab man stood over a young naked boy tied to a cot. The child bled from several cuts. The drunken eyes, the wicked grin, were something he'd never forget. The man raised the knife and lunged. Stryker's bullet drilled a hole through the brutal animal's brain, who was dead before he hit the ground. He freed the boy. *Never got his name. Never saw him again.* The prosecutor suggested the child never existed.

Thick brush outside the fence and up the back of the knoll slowed his progress. Three hundred plus yards from his target didn't require stealth, but noise discipline had become second nature. He checked his GPS once more before the climb to the top.

He'd never married; the Army was his bride, the life he chose. But they'd kicked him out, Dishonorable Discharge. Stripped of rank, six months in the stockade, no pay, no benefits and not so much as a thank you. His defense attorney told him that, if not for his exemplary record, he'd be in Leavenworth for life. *I didn't know the naked man was an Iraqi officer—on our side. I still would've shot him. Right and wrong were clear to me—but not to the Army. Ha.*

From the crest, he studied the distant house. The left half was all windows, but the lights were low. Stryker used his knife to clear brush from his field of fire and moved a few rocks to make a comfortable place to lie. Small in stature, he didn't need much space. A prone position with the bipod made for an easy shot. According to Leach, the lady had white, white hair, a thin build and used a walker.

He studied the windows with his scope. A couch against the windows faced into the room. Heads of two people appeared above the back. From the hairstyles, he guessed women, but the lighting didn't help him decide if one had white hair.

A dark pickup waited off the road for the gate to open and then drove up to the right side of the house. He adjusted the focus. The truck he recognized as the one used by the private investigator. The driver walked into the garage. Stryker swung back to the lighted room in time to see a man enter. After the new arrival leaned down to one of the women, the man went into what appeared to be a kitchen. Stryker watched and waited to identify his target.

Later, a sedan arrived at the gate and drove up to the house. The large driver and a passenger strolled off into the darkness behind the house. On his first reconnaissance, he had spotted stables and corrals behind the dwelling. The couple returned after a few minutes and entered the garage.

Stryker wiped his strong eye, blinked and sighted on the room where everyone gathered. Maybe the white haired woman hadn't joined the others yet. The larger man he could track, but with people up and down, back and forth, target identification became difficult. A long time had passed since he'd worked with a spotter, but his current profession required him to work alone.

Thrown out of the Army, he had no future. Who needed a shooter? Flat broke and depressed, one day an old friend from his unit had found him at his parent's Colorado farm. A business manager for a huge public employees' union, his friend had offered him an opportunity to use his skills and to earn more than he'd thought possible. A poor farmer to most, Stryker became a code name known within a small circle. To right a wrong, this principle justified his first hit. Over the years, justification had been pushed aside. Tonight, he lay in wait for an old woman. His employer didn't bother with a reason. He didn't think to ask.

The large man waved his arms as he entered the room. *What got him worked up? Pacing around, waving his arms, upset about something. Maybe the old gal is back in another room.*

He rolled from the rifle to relax from the strain. The eye doctor had noticed cataracts during his last exam. Early stages, but they could affect his vision. *Maybe that's why the images aren't clear.*

Chapter 30

"Sure quiet without the nurse here," Marion said. "Do this—don't do that, take this—don't eat that. She drove me nuts." She shifted her position on the couch. "I'd just get comfortable and she'd say, 'Time to go for a walk.' Oh, she meant well."

Seated at the opposite end, Anna smiled at the elderly lady's rant. "She wanted you back on your feet. We all do." The couch made Marion appear smaller. Her head stuck above the backrest, but not by much. The swelling in her face was gone, but the discoloration from the bruises remained.

"Is the security guy still here?" Marion asked.

"Yes, he's in the study with the control panel. I peeked in on him. He's got video games all set up in there."

"And we're paying him. You guys went to a lot of trouble for me."

"We would anyway, but right now there's a lot riding on your recovery."

"I do feel a lot better." She pressed spots on her face. "I talked to Nancy. She'll pick me up tomorrow and we'll get this over with."

"You sure?"

"I came out without my walker, didn't I?" She stuck her hands out. "Besides, the stupid thing kept dropping a wheel. Almost toppled over."

"Remind me to have Matt check the wheel when he comes."

"Did they catch the other guy? The one who put me in the hospital?"

"Not yet. I think Matt goes to the Grand Jury on your case tomorrow. Better. He spent a good part of the day getting ready."

"They can throw the book at 'em—for all I care. Union too."

"I agree, but I doubt that'll happen."

"So this guy—Richard Crum's his name, right?" Marion glanced over.

Anna nodded.

"He planned to get payoffs from two of us at the same time?"

"Yes, but he only got the union money."

"Shows they were up to their eyeballs in trying to stop me."

"Matt called his FBI friend. They're going to meet to see if the feds can do anything with the union."

Victor's voice boomed from the hall to announce someone had entered the gate. Anna checked the time. "My husband, late as usual."

"Does he think there's much chance?" Marion asked.

"Matt said they'd need a prosecutor with a backbone and no political ties."

"Your husband's got a steady hand on things."

"Yes, but he doesn't always mind me."

"Who doesn't mind you?" Matt beamed as he strode into the room.

"You." Anna said.

Matt leaned over and kissed his wife.

"Why're you late?"

"You remember the TV news I was in, right? I got a call from the station manager. She has assigned a reporter to do an in-depth report on our charges against the union."

"Will the FBI back off with all the attention?" Anna asked.

"Just the opposite. I think news stories might build public pressure for them to do something."

"Still need a prosecutor with backbone," Anna said.

"I'd bet a really brilliant person said that too." He smiled.

"Oh, stop it." Anna chuckled.

"You snuck up on us," Marion said.

"If you turned this sofa around, you could see the gate and road," Matt said. "But, best we don't do that yet and keep the lights down."

"Matt, I'd like some coffee. Marion?" Anna asked.

Matt caught Marion's nod as he moved into the kitchen. "Allen's bringing Beth out tonight." He raised his voice.

"Got a text from Beth. They're on the way," Anna said.

"I can't tell you anything."

"Occasionally."

"Sometimes I think you're clairvoyant."

"And don't you forget it." She accepted a cup of coffee.

"Do you two always kid around?" Marion asked.

"Kid? We're serious." Matt served her coffee.

"My husband—" She puffed through closed lips. "Always serious. Didn't joke much."

"Matt's problem is that sometimes he jokes when he should be serious."

"Incoming car." Victor again.

"Do you think the DA will get indictments tomorrow?" Anna asked.

"Probably not tomorrow because they'll have to round up more witnesses. Won't be long." Matt explained what he knew of tomorrow's proceedings.

Beth rushed into the room ahead of Allen. "Anna, you haven't been by to see me." She dropped onto the couch between Anna and Marion.

"I will when things settle down—I need a haircut and a tint on my gray." Anna fluffed with her fingers. "What brings you out here?"

"Allen wanted me to see the stables. He thinks I'd like a horse—I'm not sure." She touched Anna's hand. "Before I forget, I'm not sure I locked your backdoor when I picked up more dog food."

"Nobody bothers us up there. I thought you told me you loved horses. Always wanted one of your own."

"I did…" She glanced at her hands, "But life doesn't always go the way we want."

Anna touched her friend's hand. "You have my permission to be happy."

Beth glanced over with her moist eyes and nodded.

"I need my hair colored too." Marion patted her hair and pulled on a few strands. "I like a whiter gray. Turns this darker gray if I let it go too long."

"After what you've been through, you come by when you're able and I'll do your hair for free."

"I may just do that," Marion said. "Should have you do my hair before I deliver the last of those signatures. But that can't wait."

"Where'd Allen go?" Anna asked.

"He wanted to check on Victor." Beth said.

"So, I hear you're planning to go to Elections tomorrow." Matt's eyes followed a set of headlights on the road below. "Are you sure you're up for it?"

"I get around the house good without that walker. Get tired fast, but we don't have time to build my stamina."

"Matt, a wheel falls off of her walker," Anna said. "Maybe you could fix it for her."

Allen entered with a scowl.

"Something wrong?" Matt asked.

"It's been so quiet, Victor started gaming and not tending to business." Allen waved his arms as he paced.

"Problem?" Matt raised his eyebrows.

"The motion sensor on the knoll flickered." Allen stuck his finger toward the knoll. "But we're on the outer limit of its effective range."

"Thing acted up the first day we placed it out there," Matt said.

"Yeah, but I told him to shut his video games down." Allen waved his arms again.

"Spoilsport," Matt said.

"My eye. Said he thought he heard a noise like the bolt action on a rifle, but decided the sound must've been from his game." Allen shook his head. "Forty year old kid."

"The microphone had better range. Should we go out and check?"

Allen shook his head. "He's supposed to keep his ear glued. Let's wait."

"You're right, probably nothing," Matt said.

"Where's the bathroom?" Beth followed unspoken directions down the hall.

"You need me to come back after I take her home?" Allen asked.

"Not tonight, but I could use help tomorrow. I testify when the Grand Jury meets in the morning in Albany. Also have an appointment with the OSP homicide guys to talk about Duffy. Anna has a vet appointment—what time, Honey?"

"Not until noon."

"We're covered tonight, and Anna will hang around until Nancy picks Marion up in the morning. That is unless Marion changes her mind."

"I'm going," Marion said.

Matt smiled at her spunk as he said to Allen, "Be good if you got here mid-morning. Give poor Victor a break. We should all be back in the afternoon."

Beth carried the walker at her side as she returned to the couch. "Allen." She lowered her voice. "Go talk to Victor. He looked like a whipped puppy when I walked by."

"You're right. I got a little frustrated." Allen headed into the hall.

Beth stood the walker upside down and tested the fit of the wheels. "Heard you talk about the walker." She wiggled one wheel out of the leg with the housing insert attached. "I had an elderly customer with this same model." Beth chuckled. "She had the same problem. Almost a disaster then, but funny now."

"What happened?" Anna asked.

"She couldn't get it in her head to just roll and slide the thing. For some reason she had to pick it up and set it down as she moved."

"That's what I do." Marion smiled. "The first one I had in the hospital didn't have wheels. It's hard for me to change."

"Oh, I'm not criticizing. Just the way it happened." Beth worked the wheel back in place. "Anyway, I had her in for a permanent. I'd finished the rollers, the solution and had everything covered. Time to move her to the drier." She started to giggle, "I'm sorry. I shouldn't laugh. I got her up. She's got the plastic cap over her head, neck wrapped and the drape over her front. I drag the walker over. She grabs the handles and lurches for the drier. I'm beside her. Halfway across a wheel drops off as she jerks up on the walker. Before I could stop her, she plants the thing and rocks forward toward the low side. Close call, but I grabbed her arm and kept her upright."

Anna chuckled. "Does create a funny picture in my mind. Good thing you were close by."

"My manicurist chews gum all the time. She slapped a big gob in the leg, jammed the wheel back on."

"The gum worked?" Anna asked.

"Seemed to—I can laugh now," Beth said. "Here, let me show you." She yanked the faulty wheel out and stood over the walker. "See, really uneven." She took a few cautious steps without the wheel. "This was how she looked." Laughter from the ladies encouraged Beth to exaggerate her movements.

Suddenly, a slight thud as the window shattered. Broken glass crashed on and around Anna and Marion.

Beth crumpled forward over the walker and landed face down on the floor.

"Oh, Beth." Anna ignored the shards and leaped to kneel beside her friend.

Allen rushed into the kitchen. "Heard a shot— Oh no. He crouched low as he rushed to Beth's side.

"Get down. Everybody." Matt hit the kitchen light switch and lunged for the one lamp.

Light from the hall allowed Anna to see blood ooze into the hair on the back of Beth's head.

"Matt, get some towels," Anna said.

Matt kept low as he scrambled into the hall.

Allen eased the walker out from under Beth's body and straightened her arm. "Beth. Oh, please be okay."

A muffled groan.

"She's alive, Matt." Anna grabbed the towels. "Call 9-1-1." She blotted the blood and parted the hair to find the wound. Beth stirred. "I'm trying to be easy." The back of her head's a bloody mess. "We've got to stop the bleeding, Allen."

"Let's try to get her so she can breathe better." Allen yanked a pillow from a chair and helped Anna roll Beth to her side with the pillow stuffed under the side of her head.

"Gotta keep pressure on the wound," Anna said. "Get me another towel." She replaced the blood soaked towel and pressed.

Allen caressed Beth's forehead. "Oh, baby, I'm sorry I got you into this." He brushed strands of hair away from her face.

Beth opened and closed her eyes. "What happened?" She groaned.

"Somebody shot you." Anna was worried her friend would go into shock. With a hand on Beth's pale, cool forehead, she said, "Let's stuff a pillow under her legs."

Allen rushed to help raise the legs.

"The bullet was meant for me," Marion said from the floor. Her back was to the couch, and she hung her head.

"I can't tell for sure," Anna said as she peeked under the towel, "but it looks like a really bad cut. Don't see bone." She applied a fresh towel.

Matt crawled up and knelt beside his wife. "Victor's on the 9-1-1 call. I reached Saunders. She's on the way too."

"Think the shooter's still there?" Allen asked.

"The mic and sensor have been quiet. Until the law gets here, we better assume he's still out there."

"It's all my fault." Tears streamed down Marion's discolored cheeks. "Is she going to be okay?"

Anna yanked Matt's arm to hold the towel and scooted to comfort Marion. "I think she's going to live—with a really sore head for a few days." She placed an arm across Marion's shoulders.

"I hope so." She wiped at the tears.

"This isn't your fault. Don't go there." She shot a stern glance at Allen. "Goes for you too, Buster."

"If I hadn't pushed this ballot measure, none of this would've happened."

"If there weren't evil, power-hungry monsters, none of this would've happened," Anna said.

"Let's pray for Beth," Allen said.

Chapter 31

Black powder, electric matches, cell phone wired,
gasoline, propane, tape—Richard ran the inventory in
his mind. Because of the hour, he didn't get
everything on his list in Albany. There was no choice;
he had to find his gunpowder in Salem. Afraid of
being spotted by cops, he rubbernecked through the
city. The time of day and darkness worked to his
advantage. With pain from the bullet wound bearable,
he moved without much of a limp.

Mischief after midnight had always worked
well for him. He ventured out onto the highway and
headed for his destination. He had figured one hour
for travel time. The dash clock read three-seventeen.
He'd torch the private eye in his bed and be back on
the farm before daybreak in time for morning chores.
Might make for a good alibi.

The turn lane appeared in the headlights. He
signaled. In the last thirty minutes, not one set of
headlights had passed, going east or west. That was
one reason he chose a weeknight; the other, he didn't
want to wait.

Five miles was the estimated distance to where
he'd turn off the canyon road. He cursed the fogged
headlight lenses. Unfamiliar with the route he slowed
and monitored the odometer to find the right turn.
Richard yanked the steering wheel when the
intersection appeared in his lights. The graveled

surface and the sudden steep climb caught him off
guard. His car fish-tailed. The worn engine hesitated
and sputtered as he corrected and stomped the gas
pedal. In the dark, he couldn't tell if the sign read
Game Trail Road. Tires spun in the gravel as he
passed the end of a lane to the right. *Must be the
driveway. Pitch black in there.* When the brown beater
balked, he killed the engine and set the brake.

Unsure whether he had reached his goal,
Richard grabbed his flashlight and crept onto the
property. Inside the line of tall trees, he flashed the
light on the back and side of a dwelling. Cautious with
the light, he studied the siding on the house. *Cedar?
Make a good fire.*

No lights, no sounds. He worked his way
along the side to the front. No vehicles, nothing to
indicate the owners were home. He eased up the steps,
worked his light around the porch and in a front
window. A dog bone lay beside one of the porch
chairs. *No dogs barking.*

Richard explored the other sides of the house
and returned to the car. Behind the wheel, he
considered the options: set the place to blow now or
come back. *Safer for me with nobody around.*

Two trips and he had his gear at the back door.
With gloved hands, he grabbed the pry bar and
prepared to work on the door. A deadbolt had been
installed. He gripped the doorknob to test the play. To
his surprise, the knob turned. He pushed. The door
opened. A tiptoe tour of the first floor confirmed
Kinler was gone and had been for several days. He
flipped through the stack of mail on a table.

Other people's bank statements and financial mail begged to be opened. He whistled softly at the balances. *Better not Richard, account activity would be the first place the police checked.* He didn't want to leave his fingerprints or a connection to this fire.

In the hall, he stooped over and used his gloved fingertip to punch the computer's power button. Something fell. He shined his flashlight on the floor to identify the source of the noise, but saw nothing. *Probably kicked something.* The monitor displayed a request for the user's password. *I don't have time.*

He checked the first floor for a location to install the incendiary bomb. In the crowded pantry, he shined the light on the floor. One edge of the cover for the crawlspace access hole showed beside a bag of dog food. He shoved the bag to the back of the small room to uncover the lid.

Assembly didn't take long once he'd moved the components under the house. Gasoline, propane, black powder fuse and a cell phone igniter made a potent fire starter. Dynamite was the only ingredient he didn't have, but the powder would do. He preferred dynamite; he'd find more. The timers he used to trigger the old farmer's place worked fine there. For this job, he planned to be far away and yet control the moment of detonation. A wired cell phone to receive his signal and kick off the igniter would do the trick.

Pleased with the installation, Richard changed his mind. He had to observe his handiwork. The old gal may be angry with him for missing morning chores, but he'd work around her. He backed the car down the hill. Farther into the canyon, he selected a spot on the shoulder of the road where he could observe, but with enough distance to avoid being recognized. Parked, engine off, he leaned back to get comfortable. Comfortable indeed, he fell asleep.

Later, the compression brake on a log truck rattled him awake. Richard sat bolt upright; couldn't believe the time, eleven-ten. He wrestled with what to do. Check the house, wait, set the fire, he couldn't decide. First, a nature call. He jumped out of the car and into the bushes across the ditch.

A white pickup approached as he climbed out of the ditch. He waited behind his car and rubbed a hand over his face as a utility company truck passed. Minutes later, a car with flashers headed up the road toward him. The rural mail carrier appeared to be sorting mail as she drove past and into the canyon. He climbed in behind the wheel. *I'll need to decide soon.*

Forty minutes later, Richard spotted a minivan headed his way. He scrunched down. The van slowed and turned up the steep gravel road. It was a woman driver, from the distant glimpse he got. He strained to catch the van enter the driveway. He didn't, but he had a view of the gravel road farther up the canyon wall. The van didn't continue up the hill. Kinler drove a brown pickup in Salem. *Must be his wife or a friend. I'll wait for Kinler.*

Thirty minutes passed before the next vehicle. A light green pickup with the police type bubblegum machine lights drove up and braked in the middle of the road beside his car. There was a US Forest Service insignia on the door, and the driver had a badge pinned to her tan uniform shirt.

"Do you need help? I came by earlier—you were sleeping."

"No. I'm fine, Officer. Tired and I didn't want to fall asleep driving."

"Okay, good to be careful." She advanced several feet and stopped.

Richard tweaked the remote side mirror to spy on her. The officer studied his license plate number as she spoke into a microphone. He felt under the seat and moved the gun for quick access.

Hot and clammy, the shirt stuck to his body. He wiped at the sweat on his forehead. The meter had begun to run on his stay here. Hazel's car had to be dumped, soon. His stomach churned, queasy. If he waited much longer, the smell of the gasoline might reach the living space and whoever arrived in the van could discover his bomb. Kinler had an office; he'd catch him later with one of the pipe bombs. Richard grabbed the cell phone and hovered over the keypad.

◆◆◆

Earlier, down in the valley, Anna had kept her appointment at the veterinarian's clinic with the dogs.

"Whatever you're doing works. They're both in great shape. You can pick up the rabies certificate at the front desk."

Anna covered her mouth as a yawn escaped. "Oh, excuse me, Doctor."

"Late night?"

"If you only knew."

"Okay, we'll see you guys next year." The veterinarian scratched each dog under the chin and left the room.

Anna scooped Eddy up and carried him under her arm as she walked Sam outside and loaded them in the van. She returned to pay the bill.

Paperwork and flea tablets in hand, Anna hopped in behind the wheel. She swung the visor mirror down. Bloodshot eyes, hair a mess, "You guys made a better impression that I did."

One of the dogs raked a kennel door with a paw. "Eddy stop." He'd been a nuisance from the first day, but he was an adorable pest.

Anna sighed as she unlocked her Smartphone. A text from Allen: "Condition upgraded to satisfactory." The grip of worry, anxiety and concern for her friend, pent up over the last twelve hours, released. A flood of joy for her friend sent warm tingles across her back. Beth had experienced more than her share of sadness in life. Anna arrested the tears, plucked a tissue and wiped her eyes. *Thank you, Father.*

A woman who resembled the pug clutched to her chest startled Anna with a rap on the window. "Are you okay?" she asked through the glass.

Anna fumbled for the switch and smiled as the window slid down. "I'm fine. I really am—just very happy." She wiped her nose. "Thank you for asking."

The lady gave a strained smile and headed for the office. The pug eyed Anna with a skeptical expression. *Maybe they always have that look.* She closed the window and replied to Allen's text. "So good to hear."

Moments later he replied. "Another thing. She may have left your backdoor unlocked."

After all this, she's thinking of someone else. "Told me last night. On way home now." Anna replied. She started the engine, drove to the street and braked.

Another text from Allen. "To tell you. She now has smile front and back."

Anna shoved the lever to park. More repressed emotion escaped as she laughed. *She is going to be okay. Thank you, Lord.* She tapped a reply. "LOL CU."

The dogs had been away for several days. She interpreted their restless behavior as an eagerness to be home, something she and Matt shared with them. It was mysterious to her, but whenever they turned off the highway onto the canyon road the dogs stirred in their kennels. Then when the van turned onto the gravel of Game Trail Road the boys gave voice to being home.

Anna spotted a dark colored car stopped on the side of road, beyond where she left the pavement and too far away to catch the make. She didn't recognize the car as a local. The boys in their kennels whined with impatience. The house stood proud at the top of the driveway. Sound, comfortable and the home she and Matt enjoyed, together.

The dogs had been gone so long they took forever to reclaim their front yard. Anna bounced up the steps and into the house. Everything was in place, plus there was the pile of mail Beth had picked up at the post office. She started to pick through the stack but decided to finish later.

Sam and Eddy burst into the house and took turns being "it" in their game of tag. Anna shut the door to confine their ruckus to the house. An amused expression formed as the dogs acted out their delight at being home. She set the boys' medical papers down by the mail and reviewed her mental to-do-list.

In the pantry, she grabbed a plastic bag to carry kibbles for the dogs. The heavy bag of food had been moved to the back. *Why'd Beth do that? Not as convenient.* She measured out what she thought would last several days.

As she closed the pantry a few steps from the back door, she remembered Beth's concern and checked. Unlocked. Her friend had been right.

Sam ran around with his nose to the floor. "Silly dog, there's nobody new for you to pester. Ah, bet you can tell Beth's been here."

She flipped through the mail. The bank statement and a letter from their mutual fund had been opened. *Beth? I'll ask her.* Beside her purse, she stacked the important items from the mail, the dog food and the dairy goods near expiration. The accumulation required two trips to the car.

Carrying the last load in her arms, she called the dogs. Sam trotted to join her at the door, but not Eddy.

"Eddy!"

She caught the sound of a muffled whine from somewhere.

In the hall, across from the bathroom, Eddy had his muzzle pressed to the floor, rump in the air and tail wagging. "You're such a nuisance—pick the worse times."

Beneath the drawers on the computer desk, Eddy had his nose stuffed in the short space between the floor and the desk. "Ohhh." Anna stashed her cargo on the dining table, grabbed the yardstick hung beside the desk and dropped to her knees.

She nudged Eddy aside with her head as she fished for an object hidden in the darkness. "If this is another ball of dust, I'll make you eat it."

A cream-colored ballpoint pen peeked out as she swept with the stick. Eddy pawed the varmint out into the open, sniffed and lost interest.

"Oh, you." Anna snatched the pen and scrambled to her feet. Hair mussed, she moved to the bathroom mirror, slipped the pen in her jacket pocket to free a hand and tame her hair. As she returned the yardstick, a light on the desktop computer caught her eye. *Standby? I thought we'd turned it off. Beth?* She forced shutdown to save time and moved to the dining table to collect her purse and the selected mail.

"Let's go, guys." She waited by the open front door, but no eager dogs appeared.

"Now what?" Accustomed to inconvenient moments created by the way they indulged their dogs, she pushed the door shut. Sounds of dog paws and whines drew her into the hall. The boys danced on their toes at the back door. She shook her head and smiled at the new emergency. "Okay, I'll let you reclaim your backyard then we have to go." With her free hand, she unlocked the door and stepped out to supervise.

Neither dog tarried in the yard, but with noses to ground they streaked for the gravel road on the edge of their property. "Hey. Sam—Eddy!" She hurried across the yard, through the trees, and found the boys on the edge of the road, their noses busy around a dark spot on the gravel. *Oil?*

Cautiously Anna scanned in all directions for any strangers. Down on the canyon floor, she spotted the police lights on the roof of a light green truck stopped in the paved road. Forest Service vehicles often patrolled the area. The truck moved on up the road and out of sight.

During her whirlwind visit, discoveries she'd made hadn't registered on a conscious level. In this still moment, they hit her—the opened mail, the computer on, the dog food moved and the unusual behavior of Sam and Eddy. She slid the phone from her pocket.

Chapter 32

"Matt, where are you? I need you home—now."

"What's wrong? I'm headed for a talk with the OSP homicide guys."

"Cancel. Something's wrong here. Just a second." Anna squatted beside her purse and laid the phone on the road. She found the pocket with the leashes and coaxed the dogs close to secure them.

"Talk to me." Matt's voice played from the gravel surface.

"Wait." She raised her voice.

Anna unzipped the compartment to check for her gun before she retrieved the phone. "Matt." She lowered her voice. "Someone's been in the house. For all I know they're still around." After she recounted the unlocked door, mail, computer, dogs and things moved in the pantry, she asked, "Should I call 9-1-1?"

"Don't know if you have enough for them to send a car—I'm on my way. If I can get Trudeau, maybe he'll send a deputy to swing by out there."

"Oh—Matt, I just heard something."

"What?"

"A swoosh sound." She strained to check their house through the trees as a powerful, muffled explosion rocked her. The back door she'd left ajar flew open with the blast. Smoke billowed out. "No—no—oh, Honey. Our house—a bomb—there's fire."

"I'll call 9-1-1," Matt said. "You and the dogs stay away. I'm on the freeway—almost to the highway exit."

Anna eased to the edge of the trees, heartsick. Tendrils of flame shot out of the crawl space vents and the back entrance. Tongues of flame mixed with columns of smoke. She stiffened at the sight. Helpless, she stared. The dogs tugged to flee the smell of smoke and heat. Anger knotted her stomach. *Who would do this?*

The dogs yanked and jerked on their tethers until she followed back to the gravel road. Their home, possessions, memories—up in smoke before her eyes.

The van! Better save what I can. She clutched her purse and the mail. "C'mon guys." The dogs trailed downhill to the driveway. She dropped her purse and mail, tied the dogs to a bush, and ran up the driveway toward the house. The sirens sounded closer. The sight of flames in the windows brought tears of anger and frustration. The temperature at the van was bearable so she jumped in, drove out to the gravel road beside the house and parked uphill from the driveway and the dogs.

The first fire truck arrived as she secured the dogs in their kennels. Numb, with the house beyond rescue, she had no choice but to wait. Anna scooted back with her legs out over the rear bumper. The dogs whined. "Hush. You're okay."

Tears trickled down her cheeks. She blew her nose. Overhead, the smoky haze thickened and settled around the van. Another fire truck arrived and roared up the hill to stop above the house. The crew scrambled to attack the fire from the back.

One of the dogs raked the kennel door with a paw. "What am I thinking?" Anna grabbed the leashes, attached the dogs and led them down the hill. Below the thick layer of smoke, she found relief along the shoulder of the road. "Air's much better—huh?" She knelt to comfort her buddies.

Within minutes Matt arrived; his truck skidded to a stop beside the ditch. He rushed to meet her in an embrace. She buried her face against his chest and clung. Wrapped in his arms, his cheek brushed her hair. In a voice muffled by his shirt, she said, "We've lost everything, Matt." She wept.

Matt held tight for a moment before he said, "We've got each other."

"I know that, but everything's gone." She withdrew her arms and wiped at the tears with her hands. She sniffed as she fished a tissue from her pocket.

With his hands on her shoulders, he said, "We both know God had a purpose in this." He held her close. "We'll put our lives back together."

"Maybe I liked my house too much."

"Something we planned for years—hard not to enjoy our dream home."

Anna eased away to blow her nose. She patted his shirt. "Got you wet."

"Makes me love you all the more." He clasped her hand. "Our house, any house won't last forever."

"Neither will our earthly tents—that's what you always say when I complain about wrinkles." They kissed.

"On the way out here, I realized, instead of a dream home, we need to stay fixed on what is important to God—not our earthly possessions."

"So, this was to get our attention?"

"I'm not sure, but we got a good reminder. Everything as we know it will end like our house. Then, only those who have clung by faith to the Savior will be rescued."

"I know you're right." She moved into his arms. "Pray with me."

Later in the afternoon, the Fire Captain approached where they waited in the back of the van, each with a lap dog. The firefighter's protective outerwear rustled and swished as he moved.

"We got the fire out." He removed his headgear. "Some hot spots smoldering, but I'll have a couple of my crew hang around until the place is cool."

"Didn't want to get in your way, but we'd sure like to take a look," Matt said.

"It's not safe to go inside. The fire weakened the floor and everything above."

"I need to see," Anna said.

"I understand that. The Fire Marshal needs to investigate before anything gets moved around. Come with me."

Anna followed the men up the driveway and around the blocky fire truck. She froze at the sight. Windows broken out, front door gone and nothing but charred wood inside—darkness. Her heart sank. "Matt—I can't."

He comforted her with a hug. "You can. Together—you and I. Just like always." He put his arm across her shoulders as they approached the front stairs.

"The crew knocked the flames down pretty fast. Only place the flame broke through the roof was near the back door. That was the hottest spot."

"You saved my trees." Matt scanned the fir bough canopy above the roof.

"We did. A couple over the back got pretty scorched."

"I'll keep an eye on them. We can take them out later."

"Fire didn't undermine the porch."

"I've seen enough, Matt."

"C'mon. Just the top of the steps."

Anna held his hand as they climbed to the top. As Matt and the Captain talked, she let her eyes scan the ruins. Soot, water, debris, everywhere she looked. Everything was ruined, only memories remained.

"Look, honey! Our chairs survived," Matt said.

Anna blotted her eyes as she moved to what had been their favorite place. She gasped and her jaw dropped, "Oh, Matt!" She grabbed two framed pictures from the seat. "Our wedding picture—and our son, Chad." With the treasures clutched to her chest, she spun and sat in the chair. Their only son had died in a training accident when he served in the California National Guard during the time between the two Gulf Wars.

"One of my guys found those upstairs."

"Thanks, means a lot," Matt said

Back in the van with her pictures, Anna listened from the passenger seat as Matt dealt with their insurance carrier on the phone. Then he spoke with Nancy and his partner.

"Allen thinks Beth will be discharged tomorrow."

"Will she need help at home?"

"I told him they should come out to the horse farm and hang out with us. Nancy said we could all stay while we figure things out."

"Figure things out? Look at us, Matt. Burned out of our house, Beth's been shot, Marion nearly died—got a bomber and a shooter running around—don't know who they are—or where."

"Besides all that, Mrs. Lincoln..."

"Mathew Kinler. This is not time for your stupid humor."

"I'm sorry." He reached across the center console and clasped her hand. "It has been a tough time. Marion did turn in the last of the signatures today. There's no reason for the union to want her dead, now."

"I still can't believe union people would do this."

"Union leaders—some union leaders, not all." Matt gripped the steering wheel and stared into the distance. "Think I know the bomber. Need to help Detective Saunders find him."

"I want you to promise not to do anything stupid and get yourself killed."

"I promise I'll do my best not to get killed."

♦♦♦

"A Disaster—unmitigated disaster." Leach pressed the cell phone to his ear. He kept his voice down as he talked from the deck of his West Hills home. The view over the city at Mt. Hood was magnificent, but tonight the need for privacy brought him outside, not the scenery.

"I'll concede a misidentified target," Stryker said.

"Have you read the papers—followed the news?"

"I'm not interested in news. Your message on payment for services disturbed me. Thought it'd be best avoid your office phone and call this evening on your private line."

"Interrupted my dinner, but I don't pay for shoddy work."

"Don't toy with me, Mr. Leach. You bear some responsibility. You gave a poor target description and requested immediate service—I had no time to prepare."

"You shot the wrong person."

"I've been in this trade a long time. Have I made mistakes in the past? Sure—but very few. Never—never has a client refused to pay."

"There is a first time for everything, Stryker. The old broad turned in the rest of those signatures today. Secretary of State said the measure will make the ballot—can't kill it. If you'd done your job, that wouldn't happen."

"I did my job. You'll pay as agreed or wish you had."

"You threatening me?"

"That wouldn't be professional. I'm just saying, if you don't pay, there'll be consequences."

"Professional? You're nothing but a low-life bottom feeder. You've made a royal mess for me to clean up."

"There are few who do this work. I'll put the word out on your breach of contract."

"There's no contract."

"Any other lawyer would disagree. Mr. Leach, I'll expect payment in full as usual."

"Don't hold your breath. After a damage assessment, I may decide to remit a portion of your fee." Leach swiped away the call. *I probably shouldn't have been so hard on him. After I cool down, I'll probably pay him—give him a generous bonus too.* He slipped the phone in his pocket. *The unions trusted me to stop right-to-work. I failed to keep it off the ballot. If it passes, unions will lose money and power. I will too.*

◆◆◆

Bottom feeder, no contract, don't hold your breath. The dismissive words roiled in his mind. Stryker slid out from behind the wheel of his Land Rover. The wind hit him full force as he moved to the stone wall where he viewed the Columbia River. *Not one client had ever threatened to stiff him before.* Leach reminded him of an officer from his Army days. Arrogant, condescending and never able to accept responsibility for any failed mission.

When Leach had described the target, his first impulse had been to say no. But, he couldn't turn down the opportunity for an easy five hundred grand. Over the years, he had found some rationale to justify most of his jobs, but not this time. He remembered the flicker of relief as he'd read in the newspaper story that the woman had survived. Maybe he'd lost his stomach for killing.

He'd thought about retirement long enough. Stryker crossed the rest area parking lot, bought a cup of coffee from the vendor and jumped in behind the wheel. *One more job, one more wrong to right, then I'll head for home.* He drove eastbound on I-84 until he found an off-ramp. Stryker reentered the interstate, but in the westbound lanes. He headed back to Portland.

Chapter 33

You'd make good road kill. The barn cat sprawled in
the afternoon sun on the gravel drive between the
back porch and the barn. The barn door hung open.
She's tending her culls. He aimed for the cat and
gunned the engine. The gray feline darted for the shed
and disappeared through a hole underneath. Richard
grinned as he skidded to a stop at the door.

He grabbed his bag and climbed out of the car.
The old gal remained out of sight. The shed door
wouldn't budge. There was no lock on the door, so he
shoved with his shoulder. Something blocked his
entry. He took a step back and wound up to kick the
door.

"Hold on, Mister. You'll break your foot or
my door." She stood behind his car, hands on her hips,
dressed as before.

"Ms. Grace. Boy, am I glad you're here.
Didn't see you."

"I'm always here." She crossed her arms.
"You're fired—missed work today."

"Oh please, Ma'am." He hated to beg. "I need
this job. Please don't do this. I can explain."

"When I came out this morning you were
gone. Didn't tell me why you had to leave, no note—
nothing." She squinted.

"Mrs. Webster, please I'm sorry. You don't have your glasses. Maybe my note blew away. My mom had an accident. Your lights were off. I had to go—an emergency."

"The first time you came up—" She worked her store bought teeth. "—thought you told me your mother died."

"Not Mom, my sister."

She twisted her lips. "Weren't you living with your sister?"

"Another sister. Oh, please don't fire me." He buried his face in his hands and tossed his head to peek through his fingers and gauge her reaction. *I'll need to keep my lies straight. She's sharper than I thought.*

"You could've called."

He dropped his hands and hung his head. "I'm sorry, I know, but my phone went dead."

"Other phones around."

"So worried over my mother, I couldn't think." He pled with his hands. "I'll work twice as hard, Ma'am. Please let me keep my job."

"I'll give one more chance."

"Oh, God bless you. Thank you, thank you." *Old bat.*

She waved her arm at the shed. "You'll have to crawl in the cat door in back. I blocked the door to keep you out."

"Ms. Grace, you won't be disappointed."

"In a couple hours we got afternoon chores. Tomorrow, you got some catching up to do."

"Yes, Ma'am." He kept the subservient face until she walked away.

Behind the shed, he slithered inside through the opening in the back wall. Tufts of gray cat hair lined the edges. He stood and brushed his trousers while he glared back at his roommate. Grace had braced a two-by-four against the door at an angle, one end jammed under the knob and the other nailed to the floor. *The old gal's full of surprises. I better not underestimate her.*

Richard pried the brace from the floor. As he swung the board around to lean against the workbench, the barn cat sprang for the exit. *Hmm. Odd.* With the door open, he carried his groceries and supplies inside. A new ice chest held foodstuffs, not for preservation, but to prevent raids by a certain cat. Hard for him to know how crackers, nuts or dried fruit compared to field mice, but he'd take no chances. He still couldn't get his hands on dynamite, but he'd make do with the gunpowder. Richard used the time before chores to arrange the parts for his next projects.

Hazel had answered when he'd called. For him, she'd always been easy to read. The cops would snoop around because her car had been spotted near the last job. Although he didn't ask, she hadn't been questioned yet. If not now, he would soon be a wanted man. He needed to tailor every move he made to avoid being caught. The big shot lawyer had tracked him. Richard had outsmarted his errand boy, but he'd lost the motor home. Leach had to pay. Why Kinler had taken an interest, he didn't understand. The private eye had gotten his message, but Richard considered their business unfinished.

He held his tongue during the afternoon chores. Too much feed, not enough, hold the hose this way, don't leave the dung there. Richard figured she picked at him as punishment for his first offense.

When they finished she tossed him a bag of supper and marched to her house. He opened the sack. *Goody.* The same as before, tuna, maybe, apple and a pear. He returned to the shed and plopped on the cot.

The gray beast kept a vigil as Richard ate. The supplements hidden in the ice chest helped. Between courses he exchanged glares. If not for being on thin ice with the old lady, he would block the hole in the wall to rid himself of a roommate. He plucked a dried apricot and studied the hole at the foot of his cot. The way he booby-trapped the motor home had allowed him to escape—made him homeless, but it'd been effective. Being a wanted man, he needed an escape plan.

Through the window over the workbench, he could see the sun hanging low on the horizon. He inventoried parts on hand and sketched how he'd assemble the bombs. Incendiary devices were his specialty, but Leach required a different application, a pipe bomb. He grabbed the end cap for a three-inch galvanized pipe. *Big office, big chair, big desk, mister high and mighty orders his goon, 'squash this guy, squash that guy,' he don't care, he's safe. Ha.*

As he sorted through the drill bits, he bumped the two-by-four he'd leaned against the bench. To test his theory, he swung the board out behind him. The cat hit the hole quicker than Richard could turn to enjoy the panic. He chuckled as he resumed his project. Movement behind his car caught his eye as the cat loped toward the house. *Probably tattle on me.* The cat zigged and disappeared behind a bush beside the back porch. Richard studied the spot. *Not sure, but, kitty, you just gave me a brilliant idea. Have to check it out.*

With no time to find and surveil the residence or to gain access to his high-rise office, he'd need to hit Leach in his car. Pipe bombs were smaller than his other devices; he'd practiced with them but hadn't deployed one.

♦♦♦

The sound of a horn woke him. He glanced at his watch—he'd overslept. Three more blasts. "Okay!" Richard shouted, jumped to the window and waved. "I'll be right out."

Up late, he had found the opening in the foundation for access to the crawlspace. The way she kept the house buttoned up and didn't allow anyone inside piqued his interest. He pulled on trousers, jammed his feet into sneakers and rushed out the door. Morning mouth, hair styled by pillow, he stormed into the barn. "Sorry, Ma'am. I got sick in the night."

She helped with the feed and water and then tethered one of the smaller alpaca to a post. "I'll do the nails on one hoof. You watch."

Without glasses, she stooped low to trim the hoof, her nose so close to the nail he had to squat to learn what to cut. He didn't understand why the woman didn't wear her glasses.

It was awkward, but he managed to finish the other hooves.

"She's the tame one." Grace squinted at him. "Now we do the rest."

Some were easier than others, but by noon they'd completed over half the herd. He'd been kicked, bit and spat upon. It was a place to hide and the chance for another pile of money; otherwise he'd be gone. He stormed into the shed, ripped off his shirt and chucked it outside. "Phew!" Alpaca spit had a foul odor. Dressed in a clean shirt, he sat on the cot and raided his stash for lunch.

The old gal knew how to avoid the abuse he'd taken. She had poor eyesight, but sensed trouble before it happened. He didn't and got clobbered. The sooner he finished his business here, the better.

The sound of a vehicle drew him to the window. He peeked out. A tan commercial van had parked in front of the house and honked. As with any new arrival, the barn cat galloped toward their quarters. Grace waited on the porch as the driver opened the back doors. Richard strained to read the block letters on the driver's door. "Courier." Not certain, but his best guess.

With the back doors closed, the driver pushed a hand truck loaded with one small wooden crate. *Must be heavy.* At the bottom of the stairs, the driver spun the hand truck around and backed up the steps, one by one. *Really heavy.*

Grace escorted the driver inside and moments later they returned to the porch. Beside the hand truck, she signed something on a clipboard.

He eyed the cat curled on the chair. "Does he come here often?" Food secured, he headed back to work. He had to dump his car, finish his bombs and try to get into her house.

The afternoon had been easier. He'd only been kicked once. The best part was that he'd formed a game plan. Excited, he spent little time with his meal but snacked as he worked.

He loved to experiment and had used a different design for the booby trap on the hole in the back wall. A motion sensor placed at the front entrance simplified matters for him. He placed the switch to arm the booby trap under the window where he worked. If he spotted someone who might be a threat, he'd flip the switch, grab his bag and rush out the back. There was no delay timer, as the motion detector at the door would ignite the bomb when anything moved in the entrance.

When he finished he had three pipe bombs. One installed with his booby trap in the shed and two ready to be fitted with detonators, one for the private eye and the other for the lawyer. To power the circuit for the booby trap, he stripped the battery from his car. He smiled as he thought of the brilliant symmetry of his plan.

He stuffed his carryout bombs and the extra supplies in the backpack under his cot. Mr. Cat glared back at him. "Hope you're there in your usual place when the law comes." He snickered.

Under the workbench he found a length of rubber tubing. Outside, he siphoned gas from the car into a plastic bucket he borrowed from the barn. The tank had less than he'd thought.

After midnight, Richard coasted the car back down the driveway and stopped a safe distance from the house and barn. After all, he didn't want to burn her out yet.

He had located the telephone junction box earlier in the day. With his flashlight and tools he disabled the line. She'd never used a cell phone during his stay.

He hooked up the water hose, uncoiled it to reach the car, attached a nozzle and turned on the water. Then he made a mental rehearsal as he surveilled the house. It was dark, no lights, no sound, no movement; he'd wait until three-thirty, his favorite time. He hadn't checked on the fire department's response time. *I hope they don't send the law up here. Oh, forgot the plates.* With the license plates removed and stuck under the shed, he resumed his vigil.

Numb from the cold, he jammed his hands in his pockets and bounced on his toes. Finally, *Showtime.*

He fished the smelly shirt from the bucket of gas and tossed it through the driver's side window. Then he splashed additional fuel through the back windows. The fumes smelled potent in the heavy, humid air. Richard moved back, wiped gas from his hands and fished the Zippo lighter from his pocket. The wipe rag wadded, he made one last check of the car, pitched the rag through the window and moved back to a safe distance. After he struck the flint, the wick he had lengthened flamed. The underhand lob missed the window. The flaming lighter bounced on the ground. A moment later, a frightening whoosh sounded, the gas fumes from the car erupted and flames engulfed the car.

Richard ran to the front door pounding and shouting, and then the back door. Beside the blazing car, he held the hose ready to crank the nozzle at the right time. First, lights appeared on the second floor, followed by light in the kitchen and then Grace appeared. Without glasses, in her nightclothes and rubber knee boots, she clambered off the back porch.

"Oh, my goodness!"—a gasp for breath— "What happened?"

He trained the water in the direction of the fire. "Don't know. I think somebody tried to steal my car. Did you get 9-1-1?"

"No. My phone's dead. Oh, dear." She rocked, unsteady, no teeth.

"My phone won't work either. Where's your phone?"

"Ah, ah—ah inside the backdoor."

"We have to get a fire truck, Ma'am, here." He shoved the hose in her hand. "Keep this on the fire while I try to get your phone to work."

In a daze she shot water into the air. Some fell on the flames.

Giddy, Richard rushed through the backdoor with his flashlight. Given her size and the weight of the delivery, his prize had to be on the first floor. Door to door, room-by-room, he found what he sought in a closet. Gold coins and bars in three small wooden boxes. They had been opened, but otherwise undisturbed. He couldn't believe his good luck.

He ran from the house. She shook from the cold, disoriented. He grabbed the hose and closed the nozzle. "Ma'am, I couldn't get the phone to work." He took her arm. "You're cold. "Let me help you to the house and I'll try to put the fire out."

She didn't respond, but followed his lead.

Minutes later, he worked to get the fire quelled. He tingled with excitement. The ploy had worked better than he'd expected. His mind raced ahead on plans to remove the gold from her house.

Chapter 34

A sucker punch from a coward. Up since three, Matt's mind wouldn't shut down. The recliner provided a front row seat for the sunrise. Peaks and ridges of the Cascade Mountains appeared against pre-dawn light. The horizon appeared sculpted, colored in shades of dark gray, navy blue and black. He'd thought the chair placement odd when he first entered this room. But now, he understood.

Anna moved under the kitchen light. Her image reflected on the window to overlay his view of the horizon. No bother, he'd rather watch her, be with her. Each dog solicited attention and then resumed exploration of the new digs.

Yesterday's fire left them without a change of clothes. Nancy had opened her uncle's closet to them. Anna shopped early. A too large dress shirt, sleeves rolled up and droopy, sweat pants with room for another—the sight warmed his heart. Anna approached with a cup of coffee.

"Hi, Honey. You're up early," he said.

"Me? I didn't get up in the middle of the night." She eased into the twin chair and slid her cup onto the table between them. "I hope today is better than yesterday." The dogs filled her lap.

"Will be, but you set a low standard." Eddy joined him. "Nice of Nancy to let us have our dogs here."

"We'll need to get some clothes to wear. I threw the ones I wore yesterday in the washer—want to do yours?" She combed her hair with her fingers and shook her head. "Shower felt good."

"I haven't thought that far ahead." The dog jumped as Matt rocked out of the chair and stole a kiss. "I need a refill." He switched the kitchen light off before he returned.

"The sun will be up soon—beautiful view," Anna said. "Do you think he'll be back?"

"The shooter? I'd guess not."

"Allen messaged for Beth last night. She hopes to be released after the doctor sees her this morning. Said she's worried about us—can you believe it?"

"Sounds like her."

"I didn't ask yesterday. Did they figure out who shot her?" Anna asked.

"Nope. If he doesn't try again, doubt they will."

"I thank God he missed."

"Had to be a pro. One shot, three hundred yards, no brass. Nothing but matted grass and brush."

"When Marion's up I'll tell her she doesn't need to worry anymore. Okay?"

"Sure." Matt sipped with his gaze on the horizon. "Probably a bolt action—one lucky guy—the bullet busts the front glass, passes through the back window, and Saunders can't find the lead."

"I think Victor said the deputies had metal detectors out there," Anna said.

"Needle in a haystack."

"You were on the phone with Lucille when Marion said Nancy's uncle will stay down south. We can stay here as long as we need."

"Generous of him. I think our insurance would pay some rent. I've got to meet the claims guy at the house this morning. Need to get our video inventory from the safety deposit box." He drank from his cup.

"How's Lucille Duffy?"

"Seems okay. Still sad over Tom's death, but relieved Boyd has been charged. After I explained the plea bargain for Gerard's testimony, she understood. Of course, he's still got Marion's burglary and assault to answer for."

"What about the brother?"

"There's a warrant out for the bomb he set off at the filbert farm and Saunders will have warrants on Marion's assault any day."

"Nobody knows where he is, Matt."

He peered over his glasses. "Think we know where he was yesterday."

"Why us?"

"Me—he's after. Sick psychopath. Coward thinks he's some great avenger. We'll have to be careful until he's caught."

◆◆◆

Matt drummed fingers on the wheel as he waited for the gate to open. The day turned out longer than he'd planned. Marion answered instead of Victor.

The day spent with the Fire Marshal's investigator, the insurance adjustor and their builder left him drained. The bottom line was they had a big mess to clean up before they'd start construction. His river rock fireplace and chimney survived the fire, but maybe not the rebuild.

Matt parked his truck beside Anna's van. He passed behind his partner's sedan as he strolled into the garage.

Side by side, the ladies filled the couch along the front window. Cardboard covered the broken window.

"Beth!" Matt stooped to clasp her hand. "Glad to see you up and about." He bent over to kiss Anna, who perched on the end. "Did you get to shop?"

"I did. Beth and Allen got here before I returned."

"You bounced back fast," Matt said. "I expected they'd keep you longer."

"After the headache cleared up, I felt a lot better. Pretty sore." She lightly touched the bruise on her forehead before she bowed her head. "Made a mess of my hair." A thick gauze bandage ran across the back of her head.

"The size of the bandage makes the wound look worse. Doc used a few stitches." Allen occupied a stool at the counter in front of the kitchen. "She had a slight concussion, but they kept her longer just to make sure she had no bleeding on the brain."

"Good," Anna said. "I've heard of people dying because nobody checked."

"It's been hard to make myself presentable." Beth smiled as she toyed with her hair.

"Ha—you and me both girl." Marion laughed as she clasped Beth's hand.

Allen cleared his throat and stood. "Reason we came … ah … well—we got an announcement." He blushed and spoke to the rug. "At the hospital, I asked Beth to marry me—"

"—I said yes." Beth bounced on the front of the cushion and squeezed Anna's hand.

"Good for you." Matt shook his partner's hand. "Not surprised, but didn't expect you to pop the question this soon."

"It scared me when she got shot. I thought, wow, I might lose her."

"We talked and prayed. Couldn't come up with a reason to wait." Beth rose and embraced Allen. They kissed.

Anna clapped. "We need to celebrate."

"Nancy said there's steak in the uncle's freezer," Marion said. "He's got the grill stored down in the garage."

"You ladies talk wedding and we'll do dinner," Matt said.

He led the dogs down into the garage while Allen stayed in the kitchen to defrost the meat and work on a menu. With a bag of charcoal in hand he rolled the old kettle grill outside onto the asphalt apron.

The cloud cover had a bright spot on the western horizon. He grabbed a jacket from his truck. The heat from the coals warmed his hands as the dogs pawed his legs. "Okay." He fished two treats from his dog-walking jacket and sent the pests off to explore.

The briquettes glowed as dusk arrived.

Allen approached with a pile of steaks on a platter. "We couldn't find any sauce. I mixed up some of my own rub."

"You're full of surprises, partner." Matt slapped meat on the grill.

"Didn't think I could cook?"

"No. Didn't think you'd marry."

Allen stared at the fire. "Remember when you asked me if I was serious?"

"Yeah." Matt coughed and fanned the smoke from his face.

"When they wheeled her in behind the curtain at the E.R.—I almost panicked." Allen ignored the smoke, eyes fixed on the coals.

"You'll be good for each other. I could tell Anna's tickled."

"Matt, something else—you and Anna are a great model for me. I've told you how I grew up. Never saw a good marriage—up close. I want that for us."

"Commitment, buddy. God first, then Beth, yourself last." Matt flipped a few steaks. "If you put her first and she puts you first, can't go wrong—well, not too wrong." Matt smiled as he moved the meat around on the grill. "Always helps to have a good sense of humor—keeps things in perspective."

"I'm going to get her a horse as a wedding present."

"You're no cowboy."

"I'm not getting one."

"You're so big—if you do, better get a Clydesdale."

"I'm not much bigger than Hoss Cartwright."

"That's going way back."

"They don't make many westerns anymore."

"I think these are ready." He transferred steaks to the platter. "Did I tell you Marion got the signatures turned in? She's going to make the ballot with her measure."

"Anna told me."

"Sure." Matt passed the platter to Allen and called the dogs. "We need to figure what to do with all the papers we found in Fish's briefcase."

"You don't think the locals will do anything?" Allen asked.

"They may try, but with politicians in the crosshairs it'd be tough. Hard with all the rope-a-dope and stonewall games they play."

"I find it hard to believe nothing can be done," Allen said. "He had records of union payments for votes to kill the right-to-work bill in the House. Union money went to Boyd right after the lobbyist's house fire and Duffy's death."

"I remember the information on that lawyer too—Leach. I think we'll take the whole package to my FBI friend. Told him I wanted to see what he thinks."

"Won't he run into the political buzz saw?"

"Maybe not with state politicians involved. Now—DC? Different story."

Matt surveyed the buffet line Anna had arranged. "Good job, Honey." He placed his arm across her shoulders and kissed her cheek.

"Allen helped," she said. "By the way, they're staying the night. You guys can sleep out here and Beth and I will use the bedroom."

"I haven't seen the new clothes you got for me."

"I'll dig them out while you guys clean the kitchen."

"You're always thinking of me."

"I am." She smiled, patted his cheek and helped Marion with her plate.

After dinner and cleanup, the men moved into the recliners. The ladies had gone into the bedrooms.

Matt sorted through his new clothes. "I wouldn't wish this on anybody," Matt said. "The reality didn't hit full force—until today."

"If we can help with anything, just ask."

"Listen to you." Matt peered over his glasses with a smile. "You used, the 'we' word."

"Huh." Allen shrugged. "Guess I did."

"Matt, I forgot about this." Anna approached with a cream colored pen in her hand. "Eddy found it under our computer desk. You know how he does."

He examined the pen. "When?"

"The day of the fire. I put it in my pocket and spaced it. It went through the wash in my jacket."

"Webster 4 Alpacas?"

"Sounds like an advocacy group." Allen said.

"I don't know anyone with alpacas," Anna said. "I thought you might have brought the pen home—or maybe it's from our friends with the llama farm."

"They've been at church, but haven't visited our place recently."

"Didn't dawn on me until now," Anna said. "The guy that burned our house may have dropped it."

"What do you think?" Matt passed the pen to Allen.

"Didn't come from me or you," Anna said.

"How would Richard Crum get hooked up with alpacas?" Allen swiped and tapped his Smartphone.

"How'd he get hooked up with filberts?" Matt asked.

"Excellent point, partner." Allen scrolled on the phone. "Here's a site for an alpaca association in this state." More flicks and swipes. "The name on this pen doesn't show on their list. Here's a contact link. I'll send a request, see what happens."

"Pretty late." Matt checked the time.

"I'm off to bed." Anna kissed Matt. "Beth zonked out while I sorted clothes."

"I'm not sure." Allen stared out the windows into the night. "Didn't Gerard tell you or the cops, his brother had another elderly victim? A fruit orchard or something similar."

"Yes. Orchard owned by an old woman."

"Wow!" Allen worked his phone. "Got a reply—no record and knows nothing of Webster 4 Alpacas. This is from the daughter of the founder of the association. She'll contact her mother who knows everybody involved with alpacas in this state."

"Good, but we still can't be sure this pen came from Crum."

Chapter 35

Got to be a way. Richard spread hay along the trough. Grace didn't answer the door this morning. *Should've hosed her down and let hypothermia solve the problem.* He checked the animals' water. After the fire died down, he'd slithered and crawled every square foot of space under the house and failed to find a way to the first floor. By daylight, he had returned to his cot for a couple hours of fitful sleep. The "siren's song" of gold echoed in his mind; he couldn't relax.

He had used his phone to call a tow company. They agreed to haul the burned-out carcass of a car to the junkyard. Her phone remained out of order. The longer he waited to reconnect the line, the longer she'd be cut off from outsiders. He finished morning rounds and headed back to the shed. En route, he checked for the tow truck and Grace.

Transportation had become a problem. To find a decent rental he'd have to go to Albany or Corvallis. It was doubtful he could coax Grace into dropping him off that far away, unless she wanted to be rid of him.

Got to look like an accident. I've got to be long gone with the gold when they find her. Richard cranked out ideas and one scenario after another while he sat on the cot. *Door can't be damaged. Maybe shoot herself—fall down the stairs—hair curler dropped in a tub full of water. She probably doesn't own a curler.*

He jerked the ice chest out to grab a snack. The cat stared. Richard sprung for the feared board. Before he swung, the gray ghost disappeared out the back. He peeked out the window. The critter galloped toward the house, but veered right into the barn as Grace shuffled out. Wrapped in a thick bathrobe with slippers on her feet, she motioned for him. He grabbed a cracker before he hurried outside.

"Are you sick?" He didn't have to ask.

"Need you to get me some cough syrup and a few things." She had a coughing fit.

"No car."

"Use my truck." She clutched her sides as she coughed. "I'll get my keys—and some money." She croaked.

Before he left the driveway, the significance of this development hit him. So pumped, he fought to control his excitement. Richard eased off the gas pedal. He'd hoped to win the lottery one day; this may be the next best thing. The key ring she handed him for the truck also had the house keys.

In town, he'd have the keys on the ring duplicated. *Keys to the house, her truck—now, how to deal with the old woman.*

♦♦♦

"Check this out." Allen slid his phone across the table to Matt. "Nice of her to get back so quick, but it may not be much help. She's never heard of Webster 4 Alpacas."

Matt elbowed his cereal bowl to the side as he read the message. "She does recall an old breeder named Elmer Webster, but he's deceased."

"Wonder where he lived." Anna spread marmalade on a piece of toast.

"I'll ask her." Allen worked with his phone. "If she met him through the alpaca organization, must have been in Oregon."

"Maybe there's an obituary," Anna said.

"I've been searching." Matt tapped the screen on his phone.

"After breakfast, you still want me to change the dressing on your wound?" Anna asked.

"Sure, we go back to the doctor tomorrow." Beth drank from her coffee.

"Here's one." Matt read from the screen. "Eighty-nine. This Elmer had bred champion alpacas. Lists a wife, Grace. Don't find an obit for her."

"What paper?" Allen asked.

"Albany. Died about three years ago."

"Here's an old address for Elmer, Upper Springs Road—east of Scio. Don't find a listing for Grace Webster," Allen said.

"Marion, you live south of Scio," Matt said. "You ever hear of this Webster?"

She shook her head. "No. We moved down there over ten years ago."

"I better contact Saunders and pass this info along. Hate to give her something so vague, but maybe they don't have anything better on Crum," Matt said.

"We might be able to flesh this information out with a trip to Scio," Allen said. "I've got time. Beth, you said you were just hanging out today, right?"

"Anna's going to put on a fresh bandage and work on my hair," Beth said.

"I'd feel better if we gave Saunders something more definite to work with," Matt said.

"Matt," Anna said. "I know you."

"Oh, Honey. We'll just sniff around a little."

"You promise, if you find this Crum, you'll back off and call the sheriff's office."

"Promise."

Over an hour later, Matt drove along Upper Springs Road for a second time as Allen called out the occasional address numbers. "Doesn't make sense. Should be right here." Matt paused in the middle of the road.

"I'll double check the number." Allen flicked, swiped and tapped.

"Let's wait and catch the farmer on that tractor on his next pass." Matt drove a few hundred feet, through an open gate and into the field. The tractor towed a sprayer.

"Wind's in the right direction for us," Allen said. "Get out of here if the wind changes."

As the tractor drew near, Matt jumped out and rushed to the edge of the crop field. He waved his arms in scissor fashion over his head. The sprayer stopped before the tractor reached him.

"What's up, boys?" The man, not much taller than the rear wheel behind him, had been around a good number of years. He stuffed his hands behind the bib on his coveralls.

"We're trying to find Elmer Webster's place," Matt said.

"Well," He brushed the ball cap off his head and spit brown gook on the ground. "Figure we're about where his front yard used to be."

"The house is gone?"

"Yep."

"Did you know him?"

"Yep. Died."

"His wife?"

"Yep, IRS took everything she had. Gracie sold out. You're not government are you?"

"No," Matt said.

"Good, 'cuz she don't care much for government."

"Did they raise alpacas?"

"Yep, nice ones."

"They ever use Webster 4 Alpacas as a business name? The number four."

"Beats me."

"Where'd she go?"

"Beats me. Folks in town at the feed store might know?"

Matt headed for Scio. "Not much progress, confirmed Elmer's old address."

"And Gracie got an IRS beat down," Allen said.

They parked on the main drag and strolled back onto the side street in front of the feed store. A man with ample girth leaned on a broom near the entrance. He wore a red flannel shirt and jeans and had an unshaven face under a straw hat.

"Hi," Matt said. "We're trying to find someone."

"I know about everybody from around here." His belly shook as he chuckled. "They call me a one-man-rumor-mill."

"Elmer Webster," Matt said.

"The alpaca guy. He's dead."

"What about his wife?"

"She inherited some tax problems. Sold out."

"Would there be any business records with an address for her?" Allen asked.

"Oh, you'd have to ask inside. I'm just here to buy this." He waggled the broom.

"Thanks." Matt motioned to Allen. "Let's go in."

"Wait," the man said. "Here's my wife. She's friends with Gracie Webster."

A slender women climbed from an old red pickup parked across the street. She left the engine running. Gray hair was tucked under a white Mennonite cap, and the skirt on her long-sleeved dress brushed the top of her sneakers.

"Ferron, we're late," she said.

"Ester, these men asked about your friend, Gracie."

Her eyes darted from Matt to Allen and back. "You with the government?"

"No, Ma'am," Matt said. "We heard she had a way with alpacas. Wanted to talk with her is all."

"We don't want anything to do with the government—especially the tax man," Allen said.

"Us neither." Ferron held his hand to the side of his mouth. "Gracie and us, we have our own Constitutional driver's licenses. Don't use government issue."

"IRS dogged poor Elmer to his grave," Ester said with mischief in her eyes. "Tried with Gracie, but she outsmarted 'em."

"How so?" Matt asked.

"She sold everything. Tax man took most of what she showed." Ester narrowed her eyes. "Didn't show everything."

Ferron chuckled. "Rumor around here—when she left she had an armored truck as a moving van."

"Stop that—not funny." Ester glared at her husband.

"Ester, you know where we can find Gracie?" Matt asked.

She fished a small notebook from the folds of her skirt and leafed through the pages. "I got no address, only a phone number, but I haven't called for maybe a year." She read the number.

"Does she live alone?" Allen asked.

"Yes, but she usually has a hired hand around," Ester said.

"She posted a notice for hired help on the board inside about a month ago," Ferron said.

"That's how she finds help," Ester said. "Posts here, Jefferson, Lebanon—all around."

"Ester, did Gracie and her husband ever have a business that had a name like Webster with the number four and alpacas?" Matt glanced at Allen who headed for the store entrance.

"That's what got them in tax trouble." Ester tucked her notebook away. "Elmer had a non-profit with that name. He had pens, hats everything made up. I may still have one of those pens. I don't think I ever knew what he was up to, but everything fell down around his ears when the IRS came along. Gracie believed that's what killed him."

Matt bid farewell and joined Allen as they headed for the truck. "Did you find a notice?"

"Yes," Allen said. "Same number. Ask for Grace."

Matt tapped the number on his phone as he waited beside the truck. "The call won't go through. Maybe disconnected."

"Must've been good six weeks ago according to the date on the notice she put up in there."

"Do you think you can pull up an address from the number?"

They climbed in the truck. Matt stared ahead as he waited. "We need to decide whether we should cut the sheriff's office in now or later."

"Let my Smartphone decide." Allen flicked and tapped. "If I get an address we take a look see—if I don't, we let Saunders find the address."

"If I get in hot water with Anna, do you think, 'Honey, the Smartphone made me do it,' will work?"

"I doubt it." Allen stuck the phone out for Matt. "Bingo."

"Get the directions. We'll just do a drive by." Matt started the engine.

"Yeah, for all we know she's gone—phone's disconnected."

"We certainly don't know if Richard is there," Matt said.

Chapter 36

Yeah, I can't let her see me do this. Richard pulled over onto the shoulder of the rural road. Elated to find a rusty pair of pliers in the glove box, he ripped the sleeping pill bottle from the carton. He was unsure if the over the counter type would knock the old lady out, but he'd try. He used care to open the cough syrup. The plan relied on her poor eyesight and aversion to glasses, but the feel of the carton and bottle had to be close to normal.

The seal broken on the bottle, he swigged some syrup. Then he held it up to the light and judged there'd be room. Richard crushed the sleeping tablets with the pliers. The powder and crumbs accumulated on a piece of paper torn from a bag. Pill by pill, crush by crush, he dumped the coarse powder into the syrup. Before he returned the bottle to the carton, Richard shook it until most of the residue had dissolved.

Anger raged as he drove up the lane. The tow company had promised they'd remove the burned out car before noon. Furious, he stomped the brakes, grabbed his phone, found recent calls and jabbed the number.

After he'd vented and gained assurances they'd dispatched the driver, Richard parked near the barn door. The cat scampered up to the shed and disappeared. He jerked the keys from the ignition, jumped out and trotted over to the back porch with the cold medicines Grace ordered.

"I put the change in the bag and I broke the seal on the cough syrup for you. Those can be hard to work sometimes. Do you need help with this?"

She leaned against the doorframe as she shook her head. A cough spasm buckled her over before she moved inside and shut the door.

The sound of the deadbolt followed him from the porch. He pictured her chugging down the wicked cocktail. *Patience, Richard. Close, so close.*

In the shed, he dropped onto the cot. Sleep had been in short supply, but he'd catch up after he snatched the gold. Anxiety swept over him. The car had to be towed. He had to reconnect her phone line, but not too soon. Didn't want her to reach the 9-1-1 operator when she felt woozy.

Nervous energy kept him amped up. He knelt to check his two bags. One had the two pipe bombs for his next two hits and the other his personal essentials. With one in each hand, he carried his bags down to the truck and stashed them on the floor, passenger side. From the corner of his eye, he checked for the old woman. He fought the urge to run over and peek in the kitchen window.

The sound of tires on gravel and a revved engine drew his attention. A flatbed truck from the salvage company approached and stopped beside his old car. Richard met the driver at the car.

"Glad you finally got here," he said

"Ya, well had lots to do today. Got lost finding this place."

"The sooner you get this piece of junk off my property the better."

"Ya, sure. Got the papers?"

"Papers!" He loved this. "Kidding right? Somebody plops a car on my property in the middle of the night, torches it, and you want papers!"

"Ya, something I'm supposed to ask. There's no plates?"

"Can't help that—get this junk out of here." Richard marched up to the shed.

The cat glared as he entered. Empowered by his performance, Richard shut the door and grabbed the board to torment the cat off his perch. He smiled as the cat darted outside. Richard flopped on the cot and stared at the ceiling. Everything in place, he waited. By late afternoon, he'd know whether the sleep tablets worked. With her conked out, and him with the keys, he'd load the gold in the truck and be long gone before anyone found out.

He hadn't settled on an alternate plan if the concoction didn't work. The gun tucked in his bag down in the truck might be the only option. He stared at the ceiling from his cot. He'd wait.

◆◆◆

The narrow, paved farm road had no centerline. Matt slowed as he approached a sharp, blind uphill curve. A flatbed truck, loaded with a wreck, rounded the turn headed toward them at a reckless speed.

"Hold on." Matt veered toward the ditch to avoid being sideswiped.

Allen craned his neck to catch a glimpse out the back window.

"Take your share, buddy," Matt said.

"Matt. That burned out piece of junk looked a lot like the one Anna tangled with."

"Kidding, right?" He studied his friend.

"Dead serious."

"How close are we?"

"Little over a mile."

"We'll just take a peek, okay?" Matt reached back to adjust the holster on his belt.

The uphill entrance had signs posted, but Matt ignored them. He passed a patch of burned and scorched ground. "This may be where that car came from," he said.

Allen nodded.

Ahead, on the right, sat a two-story farmhouse; to the left an empty pickup was parked in front of a barn entrance. A gray cat sprinted from the barn and up the driveway; it disappeared under a shed.

"What'd you think?" Matt parked near the bottom of the porch steps.

"Alpacas in the pasture over there," Allen said.

"You wait. I'll check." Matt jogged up the steps and knocked. No response. He knocked again and dialed the number from the Mennonite friend. He pressed his ear to the door. With a shrug, he returned to the truck. "Disconnected. No ring inside. Maybe no one's here."

"No harm in a walk," Allen said.

Matt sauntered toward the pickup and barn while Allen moved along the side of the house. The truck window was down, so Matt peeked inside. There were no keys, but a small backpack and duffle sat on the passenger side floor. Tempted, he decided no.

In the barn, stacks of hay sat in front, and there were several alpaca in back, but no humans. Matt moseyed back outside beside the truck. Allen had his face pressed to the glass in the backdoor.

His partner spun with a frantic motion. "Matt, get over here."

Matt hurried to the porch, as Allen drew his gun and broke glass in the door.

He reached the top step as Allen stuck his arm inside to unlock the door. "We got somebody on the floor in here."

Matt followed and knelt beside an elderly woman who lay face down. Allen checked for other occupants. The pulse in her neck was weak and slow, her breathing shallow; her forehead felt cool and clammy to the touch. "Help me roll her over," Matt said.

"We need to call 9-1-1." Allen pressed the phone to his ear as he helped with one hand.

"Careful. Not sure we should do this, but we need to find out what's going on." Matt held his arm under her head. "Gracie?"

Her eye lids fluttered, "Who?" She coughed and then vomited.

Matt rolled her to the side and cleared her nose and mouth until she resumed breathing. He removed her dentures.

Allen took the dentures and tossed him a towel.

"We've got a very sick woman here," Matt said.

"This doesn't look right." Allen held a bottle to the window. "There's something in this cough syrup—like mud."

"You think she took any?'

"Someone did. Just a sec." Allen listened to the operator. "We don't know what happened," he said into the phone.

Matt rushed into the front room, grabbed pillows and a comforter and returned. As Allen talked, Matt moved the woman into a comfortable position on her side. She stirred.

"Gracie?"

"Water." She coughed.

"Allen, wet a towel."

Matt eased the wet towel against her lips. "Better not drink yet. We've got help on the way. Hang on."

She sucked on the towel and worked her jaw.

"Anybody else here with you?" Matt asked.

Her eyes opened. "To … To—by."

Matt flashed Allen a puzzled look. "Toby?"

Allen shrugged. "Operator says, keep her comfortable, warm and awake if we can. They're on the way—twenty minutes."

"I got a hunch," Matt said.

"Me too, but I need to stay with the operator if I can."

"Can you tend her for a minute?"

"Don't do anything stupid—he's a bomber."

"Coward's probably in the next county." Matt didn't mention the bags in the truck.

◆◆◆

Minutes earlier in the shed, Richard had sprung to the window at the sound of tires on the gravel. He froze at the sight of the brown truck. Chills ran down his spine. He took a deep breath and gave a long, slow exhale. *Be calm.* He leaned low over the workbench to peek out through the corner of the window.

His eyes followed the private detective up and down the steps and into the barn. He slid a coffee can with odds and ends over to give cover as he tracked the men.

The big man moved up on the back porch. *The old woman didn't show. Maybe she's out.*

Oh, oh, he's spotted something. Probably the woman. If she's dead, I can lay low and get the gold after they've hauled her off. His stomach churned as the men broke into her house. *Too bad I don't have my gun. I'd shoot the trespassers.* Beads of sweat formed on his forehead. *What's taking so long?* Richard backed away. The feral creature glared from the chair.

I could arm my booby trap and boogie. He checked the window and backed out of sight. *Be a waste, if I blew up someone of no interest to me. Kinler, he'd be worth the wait.* Richard glared at the cat and settled in behind the coffee can.

Outside, the man he hated returned to the driveway. *Waiting for the hearse? Don't seem in a hurry.* Sweat ran down his forehead as Kinler moved over and faced the passenger side of the truck. *If he opens the door, I'm out of here, cut my losses.*

His blood turned cold when Kinler faced the shed. *This is it.* He slipped away from the window to check his exit. The cat eyed him. *Your big day, cat.* Richard slid the cot along the back wall and flipped it on a side to cover the opening. *Stupid animal has no clue.* He snuck a peek. The man stood focused on the shed. *Oh, yeah. Wish I had an invitation.* His heart raced with excitement, his nerves felt electric. *I'll make it easy for you.* He smiled at his inspiration as he turned the knob and eased the door ajar. He thought through his steps. Flip the switch to arm the bomb, move the cot enough to get out, trap the cat inside and beat feet.

Another peek—Kinler was closer, but he'd paused. Richard flipped the switch to "on" and moved to the cot. *Wait, what if a breeze moves the door? Don't want a premature blast.* His brilliance warmed him. He grabbed the handy board to steady the door.

A gray flash of fur as the cat streaked past and out of the shed.

The blast dammed Richard's last words.

Chapter 37

Smoke billowed from the ragged hole, once a window. Flat on his chest, Matt lifted his face from the graveled dirt, stunned by the blast. He coughed smoke from his lungs and spit grit from his mouth. The door lay flat on the ground outside the entrance. Holes riddled the front wall, punched out by flying debris.

He pushed to a crawl position. Everything was dead quiet, except for the ringing in his ears. He shook his head. Strewn on the ground were pieces of glass and debris. Matt sat back on his heels, straightened his glasses, and brushed soil and dust from his palms.

"You okay?" Allen approached from behind.

"Yeah, I think so." Matt massaged his ears and worked his jaw to clear his hearing. "Some explosion."

"Did he get away?" Allen asked.

"Don't know. Not out the front. The only thing I saw before I hit the ground was a gray cat rocket out the door." Matt traced the cat's path with his eyes. "Must've survived."

"Did you see Crum in there?" Allen asked.

"No." Matt got to his feet and brushed the dust and grit from his clothes with his hands. "I stopped back there." He jabbed his thumb back over his shoulder. "I thought I heard something in the shed. Wasn't sure, but I had one of those feelings— somebody inside, danger. Ever happen to you?"

"Maybe—I think I know what you're talking about."

"I could feel danger—so real, I'd decided to go back and talk to you, but, something told me to get down. Don't remember hearing anything or seeing anything, but I dove for the dirt. Good thing."

"You're bleeding—your forehead."

Matt found his handkerchief and wiped his forehead. "Ouch." There was a sharp pain over his eye.

"Let me." Allen examined the spot of blood. "Hold still." He pinched at the small wound. "There." He showed a splinter of glass.

"Thanks." Matt pressed the wound as he approached the blown out shed. "How's the old woman?"

"We both jumped when the bomb blew, but she's no worse. My buddy at 9-1-1 also heard it," Allen said.

"Cavalry's on the way?" Matt stopped at the entrance and leaned forward to survey the damage. He said, back over his shoulder, "Allen, call your buddy. We got one deceased."

"Richard?"

"Can't tell. Medical Examiner's going to need dental records—maybe fingerprints. Hard to say."

Allen stepped up to view the inside as Matt moved away.

"That bomb was loaded with shrapnel," Allen said. "Meant to kill, not just blow things up."

The sound of the siren stopped before the ambulance turned off the road. Emergency lights remained on as the driver parked beside Matt's truck and jumped out.

Matt followed as Allen hurried down the hill. Allen motioned to direct the paramedics to the back door.

While the others went in the house, Matt called Deputy Saunders.

Drained and tired, Matt meandered to the farmer's truck by the barn. He leaned his back against the side of the bed as he talked and scanned his surroundings. Movement near the front wheel caught his eye. The gray cat rubbed against the tire. Matt squatted and extended a hand as he spoke on the phone. *Purring?* The cat retreated to the front of the truck, out of Matt's view.

After he finished with Saunders, Matt stood and called Anna.

"Where are you guys?"

"We found the alpaca farm where that pen came from. Good thing too. We found the old lady on the floor in her house—very sick. Called an ambulance. They're here now." The cat jumped onto the hood where it sat and stared at him through the windshield and the open passenger side window. "Think I got a new friend."

"What are you talking about?"

"One lucky farm cat's trying to make friends with me."

"Is the lady going to be okay?"

"Yeah, I think so. But, the guy who torched our house? He's not okay."

"Matt—If you got yourself into a mess, I—"

"Honey, be calm. It's complicated. He was in a shed uphill from the farmhouse and we didn't know. Not until he blew himself up."

"You promised, Matt."

"Honey, we were just trying to find this Mrs. Webster and—everything spun out of control."

"I get so mad at you. You're always doing this to me. You've always got some excuse."

"As I recall, I promised not to get killed and to back off if we found Crum. I didn't break either of those."

"Don't parse my words."

"Anna, look—Allen and I are safe and we'll be headed home soon. I'll tell you how everything happened."

"I love you and want to grow old with you, Matt."

"I love you too, Honey. I'll finish up here so I can come home."

He eased the phone into his pocket and with slow movement approached the cat. The cat spun and leaped from the hood. Left at the passenger window, Matt spotted those two small bags again. He opened the door.

With the blade of his pocketknife he sorted through the duffle and found a Browning pistol, Crum's assorted identification cards and a bundle of currency. He opened the main compartment of the backpack. At first glance, he stepped away and moved over to the back porch. He called Saunders to tell her they'd need the bomb squad.

"Excuses—excuses, you've always had an excuse." Anna forced the lid on the teakettle, spun from the sink and moved to the stove.

"Careful, they might hear us."

"You can't hide behind them." She shot him a cross glance and twisted the burner knob. "Beth went down to the stables with Allen and Marion's napping."

"Good. Sit and I'll explain what happened." He grabbed a chair for her at the table.

"That's the problem, Matt." She placed her hands on her hips. "Always a justification, always some explanation." She planted herself in the chair.

"Always?" He slid into the chair beside her.

"Don't be cute." She plucked a tissue from a box on the table. "You do this a lot."

"I'm not—I don't think it's fair to imply I do the wrong thing on purpose and then make excuses."

"That's not what I'm saying. It's not fair for you to leave me alone to wonder—is this the time he won't come home?" She blotted the corner of her eye.

A throat cleared behind them. Allen and Beth stood near the hall entrance. "Excuse us," Beth said.

"We hoped to get some fresh coffee, but don't want to interrupt," Allen said.

"How much did you hear?" Anna wiped her nose.

"Well—" Beth's eyes darted to Allen and down. "Not too much."

Allen chuckled as he laid his arm across Beth's shoulders. "She's not a seasoned liar like me. We heard enough to know you're having a family discussion."

"Well, come over and join the family," Matt said.

"I'll finish the coffee—the water's hot," Beth said.

"I haven't done a good job explaining what happened," Matt said.

"No, he hasn't," Anna said. "I don't think you guys need to sort through our dirty laundry with us."

"Sounded like this is something Allen needs to hear." Beth spoke from the stove.

"We've had this discussion before." Anna dabbed her eyes. "When he worked as an FBI agent I had to accept the fact that he had a dangerous job. But now he's retired and not supposed to be doing dangerous things." She placed her hand on Matt's. "He's had a hard time learning new tricks."

"Honey, you know I don't go looking for danger. I ... both of us want to help people. You'll have to admit, some of your own projects have turned dangerous for us."

She squeezed his hand before she reached for another tissue. "I do remember a few occasions." With the hint of a smile, she said, "Maybe we should let God take care of things while you and I stay home."

"—Could, but what if He wants you or me to have a part in His taking care of things?"

"What if I wish He'd use someone else?"

"Honey, I understand why you might get angry. But, it's a lot easier to find mistakes with twenty-twenty hindsight. What a Monday morning quarterback does."

"Matt." She slapped her hand on the table. "I'm not a Monday morning quarterback."

"Sorry." Matt clasped her hand and met her eyes. "Poor choice of words."

"Here's coffee." Beth placed the carafe and cups down and joined them.

"I'm the first to admit I make mistakes—" Matt said.

"—Except when I point them out first." She smiled.

"True." He nodded. "I'd just want you to remember, Allen and I made decisions and acted on what we knew each step of the way. We had the pen and a possible address, and when we got there—no house or buildings. With old man Webster dead, the farm gone and no wife, we'd hit a wall.

"Lucky we ran into the town's gossip and his wife," Allen said.

"She had a phone number, 'old,' she said. When we called it was disconnected," Matt said.

"Crum had done that, but we didn't know," Allen said.

"Anyway, Allen finds an address, but we don't know if the old lady is there or anybody else."

"Certainly not a bomber," Allen said.

"Anyway, we get there and Allen spots the woman out cold on the floor. Good thing too, otherwise she might've died. Now, she's going to be okay after the pneumonia clears up. He'd drugged her."

"I am glad you were there to help," Anna said. "Just—I don't want to lose you."

"Honey, I thank God every day we are together. I don't do dangerous things on purpose—but we've done some good. We helped find who killed Lucille's husband, rescued the filbert farmer, helped Marion and Darla. Things kind of snowballed on us. I don't sit down and ask, how am I going to upset Anna today?"

"I know you don't." She leaned over for a kiss.

"Alright, you love birds." Marion joined them at the table. "Heard you out here."

"Hope you didn't eavesdrop on our spat," Matt said. "I need to take this call—Saunders." Matt rose and moved into the main room.

"I'll never tell how much I heard." Marion accepted coffee from Beth.

A few minutes later, Matt returned. "Interesting call. Allen, you remember Leach?"

"Big union lawyer—mover and shaker," Allen said.

"A janitor found Leach dead in his office last night. It's not public yet, but there was one shot to the forehead. The cops think he had been at his window, because the shot broke out the glass. The shooter probably hid on a high rise nearby.

"And as it is appointed unto men once to die,

but after this the judgment;"

Hebrews 9:27 (KJV)

THE END